WHAT WAS MILD-MANNERED MUSICIAN MIKE DE WOLF DOING

clad in the costume of a Spanish grandee, waving a rapier he barely knew how to use, ducking cannon balls and embracing a ravishingly beautiful English lady, while listening to the typewriter that was pounding out his fate?

WHAT WAS SCHOLARLY PROFESSOR JAMES LOWRY DOING

dealing with a phantom spirit from the prehistoric past, trying to find a missing artifact that he had been warned meant his doom to recover, and moving ever closer to the most horrifying discovery that a man has ever made?

You will never guess the surprises that await you in two of the most astounding novels ever written—

TYPEWRITER IN THE SKY/FEAR

L. RON HUBBARD
FEAR &
TYPEWRITER IN THE SKY

IHE

POPULAR LIBRARY • NEW YORK

Published by Popular Library, CBS Publications, CBS Consumer
Publishing, a Division of CBS Inc., by arrangement with the author's agent, Forrest J. Ackerman, 2495 Glendower Ave., Holly-
wood, Ca. 90027

July, 1977

ISBN: 0-445-04006-8

CONTENTS

TYPEWRITER
IN THE SKY

CHAPTER ONE

Horace Hackett, as one of his gangster characters would have said, was on the spot.

About three months before, Jules Montcalm of Vider Press had handed to Horace Hackett the sum of five hundred dollars, an advance against royalties of a novel proposed but not yet composed. And Horace Hackett, being an author, had gayly spent the five hundred and now had nothing but a hangover to present to Jules Montcalm. It was, as one of Horace Hackett's heroes would have said, a nasty state of affairs. For, be it known, publishers, when they have advanced sums against the writing of a book, are in no mood for quibbling, particularly when said book is listed in the fall catalogue and as there were just two months left in which it could be presented to the public.

Horace Hackett was popular but not popular enough to get away with anything like that. He wrote novels of melodramatic adventure for Vider Press, at about the rate of one a year—though he also wrote gang stories for Pubble House and love stories for Duffin & Co. Just now Horace Hackett was furiously fumbling with facts in an attempt to explain to Jules Montcalm just why it was that no manuscript had arrived as per contract.

Jules Montcalm, being a publisher, did not believe authors. In fact, it is doubtful if Jules Montcalm ever believed anything beyond the fact that he was probably the one genius in the book business. He had, let us say, a sus-

9

picious eye. This he had focused upon Horace Hackett and Horace Hackett squirmed.

They were in the living room of Horace Hackett's Greenwich Village basement studio apartment, a darkish place well padded with sheets of forgotten manuscripts, unanswered letters from bill collectors, notes from the ex-wife's lawyer asking for alimony, empty brandy bottles, broken pencils, a saddle somebody had sent from New Mexico, several prints of furious revolutionary battles, three covers from some of Horace's magazine serials, crumpled packages of cigarettes—all empty—a stack of plays somebody had sent—just knowing that Horace could advise about them—newspapers which dated back to the tenth battleship Germany had claimed to have sunk, a number of scatter rugs from Colombia, where they had begun life as saddle pads, three empty siphons, a dun from the company which had foolishly financed Horace Hackett's car and a piano at which sat Michael de Wolf.

Horace Hackett did not appear disturbed. In fact, he was airy. This thing, his attitude plainly said, was a mere bagatelle. Why, the business of dashing off that novel was so simple and could be done so quickly that one wondered why another one should think twice about it. But down deep, under his soiled bathrobe, Horace Hackett knew that he had never been closer to getting caught.

Mike de Wolf, at the piano, was grandly oblivious of the pair. His slender fingers were caressing a doleful dirge from the stained keys, a very quiet accompaniment to his own state of mind. Mike had a chance to audition the following morning, but he was pretty certain that he would fail. He always had, hadn't he?

Jules Montcalm, with the air of a hunter who has just treed a mountain lion and is now training his rifle to bop it out of the branches, leveled a finger at Horace.

"I don't believe," said Jules Montcalm—whose real

name was Julius Berkowitz—"that you even have a plot for it!"

"Heh, heh, heh," said Horace hollowly. "Not even a plot. Heh, heh. That is very funny. Mike, he doesn't even think I've got a plot for this novel!"

"Well," said Mike de Wolf, not turning, "have you?" And he ran into a more mournful set of chords than before.

"Heh, heh. You don't think for a minute that Mike means that, do you, Jules? Why, of course I've got a plot!"

"Uh-huh," said Jules. "I bet you can't even begin to tell me about that plot!"

"Here, have another drink," said Hoarce, getting hurriedly up and pulling his dirty bathrobe about him while he poured Jules another drink.

"Well, if you got a plot, then why don't you tell it to me and stop saying 'heh, heh, heh'!" Jules had scored.

Horace sat in the chair, still airy, and he managed to put an enthusiastic light behind his pale-blue eyes. He leaned forward. "Why, this is one of the greatest stories I ever did! It's marvelous. It's got everything! Drama, character, color—"

"The plot," said Jules.

"It's sparkling and exciting, and the love interest is so tender—"

"The plot," said Jules.

"—that I almost cried myself thinking it up. Why, its a grand story! Flashing rapiers, tall ships, brave men—"

"I already said that in the catalogue," said Jules hopelessly. "Now I want to hear the plot. I bet you ain't got any plot at all!"

"Mike! Here I am telling him the greatest story ever written—"

"You haven't written it yet," said Mike without turning.

"He's a great kidder," said Horace to Jules. "Heh, heh."

"The plot," said Jules.

"Why, sure. I was just going to tell you. It's about pirates. Not pirates, you understand, but buccaneers. Back in the days when England and France were fighting for a toehold on the Caribbean and the dons had it all sewed up. Back about sixteen hundred, just after the time of Drake—"

"We got all that in the catalogue," said Jules. "The plot!"

"Well, it's about a fellow called Tom Bristol," said Horace, thinking so hard that he squinted. "Yes, sir, it's about a fellow named Tom Bristol. A go-to-hell, swashbuckling, cut-'em-down, brawny guy who's the younger son of a noble family in England. He's a gentleman, see? But when he gets into the King's navy he don't like the admiral, and when he's given command of a ship he fights the battle his own way, and that makes the admiral mad, and so they cache Tom Bristol from the service, even though he won the fight for them. He's too smart for them, see? And he's too hotheaded for the discipline, and so his old man, the duke, boots him out and tells him never to come back."

"Like all the other pirate novels you've written," sighed Jules.

"Like— Say, don't you think I've got artistic temperament? Do you think I've got just one story? Why, the sales on my last book—"

"Don't try to get out of this by getting mad," said Jules. "The plot! His old man, the duke, kicks him out—so what?"

"Why, so he comes to the New World. Out to St. Kitts. And there he runs into this girl. Her old man is the merchant prince of the English. He's got stacks of money that he's made by trafficking with the buccaneers, and he's

12

really kingpin in the West Indies. And because society in St. Kitts was very swell, why his daughter is there with him."

"With blond hair and blue eyes and very sweet—" said Jules hopelessly.

"No!" said Horace, thinking faster. "Hell, no! She's a wild cat, see? She's turned down half the lords in England because she's looking for somebody that's really a man. She can ride to hounds and shoot better'n a musketeer, and she's a gambling fool. And she figures all these noblemen are just soft-bellied bums. No, sir, she'll never give her hand to any guy that can't beat her at any game she tackles, and she's never met such a guy. So—"

"Well, that's different enough for a heroine," said Jules. "But you know what they always say. It takes a good villain to make a story. And if you go making the villain like you did in 'Song of Arabia,' people are going to say you're slipping. Now a good villain—"

"That's what I'm getting to," said Horace, pretending to be much offended. "But you wanted the plot, and I'm giving you the plot. Now, listen. This guy Tom Bristol and the girl get together, and they like each other, but it looks like this business in the West Indies is going to fold up for England and the girl's old man because Spain is getting mighty tired of it, and so the dons figure out it's about time to wipe out all the buccaneers. So in comes this villain business. Now listen. I got it. This villain is the lord high admiral of the Spanish navy in the Caribbean, see? And this Tom Bristol mixes it up with him.

"Well, the girl's old man doesn't like Bristol because Bristol isn't rich and he hasn't got a title, and so the old man thinks he'll polish off Bristol by telling him that if he knocks hell out of the dons—why, he can have the girl. And so Bristol is fitted out with a ship to knock off a couple of Spanish ships, and with a crew of buccaneers he goes slamming off to meet this admiral—"

13

"That's thin," said Jules. "You gotta have a good villain. You gotta have conflict."

"Well, haven't I got it?" howled Horace.

"You ain't got any villain," said Jules.

"Now, look," said Horace, "I'm telling you all about it. I'm getting to this villain. He's the lord high admiral of his Catholic majesty's navy in the Caribbean. And he gets it in for Bristol, too, and so they proceed to knock hell out of each other all through the book; but, of course, in the end, Bristol kills the Spanish admiral and gets the girl."

"Spanish admiral, sure," said Jules. "But what kind of a guy is he?"

Horace was stuck for only an instant. There was Mike, sitting at the piano, playing dolorously. There was no gauging what Mike de Wolf's ancestry really was, but it was certain that the Irish side of his family had been enjoined by one of the dons who, defeated in the armada, were flung up on the coast of Erin to give the Irish race occasional black hair and dark eyes. Whence came the strain which made Mike what he was, he certainly could not be told from a don. Horace had his inspiration.

"Why, there's your villain," said Horace. "Now what more can you ask than that, see? Mike! Now look, Jules. Look how narrow and aristocratic his face is. Why, his nostrils are so thin that you could see light through them. And his complexion is as pale as alabaster. He's beautiful, see? He's tall and graceful, and he's got manners that'd put a king to shame. And he's got a well of sadness in him which, combined with his beauty, makes the girls fall for him in regiments. He looks delicate, but by Heaven, I've seen him lick guys twice his size and weight. There's your Spanish admiral. A romantic! A poetry-reading, glamorous, hell-fighting, rapier-twisting, bowing beauty of a gentleman, all perfume and lace and wild cat. There's your Spanish admiral. And he falls in love with this girl

14

when he gets shipwrecked on the island where she lives and she doesn't know he's a don because he's so educated he can speak English without an accent—"

Mike had begun to glare. "You leave me out of this."

"See the fire flash in that dark eye?" said Horace to Jules. "Can't you see what he'd think of a swashbuckling captain from barbaric England? And when he gazes upon this girl who has saved his life he loses his heart to her. And not only does it become a battle between them for empire, but a conflict for a woman."

"Well—" said Jules doubtfully, "it *sounds* pretty good. But the color—"

"The color will be perfect!" said Horace. "I know the Caribbean like I know the keys of my mill. Can't you see it now?" And he really was taking fire about the idea. "This Mike, as the Spanish admiral, will wow 'em. He's the perfect character!"

"I said to leave me out of it," said Mike. "I've got to audition in the morning, and I don't feel any too good as it is."

"Nonsense," said Horace, and faced Jules. Horace girdled the bathrobe about him and began to pace up and down the floor amid the scatter rugs from Colombia. "So there's the novel. It begins with this Bristol getting the boot like I said, and then, when he's en route to the Indies, we cut the scene and we find ourselves on St. Kitts. No. We find ourselves on the deck of the *Natividad,* flagship of the Spanish fleet. This Mike is on deck, and the captain is telling him that the rest of the fleet's been scattered by the gale, and that the island off there is St. Kitts. Well, just as they're looking at the island, Mike's telescope picks out a couple of piñnaces coming out from the land. They've got a lot of men in them, and as the sea is calm and as the wind after the storm has died, why, there's no getting away from them. So this Mike says to the captain—and boy, have we got a story here!—he

15

says: 'Pirates! Clear for action!' And so they begin to clear for action. Mike—"

Mike was trying not to listen. At the beginning of this he hadn't been feeling any too well, and now that Horace kept talking about him being on the deck of a ship and all that— Damn him, what was the idea of sticking his best friend into a story, anyway! There were a lot of things about Horace that Mike didn't quite like, such as drinking a cup of coffee halfway and then dropping cigarette butts into the cold remains, and wearing a bathrobe which hadn't been washed since Horace found it five years ago. And Horace, when he took off on a plot, was far too much to bear.

The story went on, but Mike closed his ears. He felt a little faint. An audition in the morning and, if he made it then he'd be playing piano for the Philharmonic. No wonder he felt that way. But he wouldn't drink. Maybe Horace had an aspirin in the bathroom.

Unnoticed by the other two, Mike got up and tottered toward the bathroom, tagged by Horace's ringing tones. It was quite unusual for Mike to have anything go wrong with him, for his reputation, for all of his apparent pale visage, was that he could be killed only with an ax. This worried him. And the condition was such that he soon found himself barely able to navigate.

Foggily he fumbled for the aspirin in the medicine chest, and, failing to find it, reached for the light. The metal string eluded him, and he sought to support himself by leaning against the washbowl.

He made contact. A blinding one! The light short-circuited with a fanfare of crackling!

Paralyzed and unable to let go, Mike sagged. He could still hear Horace as though Horace's plot was coming from Mars. He began to shiver and slump, and then, very quietly, he fell forward against the tub. A few seconds of consciousness remained to him, and he dimly sought to

16

pull himself up. He reached out with his hand toward the edge of the tub, and then came a surge of terror which momentarily gave him animation.

Even as he reached out with that hand it was disappearing!

From fingertips to wrist to elbow!

Vanishing!

With a quiver, he shifted his fading gaze to his other hand, but it, too, was missing. And his legs were missing and his shoulders were missing—

There wasn't anything left of him at all!

The room was wheeling and dripping. He sought to howl for help.

But he didn't have any mouth with which to howl.

Michael de Wolf was *gone!*

Some time after, Jules, much pleased about the plot now, got up to take his leave.

"That ought to make a fine story, Horace. When do you think you'll have it finished?"

"Oh, maybe six weeks," said Horace. "Maybe a little longer."

"Good," and then Jules looked around to say good night to Mike. But Mike was not to be seen. He never wore a hat, and so there was no way to tell whether he remained in the apartment or not.

"He beat it, I guess," said Horace. "He's probably sore about my using him as a character in this story."

"He's a good one, though," smiled Jules. "Well, good night, Horace. I'll call from time to time to see how you are getting along."

"And I'll be getting right along, too," said Horace. "In fact, I'm going to start in on the first chapter right away."

Jules left, and Horace pulled his mill to the forward part of the desk, brushing the alimony duns into the wastebasket, and soon there was no sound in the apartment beyond the rapid clatter of typewriter keys.

CHAPTER TWO

There was roaring in his head and bitter water in his mouth, and all around him white froth and green depths intermingled furiously. Something crashed into his side, and he felt himself lifted up and cast down into silence, immediately afterward to be torn in all directions by a savage, snarling cyclone of spray and undertow. Again he was slammed brutally into fanged rocks and heaved up and over, to land upon soggy solidity.

The next wave mauled him and tried to get him back, but he still had enough wit about him to dig his fingers into the sand and essay a crawl to a higher level. After that the surf, booming about its losses, only reached his feet.

Mike de Wolf was ill. He had swallowed a gallon or two of the sea, and his stomach disliked the idea. There was blood on his hand and upon his cheek, and his head ached until he had no memory whatever of what had happened to him. Exhausted, he could not move another inch up the strand. Far off sounded a rattle of musketry, but it fell upon disinterested ears. The world could have ended at that moment and Mike de Wolf would not have cared.

How long he lay there he had no way of knowing, but when he came around, the back of his neck felt scorched and he himself was hot and gritty and bothered by the flies which hovered above and settled upon his wounded head. There was no further sound of firing. Instead, there was a faint whir, reminiscent of a typewriter, which seemed to come out of the sky.

He groggily sat up. Something within was telling him that if he stayed there he would invite even further disaster. But—where else could he go?

Immediately before him were a toothy series of rocks awash in a restless sea. To his right, a craggy point reached up and out, a brownish silhouette against a crystal blue sky. Reaching away illimitably was the sea, quiet and sparkling and full of the whole spectrum.

Where was he, and why?

He turned his head and winced at the pain it brought him. Behind him lay a tangle of brown and green foliage, a wall reared up out of the gleaming yellow of the sand. This beach was not deep, and it ended at one end with the point and at the other with a tumble of gray-blue stones.

He tried to rise and abandoned the effort as impossible, at least for a while.

What place was this?

A few pieces of wood were being nagged by the grasping waves. They were round and broken, and lines trailed from them. And now that he had seen them he also saw more wreckage adrift upon the waves.

Suddenly he was beset by an incredible memory. He had been standing on the deck of a galleon when two pinnaces had surged up under oars to begin to hull the tall vessel 'twixt wind and water and to sweep the decks with musketry so diabolical in its accuracy that four helmsmen in a lump were beside the wheel. And then he remembered spars coming down in a deadly rain and a musketeer in the tops diving for the sea and striking the deck instead. And the scupper ports had opened their leather mouths, and from the sodden slain a series of red rivulets gathered into one and drooled into the sea. The galleon's list had increased, and then, alone upon the quarterdeck, Mike had seen half-naked men, burned black with sun

20

and powder, come swarming aboard, smoke sweeping back from their linstocks—

He was crazy—that was it. He'd eaten too much lobster and had had a nightmare, and it had driven him crazy. How else could one account for it?

He recollected dimly that a man in a plumed hat had bowed to him with the words: "Your lordship commands that we open fire?" And that had been the start of the chaos.

Mike held his head in his hands, for the world was beginning to wheel and dip once more. His feeble attempt to understand his condition and his weird displacement had been too much for his sun-scorched brow.

"Your lordship?" Now why in the devil had anybody said that to him?

The sun—that was what was making him feel this way. He had to get out of it, no matter what the struggle cost him.

He was reaching forward with his right hand to take another step when the sand fountained almost between his fingers. He snatched back. A report came to him, and then several more. He stared at the rocks at one end of the beach and saw smoke spouting thickly.

Somebody was shooting at him! And he wasn't even armed!

The pain in his head vanished and he scuttled with all speed for the green-and-brown cover. When he reached it, a bullet-plucked twig smote him stingingly upon the cheek.

There was a yell, and the thudding of approaching feet. "There he went!" "In there!" "Get through and cut him off, the swine!"

A pistol slug plowed earth beside his foot, and he crawled faster. Who the devil were these people, and why?

"Get behind him!" roared someone.

21

"Aye, aye, Dirk!" came from within the woods.

The sound of a horse came from the other direction on the beach. Men were threshing through the tangle and shouting to one another, coming nearer and nearer.

He felt like a rabbit, having no arms whatever. If only he had a gun or—

Clank!

He felt himself smitten about the waist, and lo! he had a buckler and sword! The rapier lay naked in the sling, without a scabbard, the way bravoes wore them of old. The hilt of the weapon was gold, and studded with round-cut precious stones. And in clear letters on the steel was stamped "Toledo," and "Almirante de Lobo."

Mike stood it as long as he could. The inanity of the business made him angry and the thought of lying there like a badger to be torn up by hounds gave him strength enough to rear up and grasp the hilt of the long blade and haul it free from the buckler. He took several stiff-legged strides and came out upon the sand.

Four dark-visaged swashbucklers, weapons alert, confronted him.

"There you are!" cried the black-bearded giant. "Hallo-o-o, Red, we've got the don!"

The point of the rapier licked the air. "You'll never take me alive," said Mike. "Use your pistols, you English dogs, or I'll spit you like a roasting chicken and feed you to the sharks!"

"By gad, he's got spunk!" said Dirk, the giant, merrily. "I'll take you on meself, me bucko, and send your ears back to 'is most Catholic majesty with the compliments of me bully boys. Lay on, me lace-petticoated papist, and 'ave a taste o' Manchester steel." Dirk's cutlass flashed before Mike's calm face, and the others, drawing, rushed forward.

Assailed from four sides and, presently, from eight, Mike sent the rapier singing into the throat of one and then into the heart of another before the weapon was struck from his hand. Bare-breasted to their steel, he stood erect to receive it. And the six, with a yell, dashed in.

"*Stay!*" came a clarion voice. "Back, you gutter sweepings!" And Mike was stunned to see a great bay horse come thundering into their midst to send them sprawling, but to miraculously miss him. And he was more than stunned to see its rider.

A flame-headed woman, imperious and as lovely as any statue from Greece, was upon the bay's sidesaddle. Her white linen gown was sewn with pearls about the throat and a wide hat dangled from its silken strap at her back.

"Back, I say!" she commanded. "You, Dirk! Have up the gentleman's sword and give it to him by the blade—if he'll permit a fatherless varlet to touch it!"

Mike accepted the hilt of the weapon and slid it back into the buckler.

"Begone, you wretches!" cried the girl. "Or I'll ha' ye flogged from St. Kitts!"

"Your father—" hesitated Dirk.

"Handle yer bloody business, you fumbling oaf, and I'll handle my father! Get ye hence afore my groom puts spirit into ye wi' the cat!"

They fell back away from Mike, and a Nubian nearly seven feet tall coming up with chest heaving and skin agleam flourished a nine-tailed lash until it screamed avidly.

Dirk and his men retreated in good order, looking back as they went, sour about the loss of a don. Fifty paces away, Dirk drew himself up and cried: "He's a Spaniard, your ladyship, and ye'll ha' a sorry time keeping him against the town!"

"You'll have a sorry time swinging from a gibbet!" cried her ladyship. "Get hence!"

The sailors went straggling out of sight beyond the boulders at the far end of the beach.

Swish!
Swirl!

Mike was cloaked in black silk! And upon his head was a wide-brimmed hat with an enormous plume!

Mike felt weak and shaky, but he swept the miraculous hat from his bare head and bowed deeply to her. Midway in this operation the world's light went on and he pitched forward on his face into the sand, his fall cushioned by the corpse of a sailor he had slain.

CHAPTER THREE

Mike luxuriated in the huge bed. The four posts were tall sentinels guarding his rest, and, if they were not enough, the doors to the place were massive enough to stop a battering-ram. It was comparatively cool even here inside the netting. His head was bandaged, and his side was taped, and he smelled of rose water. He was only half awake, and so his surroundings did not particularly startle him, for Mike had slept in many a bed in many a clime.

After a while he'd get up and practice a while and then maybe call Kurt von Rachen and have a round of golf. Summer seemed to be here in earnest. Almost tropical, it was.

A set of hinges creaked and a round black head was thrust through the door. Then, more bravely, the servant, clad only in a white gown, came shuffling to the bedside to lift the netting and slide the tray onto the silken coverlet. He patted up the pillows behind Mike's head and helped him sit erect and then placed the tray on his lap. As quietly, the servant went away.

Mike was coming around now. He tried to remember what friend he had who owned a place like this and had black servants. But evidently—

The memory of the encounter on the beach brought him upright so hard that he almost spilled the tray. He looked at the netting and then at the coverlet and then at the massive stone room. Somewhere a surf was beating, and nearer palms were clattering languid fronds.

25

Where the hell—

He caught the tray just in time to keep from losing it. There was a fragrant melon, cool and luscious, a bottle of Madeira, a few sweet buns and a small pot of coffee. And propped against the coffee was an envelope.

Mike picked it up and read: "To the gallant captain."

"Huh," said Mike. He smelled it and found that it was old English lavender. "Hm-m-m!" said Mike.

He broke it open and found a copper-plate hand had written:

Sir;

I am grieved at the discourtesy which greeted ye upon our land and beg to tender my sympathy and the hope that your woundes paine you not this day. It is not the waye of the English to morder theyre captives particularly when they have beene gallant and strong in conflicte. Please accept our guarantye of our protection and hospitalitey as a smalle pyment for the injustices and horrores through which ye have been brought low. If I may so humbly request, should youre fever not be too great, I plead to attend you in your chamber come the afternoon.

Lady Marion.

Mike smelled the letter again and then laid it carefully beside his pillow. He poured himself a stiff jolt of wine and downed it while he poured.

He had been in many a strange situation in his life. As a matter of fact, his life had been full of strange situations, for he had long pursued a course of dabbling with anything which happened to attract his eye, and then, when he had failed in it, to go on to something else. Music had been the only stable commodity in his restless existence, and—

Gosh! That audition!

He'd worked hard for months to get it, and he'd practiced his fingers to stumps to prepare for it, and now—

He made a sudden effort to get up, but it made his head throb and he sank back. Might as well have some more wine, he mused. And he did.

Where was he, and why was he? And had it been he who had lain two sailors low with a rapier?

Again he was jolted. In his realm, men who killed people usually wound up with a rope about the neck!

And, as if in answer to his misgivings, there came the sound of voices from the yard below, voices which swelled into a wave of anger. Mike listened tensely. He could not tell what the words were, but he could make out a single voice which seemed to be trying to placate the mob. Shortly, amid jeering and catcalls, the babble melted away, leaving only the surf and the palm fronds.

The black head was poked in the door again and the servant soft-footed up for the tray.

"What was all that racket?" said Mike.

"Them people from de town," said the Negro.

"What did they want?"

"Dey say mahstah more better give up Spaniard, suh. Dey say dey like hang Spaniard."

"Spaniard?"

"Yas, suh," drawled the Negro. "Dat's you, suh?"

Mike blinked. "B-but why do they want to hang me?"

"Ah guess it's on account of you is a Spaniard, suh."

"Spaniard! I'm no Spaniard!"

The servant's eyes went very wide. "You isn't, suh?"

"Hell, no! I'm . . . I'm an Irishman!"

With effort, the servant brought himself back to the instructions he had received. "Missy Lady say she want know answer, suh."

"Tell her I'll see her right away," said Mike.

Lady Marion! If that had been Lady Marion on that bay, haughty and commanding and beautiful to the point of pain, Mike felt that his luck was definitely in. What a woman!

Immediately, Mike being Mike, he cast about to find some way of making himself a little more presentable. He smoothed at his hair and was startled to discover the bandage and to find how his head was throbbing under it. And when he moved, his side throbbed, too. He'd been banged up, it seemed, but just how he could not exactly recall. He knew that the ache in his skull was probably the reason he could not think straight. He felt he ought to be much more alarmed than he was.

Well! If Lady Marion was going to pay a call, he certainly did not want to be found in bed, undressed. At a cost of many winces, he got up the netting and put his feet on the floor. What a strangely furnished room this was! Massive chests all studded with golden nails, tapestries covering the stone walls, a shield and a battle-ax decorating the space between the windows.

Mike gave his attention to the problem of clothes. There on the chair was a pile of garments, evidently smoothed out and intended for his accouterment. Mike hobbled to them and picked them up, examining them with definite dismay. Silk stockings, black and sheer, puff-sided knee breeches, also black, and a shirt to match. And lace! There was enough lace on the cuffs of that shirt to wrap a damsel from head to toe. It was beautifully worked with gold points along the edges, but it didn't seem to Mike that lace was quite the thing to wear when meeting a lady. The lace collar was pointed to stand up behind the head, and it also was heavy with gold. And the white doublet and the white half cape were braided and gold-buckled until they weighed pounds. What a weird outfit!

And yet, as he looked at it, it seemed familiar and even proper. Despite the fogginess of his head, he felt that there was something about this which harbingered a discovery of a new past stretching, forklike, behind him.

He dropped the clothes and went searching for more

28

appropriate gear, but nowhere could he find anything even slightly resembling tennis slacks or polo shirts.

The black servant came drifting in with the noise of a shadow. He expressed no surprise at seeing Mike out of bed; rather, he expressed surprise that Mike would seek to dress by himself.

"I help," said the servant. "Missy say when you send me, she come." And he solemnly began to sort out the clothing on the chair, selecting the breeches as first.

Mike stared at them in dismay. They were silly-looking things. The cape he could understand, and even the doublet. But those breeches and that silken hose—

"Ole man sea raise ole Harry wit dese silks, suh. I try mah bes' to fixum, but dey don' fix so good."

"Was . . . was I wearing those yesterday?"

"Oh, yas, suh. 'Deed you was, suh. We wouldn't have no Spaniard fashions in dis yere house, suh."

The boy seemed determined to put them on him, and Mike was too groggy to resist. He was shaved and steamed and hauled at and tugged at until he closed his eyes with complete resignation. The pain in his side was terrible! And when this black boy girded up the hugely buckled belt about the doublet, Mike nearly yelped.

After a while the servant backed off from adjusting the gigantic gold buckles of the shoes and produced a brush to go to work on what of Mike's hair appeared below the head bandage. It seemed to Mike that there was quite a bit of that hair.

At last the black boy helped Mike to a full-length mirror. Mike had thought to find himself very strange, and he was astonished to discover how very usual he looked to himself. In fact, it seemed to him that if he hadn't looked so, it *would* have been strange.

The mirror gave back the tall, supple image of a Spanish gentleman, aristocratically handsome head backed by the upstanding lace collar, pale but strong hands barely showing under the folds of gorgeous lace, slim and shapely legs backed by the flowing cape which dropped from one shoulder. He was Mike de Wolf, but somehow he wasn't Mike de Wolf. There was a commanding poise about him which was an intensification of his usual manner, and in his face showed a pride of being and a consciousness of station which the old Mike de Wolf would not have had at all. He was grand and handsome and dashing, and, all in one, he was quite confused about it.

The black boy dropped the wide buckler over his shoulder and secured the sword in it. Mike almost failed to note that there was something unusual about that sword today. Its hilt was of unfaceted precious stones, set in beautifully wrought gold, and its scabbard was ornamented by two golden serpents, one on either side— The scabbard! Yesterday it had no scabbard, and Mike knew enough about swords and rapiers to know that each was fitted to its own. And he was certain, now that he thought of it, that he had not been wearing this cape when he had come through the surf.

Strange, but he could swear that he heard a typewriter running somewhere.

"You may now summon your mistress," said Mike, and as he watched the boy to the door he wondered a little at his change of speech. How grandly formal had been those words, and how melodious his tones. Truly, wherever he was and why, there were some improvements which he could not discount.

He stood by the window, looking far out across an unfamiliar sea, one hand resting on the hilt of his sword, the other lightly touching the draperies at the height of his head. It was an easy, graceful pose.

The door opened and Mike did not immediately turn. He heard the rustle of silk and then the lady was bowing. He bowed low in return.

"I am indebted to your ladyship for my life," said Mike.

"And I, your lordship, am ashamed for the conduct of those sailors." She spread her loose skirts out as she sat in a carven chair and smiled upon him. "I trust your lordship is much recovered from the ill effects of the sea?"

"Thank you for your tender concern, milady. I am a little weak, but otherwise quite well." He made a slight motion toward the yard below. "I seem to be guilty of bringing threats upon your house."

"Lord Carstone cares nothing for that. He would not have you Spaniards think us murdering barbarians, and he is gone even now to have a pinnace brought up into the cave of yon point to take you to safety—providing, of course, that your people can furnish some slight ransom to remove the stain of guilt from his lordship."

Mike was bewildered at the next words which nearly left his lips. And those words were: "Milady, I am Miguel Saint Raoul Maria Gonzales Sebastian de Mendoza y Toledo Francisco Juan Tomaso Guerrero de Brazo y Leon de Lobo." But they went no further than his mind. Instead he heard himself say:

"Milady, please disabuse yourself of this belief that I am a Spaniard. True, I come before you clothed as an accursed don, and true, I was aboard the *Natividad* during the action, but I, milady, have the honor of being Michael O'Brien, an Irish gentleman of family, at your service and indebted to you for your hospitality."

She looked incredulously at him, at his Spanish cape and Toledo sword, at the pale aristocracy of his visage and the slender body within the silk.

"Not a Spaniard? God's breath, milord, you jest!"

"That I resemble a don, I avow. When the great armada of his most Catholic majesty was smashed by the brave English a few decades ago, my grandfather was cast up on the shore of Ireland, storm driven and perishing. He was taken into the castle of Lord Dunalden, and there met my grandmother, his future wife, an Irish gentlewoman. I am the last of their family and, much against

31

my own wishes, I sought my fortune in Spain. I was being sent here to the West Indies to take command of a mine when our fortunate accident took place off this island. I care nothing for my Spanish forebears after I have been with them. I repeat, milady, that I am an Irish gentleman, unfortunately part Spanish, thrown upon your mercies and your hospitality. If I must pay ransom, then let it be sufficient unto the dignity of a Dunalden."

Plainly, she was fascinated by him. Her tawny eyes examined him more minutely, and her lips were a little parted with wonder at him.

"Then . . . then you were not in command of that Spanish vessel?"

"I was not, milady," said Mike, and knew that he lied, but was powerless to correct that lie.

"You . . . you are a Dunalden?"

"Aye, milady. That I am also Spanish is only a whim of the Almighty."

"Prithee, milord," she said, standing, "have no fears of your treatment in this house. You are welcome as long as you like, for we must be given a chance to wipe away this ill-considered insult. Lord Carstone will be pleased at your presence tonight at supper. And now I must not further weary you. Good afternoon, milord."

Mike bowed deeply and felt his side was being torn out of him. He watched her as she went through the door, side or no side, for she had a graceful, regal way of walking which made him warm all through.

When she was gone he sank down on the bed and lay out at full length. God, what a woman! She was about five feet nine—some four inches shorter than Mike—and she had the poise of a queen. But she needed no crown. She had been born with it—her hair. How long and lovely she was! More of flame than of flesh. And those eyes— When they raked him they bathed him with ecstasy! Never had Mike—even Mike!—seen a woman like her.

And then, slowly, thoughts of her became confused in

his own puzzle. Where was he? Why? And what time? Surely no woman had worn clothes like that since the early seventeenth century. Pearls in her hair where they made her coiffure flame the more, a great lace collar about her sweet throat to make her skin seem all the more white by contrast, a tight-bodiced gown which set off every curve of her delicious figure— She was something out of Van Dyck! All blue of gown, cream of lace, red of hair. And his thoughts drifted back slowly again to his problem.

Evidently, Mike decided, he had received a knock on the head which had brought on delusions. Yes, that must be it. And he felt sorry for himself. Besides, his head did ache dreadfully, and he loosened his collar and shed his cape in order to relax and try to sleep. Maybe when he woke, all this would be gone and he would be back in time for his audition with the Philharmonic. He'd have to tell Horace about this. Might make a good yarn for him—

He sat upright so abruptly that he nearly tore his head off.

Horace!

Horace Hackett!

Why, he'd been talking about buccaneers and the West Indies and Spanish gentlemen and a hero named Tom Bristol— The light cord, the vanishing limbs— And Horace had said Mike was the perfect part for the villain of the piece— And Jules had grinned and agreed—

Horace Hackett! And his novel, "Blood and Loot," a tale of buccaneering on the Spanish Main when the English and French sought to stem the tide of the Spaniards and wrench from them some of the riches grasped in the early days of discovery.

"Blood and Loot," by Horace Hackett!

Then Mike grinned wearily. Well, that was that. He'd been listening to the plot, and he'd gotten a knock on the head, and now, of course, he was dreaming. Well, 'twas a

33

pity to abandon such a lovely lady, but a dream was only a dream, and one had to get some more sleep to audition at the Philharmonic. Ho-hum. And Mike de Wolf, convinced as a dreamer is always convinced that he was not even awake, went off to sleep.

Some hours later Mike awoke and the room was dark. A few stars twinkled in the rectangle of open window, and the surf was quiet. The palm fronds no longer rattled. Mike, yawning, reached for the table where he always kept his cigarettes, but there was no table. He reached farther. Still no table. Instead, his questing hand connected with a bell cord, and to steady himself he gave it a strain. Somewhere near a bell jingled, and the black servant slid in, carrying a taper.

Mike stared at the fellow in disbelief. He had sold himself the dream idea so completely—

"Supper ready in mos' an hour, suh," said the boy. Like a white-gowned ghost he went drifting through the room, lighting tapers. One by one the objects appeared which Mike had seen before. And then, looking down at himself, he saw that, while his shoes had been removed while he slept, he was still clothed as before.

"Boy!"

"Mah name Jimbo, suh."

"Boy, what's the date?"

"Don' guess Ah knows whut you is talkin' about, suh. We ain't got no mo' eatin' dates, iffen that's whut you mean."

"The date," persisted Mike. "The month, the day, the year."

"Seems like I heerd somebody say this was somethin' like sixteen hunnert and forty, suh, but Ah wouldn' know."

"What?"

Mike was so startled by the statement that the boy, Jimbo, almost dropped the taper.

"That's three hundred years ago!" wailed Mike. "That's impossible!"

He slumped back on his pillow and stared groggily at a lizard which walked upon the ceiling, stalking a fly. Sixteen hundred and forty! Those clothes matched the date. So did his rapier, the ship yesterday, the sailors, the Lady Marion's speech, and her clothes—all, all added up to sixteen forty! And yet—somehow it wasn't.

He had heard of time travel, and he'd also heard of lunacy, and the way he felt right now, he was more willing to grant the latter. Was this a movie set, made of cheesecloth and propped with sticks? That thought brought him up and made him kick the wall, but, hobbling about and nursing his wounded toe, he decided that it was not a movie set and made the decision with profanity.

When Mike quieted he fell to wondering on the battle of yesterday. He remembered it very clearly now, recalled the soul-shaking thunder of cannon and the nasty sight of men being torn in half by chain shot and the all-too-real screams of suddenly shattered humanity. That battle had been no fake. And when he had run his rapier through those sailors on the beach that had been honest-to-God blood, and their death throes could not have been simulated.

Something else was coming over him now, a sort of strange belief in all this and a belief in his own part in it. Time travel? Well, if it was time travel, then how was it that he had managed the ship out there, knowing all its parts, giving the necessary orders, feeling a hatred toward the enemy which would never have existed in the heart of one who was wholly strange to the scene. No, he was not strange to this place or this time, for he had memory of it which, dim though it was, ran currently with his own life memory. And yet the memory did not seem anything from the past but from the immediate present.

Again he tried to lay aside the thought that this was "Blood and Loot," product of Horace Hackett's fertile if somewhat distorted imagination. These names, his own character, even this plot— Oh, no! My God, not that! Why, that would mean that he was Horace Hackett's villain in truth and in the flesh. And it would mean that he was in a never-never land where anything might and probably would happen. Where time would be distorted and places scrambled and distances jumbled and people single-track of character— Oh, Lord, not "Blood and Loot."

A horrible thought took him then and froze him to the bed. Horace Hackett's villains always suffered a frightful fate!

No, no, no, no, no, no, no!!!!!!!

Not "Blood and Loot"!

He was just going through a delusion brought on by that electric shock. He was just living in his own dreams after hearing Horace Hackett outline a plot. This place could not exist at all, either in time or in space.

Still—and he attempted to fend off that gruesome conclusion—he was definitely awake and sufficiently in his right mind to realize this was all wrong.

And if this was the Spanish Main in the year 1640, and if these people were English gentlefolk, and if those sailors had been Brethren of the Coast, and if he *was* Miguel Saint Raoul de Lobo, almirante of the fleets of his most Catholic majesty, then, b'Heaven and gazooks, this was the last island in the world where he should be! His strangely entangled memories gave off some facts about what happened to captives in this undeclared war.

He'd escape, that's what he'd do. And instantly he was reminded within himself that there were Caribs on this island in the interior, and that Caribs thought white flesh a luscious banquet. And besides, he couldn't escape, for what did he know about these guns and sword fighting and sailing a ship? If he tried to fight free, that would be

36

the end of him. In the interior he would be eaten. At sea he would drown. If he stayed here he'd be discovered and strung on a gibbet—

No, no, no! This wasn't Horace Hackett's "Blood and Loot"! It couldn't be! It was just a nightmare. It *had* to be!

Jimbo fixed him up again and then helped him down the stairs. Mike was pleased to find that his side hurt much less and that his head did not ache at all. And again there was that sound of a typewriter.

He walked through a long hall and into a room where tall candles gleamed above gold dishes and crystal, and found Lady Marion there before him. He bowed elegantly to her—amazed at this graceful accomplishment of his—and she curtsied deeply back. His eyes were so taken up with her—for her gown was now amber, like her eyes, and cut very low at the front and back—that he failed to see Lord Carstone until a "Harumph! Har-r-r-umph!" appraised him of that presence. He bowed again to Carstone.

The fellow was almost as broad as tall, an overly upholstered giant sculped out of lard. Great gold chains gleamed against a flowered vest and green-and-red patterned coat; his calves bulged out of strained white stockings, and there were artificial roses on his shoes. His wigged head was a lump of putty sunk into a huge roll of cotton. All seven chins wabbled as he spoke.

"Milord," said Mike, "I am pleased at last having the pleasure of meeting my gracious host."

"Harumph, harumph," said Lord Carstone. "M' daughter tells me yer Irish, sir."

"I have that honor, milord."

Carstone inspected him. "Damme if ye don't look like a don. Well, well! Harumph, har-r-r-umph, my error. M' pardon, sir, and I bid ye welcome to my house. Gog's wounds, Marion, my wench, if he doesn't look like a double-damned don, at that! Well, no mind, no mind. Sit yer-self down and have at it, m' boy."

Mike seated Marion at the foot of the board and took his own station in the middle, but dinner was not yet to begin, for, with a clank and a creak, there entered a scar-let-coated, gold-braided, white-wigged, powdered fellow of about middle age, whose bearing and address were those of a soldier.

"Hah, capt'n!" said Carstone. "In time, I see, for din-ner as usual, eh? This is Michael O'Brien, an Irish gentle-man that we mistook for a don. Sir, Capt'n Braumley."

"Pleased and honored," said Mike, getting up and bowing. The captain bowed doubtfully and took his seat, with a clatter of weapons, across from the guest. Captain Braumley's battle-battered face was a little antagonistic.

"So it's Irish, is it? Blast m' blood and bones, what's this?" He looked hard at Mike. "Can't say as I've any belly for sitting to dine with a Spaniard papist!"

"Ye'll keep yer evil tongue in yer cheek, sir," said Marion with lifted chin, "or I'll have ye taught better manners by the gentleman himself. He's no common gut-ter-bred soldier!"

The captain choked on that one and became purple-hued. Mike had never seen anyone really turn purple from embarrassment before, and it was really amazing to see it. Bright purple.

"He's a gentleman, and he's at m' board," said Car-stone heavily, "and if ye can't be civil, he's welcome to run you through a time or two."

The fact that they both insisted on the fact that Mike was a gentleman seemed to mollify the captain at least to the point of civility. That the captain was not a gentleman he soon proved by his address to his dinner, which was as overbearing as his presence on a parade ground, and quite as loud.

"Forgive 'm," said Carstone to Mike. "You do look damned like a don. Fact, they're talkin' o' catchin' and

38

hangin' ye in the public square and burnin' ye in the bargain, so don't be too hard on the captain."

Being a gentleman was evidently important, thought Mike. But it didn't make one immune from villagers.

"Hanging and burning?" he said, spoon poised over his soup.

"Aye. Ye killed two sailors, I hear, and a damned capable piece of work, too, what's more. Throat and heart. Have you teach the capt'n here a trick or two with the sword, eh?"

The Captain glowered, but went on with his frontal attack, evidently supposing his beef still on the hoof.

Dinner sped by, plate by plate, and Mike was becoming groggy with the profusion of various kinds of meat when, at last, the parade stopped and the rear guard of wine began to come up.

"So yer Irish," said the captain.

"Aye," said Mike. "An' I take my mother's maiden name of O'Brien."

The captain thought he saw a joke in that and looked sly. "Was anythin' wrong with yer father's, or didn' ye ever know it?"

Carstone spilled his wine. Lady Marion went white and stood up so fast that the black servant behind her barely had time to get her chair out of the way.

"Sir," Mike heard himself say, "my grandfather was Martine Sebastian Jose Ignacio Tomaso Guerrero de Brazo y Leon, Knight of the Golden Fleece, Captain of the Cross, Lord of Toledo and Seville. My father, sirrah, was Lord Follingby, Terrence O'Brien."

"Then you *are* a don, b'Heaven!" cried the captain. "Guts and gadflies, Carstone, ye'll have a don at your board and keep him from the town! I'll have my garrison here within an hour!"

"You'll be dead within an hour," said Mike coolly. And his blade leaped from its scabbard and flashed as it

39

danced across the board. He leaped between the tall candles and jumped down in such a way as to bar the exit of the captain.

"I'll not kill you with this, for it takes no stain of filthy blood," said Mike. "But pistols, Lord Carstone, are in order for two."

"B-but you're really a don!" said Carstone.

"I choose to call myself Irish, and my allegiance is English," said Mike. "If the clod here can stomach the pistol's mouth, have them out and we'll to it!"

"You call me coward!" roared the captain, his own blade shrieking from its sheath.

Mike was forced to give way before the lightning thrusts which sought his throat. For an instant he was paralyzed by the certain knowledge that he knew nothing whatever about swordsmanship! The singing steel blades clashed with desperate thrust and more desperate parry, and Mike went up the stairs of the hall two steps. He knew he needed all his eyes for that magically shifting point which sought his heart or throat, and yet he amazed himself by saying coolly:

"Your permission, milady. The beggar seems a bit insistent."

What the devil made him talk like this? And was that sound he heard a typewriter? It *must* be!

Marion stood in the doorway of the dining room, light from the lantern there throwing molten beams into her hair. Her lips were parted in fascination, and her eyes were over-bright.

Mike went through the other's guard in a false return, leaped back, parried with a quick cutover, attacked with a flying return so swift and adroit that Captain Braumley was disarmed so suddenly that he stood staring at his empty hand while his rapier went clanging over the stones to bring up loudly against the wall.

Mike then used his blade as a whip and began to cut the low-born captain about the back and buttocks until

Braumley howled in pain and protest at the abuse, stumbling backward and striving to fend off that merciless blade with his extended hands:

"I apologize!" wailed Braumley.

"Out, offal," said Mike, catapulting the fellow through the door and down the long curving steps. And when Braumley had fallen the flight, Mike seized the fellow's sword and flung it after him.

Leaning upon his sword at the top of the steps, Mike said: "Thank your pagan god, blackguard, that you're oaf and no gentleman, else my clean blade would have drunk your blood to death!"

Braumley, moaning, picked himself out of the refuse in the yard and, retrieving his sword, slunk swiftly off into the gateway and down the hill to the town.

Mike turned with a gallant bow to the Lady Marion. "Forgive me, milady."

Her voice was throaty with emotion. "He . . . he insulted you in our house. The . . . the right was yours—"

"Then I am forgiven?" said Mike.

"Aye," she said, faint-voiced. And then she fled down the hall and closed the door of the drawing room behind her.

Mike went back to Carstone, who poured him a glass.

"Sorry, sir," said Mike.

"Oh, bosh and fiddlesticks, m' lad; these things happen. Frightful bore, anyway. Drank m' wine and made love t' me daughter. Swine, swine clear through, m' lad. Have another glass. Cawn't say I've enjoyed anything so much since my brindle bull whipped Snarling Laddy in '21. Besides, I owed him money."

"I trust I didn't frighten Lady Marion too much."

"Frighten! *Hah!* Why, m' lad, there's a wench! There, m' lad, is a wench. Damme if she didn't run away, at that. Show, all show. You'll know these women after a time. Daresay when yer as old as I am and you've known as many, you'll understand. But there's a wench, that Marion. She thinks she's sick at the sight of blood and violence, but what are women but violence and blood, what? I say, m' lad, I'd never question the word of a gentleman, but are you sure you weren't in command of that ship out there the other day?"

"I?" said Mike, smiling.

"Well, we've had a bad time about dons. Papists and all that. Lord Buck'n'h'm—Steenie, you know—made all sorts of blather over papists. He's dead, but the English are still stirred up about the dons. Now, bein' a political power, I know somethin' about it and religion—well, what's religion? I make no bones about it, damme eyes. I want what the Spaniards have, and so I'm made to preach against 'm. Y' know, most of m' trade is done with the buccaneers, and so we keep 'em worked up about the dons. Well, have another glass. A man can't help his grandfather. Lord of Toledo and Seville, you say? Well, well. I'd say there's only one don I'd like to see swing, and that's the fellow they call Miguel Saint Raoul de Lobo, lord high admiral of his most Catholic majesty's navies in the New World."

Mike felt a jolt and a realization of identity with that same lord high admiral. In fact, it was coming to him that he *had* commanded the *Natividad* in the recent action, and *was* Miguel Saint Raoul de Lobo. He felt faint, but he heard himself say, offhand:

"Yes? Can't say as I know the gentleman. What have you against him in particular?"

"Well, m' lad, I'm a businessman and a good one. England may have no right at all to these colonies, but as long as I can keep the buccaneers hard at it—the English and the French both—why, the Spanish cargoes find their way to England through my clearing house. We might as well be frank about it. It's damned good business. Spain is rich. Why should she begrudge a few millions in bullion? Eh? And these seas are swarmin' right now with English

42

and French adventurers. So business is very good. But m' intelligences from Spain tell me the dons are sick of it. They've sent an admiral, and a good one, out here. Not one of your pap-suckling pansies, but a fellow that distinguished himself in the recent unpleasantness against th' English. But I'll ha' nothing to worry about soon."

"So?" said Mike.

"Aye. Y' see, there's a young chap name of Bristol, good family but wild, cached from the navy, he was, that come out here to seek 'is fortune. Impressed Marion no end, and she gathered up his eyes and she's still got 'm. Likely lad, but wild. All steel and cannon shot, that's Bristol. Good-lookin', too. 'E come down here to take his ease with the brethren of the coast, and soon as they found out he was an ex-naval captain they gathered 'round. So, not wantin' to stop in the way of the lad, I outfitted a bit of a fleet to see how many cargoes he can bring back. I've faith in 'm, though I'd never let 'm know it. If he comes back with a good haul, why, the lads'll be tearing to go to sea at his heels again, and we've a force against Spain. If he's the boy he started out to be, why, there's even a chance that we can take a colony or two from the dons. I've given 'm letters o' mark as governor of this island, and I've offered him the hand of Marion herself if he can come back here with the head of this fancy lord high admiral dangling under his bowsprit."

"Quite a prize," said Mike jealously.

"Aye, quite a prize. If I hadn't done it, Bristol might not have tackled any Spanish first-line vessels. He'll be back here in a week or two, God willing, and he's hoping to bring home the pride of the navy of Spain as aforesaid."

"Head under the bowsprit, eh?" said Mike.

"Even that. If not now, then some day. The Spanish, y' know, sent this Miguel Saint Raoul de Lobo here to wipe up the English and the coast brethren, and what a joke on his lordship to come home under a bowsprit!"

"How . . . how," said Mike faintly, "will he know if he has the right man?"

"Why, 'tis simple. He's got some Maroons from the Panama coast that were slaves on the flagship when his lordship came over from Spain. They know him. Y' see, if we get him, we get the one man who has orders to wipe out the English, and we'll discourage another from taking the field against our thriving little colonies. Neat, eh?"

"You mean . . . mean that these Maroons will betray his lordship?"

"Betray! Why, 'tis plain to see you don't know this coast, m' lad. The Spaniards murdered Maroons until their arms were tired, and Maroons are fast friends of the buccaneers. They even wanted Bristol to go to the home where his lordship first put up and take 'm in 'is sleep. And maybe they'll do it. You can't beat a proud man like a Maroon and murder his wife and friends without him doing something about it, Indian or no Indian!"

"I daresay," said Mike, and memories were stirring uneasily where no past have been. "And this Bristol will soon be home, eh?"

"Right."

"By the way, milord, I'd like quite well to stay, but I can't have the town revolting against you because of my father and because of this Captain Braumley."

"But yer English sympathies and the word of a gentleman protect you," said Lord Carstone, all chins wagging. "And as for Braumley and all, he's no loss. I've but to say what happened. Damme, who's governor here? And you knowing Spanish—why, you can be of great help to me. In an intelligence way, you know."

Mike received the impact of the reason why Lord Carstone was being so nice to him. Mike could be so neatly used in this business that Carstone's eagerness quite blinded him to Mike's possible duplicity. A spy to the

44

Spanish, indeed. In the pay of the English! Unaccountably, Mike broiled within at the thought. But the fact was saving his life. For he, Miguel Saint Raoul de Lobo, lord high admiral of his most Catholic majesty's navy in the New World, would not last long the instant one Tom Bristol arrived home. His command of English, a thing so rare as to nearly excuse his "Spanish father," would not serve him once those Maroons laid eyes on him. He had a vision of raw-backed men dying in the sun while the lash still swooped down upon them, and gutted women lying in the charred wreckage of forest huts, and babies with their skulls smashed against rocks—Maroons! How they hated the Spanish. And with what cause!

He tried valiantly to figure an avoidance of the necessity to stay here until Bristol arrived. But a panting black brought news which saved his energy.

"Mah lord," said the black, bowing to the floor, "guard say come run and tell quick. Cap'n Bristol just now pass he fleet in by light."

And the thunder of saluting guns tore apart the night to confirm the news.

CHAPTER FOUR

In the cool, dark depths of the Vagabond Club on Fifty-fourth Street, Horace Hackett limply regarded a half-empty glass, a perfect picture of an author who has finished a day's stint and who hopes his virtuousness will be noticed. His sport coat was unbuttoned to relax his rotundity, and his pink-and-purple tie was askew; he needed a shave and seemed to be in a bad state of disrepair, hair in eyes and cuffs none too clean.

He was wholly unconscious—so far as anyone could tell—of the whisper across the room, to wit: "That's Horace Hackett, the popular novelist." And it was purely coincidental that Horace immediately sighed deeply and assumed a profound expression.

Winchester Remington Colt, the Western writer, came lounging in to the bar, his Stetson on the back of his head, his high-heeled boots loud upon the mosaic. "Gimme a shot of redeye, pard," he said to the English bartender. And because the English bartender was used to the various artists and writers and publishers who belonged to the Vagabond Club, he knew already that this meant a drink of King's Colony Scotch in soda, weak.

Winchester Remington Colt wrapped a pale hand around the glass and came striding along, having spotted Horace.

"Hello, Hackett, ole pard," said Colt. "Mind if I hunker down a spell? Reckon as how you been horse-whippin' the wordage from the way yore all tuckered

47

out." He was wholly oblivious of the whisper from the end of the room:

"That's Winchester Remington Colt, the Western writer."

"Worn to the bone," sighed Horace, extending a hand so that Colt could see how his fingers were shaking. They weren't and so Horace made them shake a little. Colt wondered if Horace had ever bothered to clean his fingernails in his life.

"Book, I suppose," said Colt. "Doing a book myself. It's about—"

"Yes," said Horace hurriedly, "a book. Deadline right up on me, practically feeding it to the presses. It's called 'Blood and Loot,' a story of—"

"Is that so?" said Colt, his Western jargon getting lost now that he was talking in lowered tones to Horace. "My story is right up against the press, too. It's a fine yarn, though. Splendid setting. Early Southwest. Unusual, too. This sheriff has a son who isn't any good, and so when everybody accuses the boy of holding up the Wells Fargo office at—"

"Sounds fine," said Horace. "Yes, sounds fine. This 'Blood and Loot' is a story of the early buccaneers. You know, lace and tall ships and rapiers and two men fighting to the death over a lovely woman—"

"Is that so?" said Winchester Remington Colt swiftly. " 'Hell on the Border' has a swell heroine. She's a dance-hall girl that's trying to go straight, see? And so when she falls in love with the sheriff's son—"

"Well, well, well!" said Horace. "That does sound fine."

They gave up and sat moodily sipping their drinks. At last the plot-recital contest which so often baffles authors died out within them and they began to chat generally.

"This is a hell of a business," said Horace. "If I had it all to do over again, I would dig ditches for a living."

"So would I," said Colt. "Work, work, work, and where's it get you. Some day you turn in a sour one and then they say, 'Colt's slipping. He's a has-been.' And they forget about all the money you've made for them and they shake their heads. And then they're convinced that you're through, and so everything you send in gets put into the slush pile and read by the fourth assistant editor, and after a while they don't even send letters, just printed rejection slips. It's a hell of a life."

"Yeah," said Horace. "Just as if everybody didn't lay an egg at one time or another. It'd be different if editors were different."

"They're all a pack of bums," said Colt. "And what makes it so awful is that they never really know what the public wants. Why, sometimes you get a story through that they think stinks, and the public eats it up. And sometimes the story really does stink, and the public eats it up just the same."

"Yeah," said Horace. "Remember 'Gone with the Wind'?"

"Huh?"

"'Gone with the Wind.' All the waitresses and bus drivers thought it was swell, and what'd it have on the ball? Nothing, that's what. Any professional writer could really have done a good job on it."

"Oh, sure. I remember now. It was about a young guy whose father was out to kill him."

"Yeah," said Horace.

"Or was that 'Anthony Adverse'?"

"Yeah," said Horace. "But the point is, editors make me sick. They burn you out and squeeze you dry, and then they say you're a has-been. I ought to buy a farm."

"Farm?" said Winchester Remington Colt, stretching out his high-heeled boots. "I was on a farm once. For a week end. Hell of a place. Woke me up at ten o'clock in the morning, they did, after me not being able to sleep all night because it was so quiet."

They felt perfectly in accord now.

After a little, Horace said: "You know, I've been running across a funny thing lately."

"Yeah?" said Colt.

"I find out that it's a lot of bunk plotting the middle of stories out straight."

"How so?"

"Well, you get them going and they pretty near write themselves. That is, if the characters are good."

"Yeah. I've noticed that once in a while. You start a story and then it takes itself out of your hands and begins to go off as it pleases. Yeah, I've noticed that."

"Sure. You lay out the beginning and know how it's going to end, and it wanders around as it pleases in the middle. Course, you know the high spots, but even those take care of themselves pretty well if you have the effect you want in mind. This one I'm doing now started out to be a straight proposition, with the hero coming in as usual and getting mopped up by the villain and then mopping up the villain. But after I got it going I found out that the villain was a pretty interesting character, too, and so the thing is going to be pretty hot. Sympathetic from both sides, see? I figure maybe a villain, as a straight villain, is pretty hard to swallow. You know, a guy isn't all bad. So the villain's got his reasons, too. Now in this story the villain is going to fall in love with the heroine and it's going to make him as decent as can be. Course, he pulls a couple of dirty tricks and gives the hero some thinking, and there's a lot of fighting around, but the thing is handling itself, if you get what I mean."

"Sure, that happened to me in 'Hell on the Rio Grande.' It just rattled itself off as though I didn't have a thing to do with it. Sure, I knew the beginning and the end, but the middle just went racing along."

"It's funny," said Horace. "I get spooky about it sometimes. It's—well, it's as if we were perfectly in tune with the story. We don't have to think about it, it just sort of comes bubbling out of us like music."

"Yeah. I remember Mike saying one time that a story wasn't any good unless it came out that way. But, then, he's nutty on the subject of music and so it doesn't count. By the way, haven't seen him. He was supposed to come over to my apartment for a cocktail party last night, and he didn't show up. You seen him?"

"No. I think he got mad at me for saying I was going to use him for a story. He shoved off, and I haven't seen him since. But what I was getting at is the way you feel about stories sometimes. It's—well, sort of divine, somehow. Here we are able to make and break characters and tangle up their lives and all, and sometimes the characters get so big for us that they sort of write themselves, if you know what I mean."

"And you get a real kick out of writing it," said Colt. "You know how it's going to end, but you surprise yourself in the middle. Sure."

"Sure. Now I know how I started it and I know the conflicts and I know that in the end the hero knocks the villain off and gets the girl, but just how it's all going to happen I'm not sure. It just sort of happens."

"Yeah. Makes a guy feel funny. Like he's a medium, or something."

"No, I feel different than that. When I go knocking out the wordage and really get interested in my characters it almost makes me feel like—a god or something."

"Yeah, I know," said Colt.

"It's a great business," said Horace.

"Yeah. Sure. Nothing like being a writer."

CHAPTER FIVE

Mike de Wolf wandered in perplexity through the governor's great stone house. A year or two before this displacement into an apparent nowhere he had cruised the West Indies briefly in an attempt to shake off a siege of melancholy boredom—he had painted a few pictures of red-roofed houses and native women with baskets on their heads, and had then tossed the canvases overboard on the decision that he would never be able to paint—and he had seen St. Kitts from the windows of an automobile hired by tourist companions—who had bored him desperately.

Now, going to the great windows of a drawing room, looking down the hill from over the battlements to the town, he was recalled to an earlier visit here. This was Brimstone Hill, then. But how strange to find this mighty fortress all built and wholly solid if the year was 1640! This great fortress, he remembered out of the tourist's guide, was built after the American Revolution! And yet he had twice checked the date, and it was agreed that the year was 1640. In addition, as well as he could remember, there was something wrong with the geography. The harbor was nearly circular, and admission to it was gained through a very proper channel all set with flashing lights. He wasn't sure, but he supposed flashing lights to be a fairly modern invention.

Where was he, and why?

Brimstone Hill in St. Kitts solved it not at all, for this

was not really Brimstone Hill, and it was not really St. Kitts. And the dates were shuffled like the numbers on a deck of cards.

Late eighteenth-century masonry in the mid-seventeenth century. A twentieth-century dilettante of the arts masquerading as a Spaniard admiral in 1640.

And if this *was* St. Kitts, then where were the French, with whom the government had been shared by the British? And where was Sir Thomas Warner, who history said had been governor and practical owner of the place at this stated period?

Certainly this sort of thing would soon drive him mad. Nothing could be trusted. The first thing he knew, somebody would pull out a cigarette lighter and reach for a telephone, the while speaking archaic English on the subject of the doings of Charles I.

He moved out upon the balcony the better to see activity in the harbor. He felt assured that if he tried to escape from this place he would be stopped and suspected, and yet—Gog's blood, as Lord Carstone would say, he didn't dare stay here and face Captain Bristol and the Maroons! There were the vessels, all lights and activity, anchor chains rattling out as they took their anchorages. Seven there were, most of them small, about two hundred tons. Their type was difficult to establish for lack of daylight.

Where was he, and why?

He hadn't moved back into history, for history had never been thus, and so any time change was out. He hadn't ascended to another plane, for too much of this was definitely human earth.

His first guess about Horace Hackett had sent a chill prickling at the hairs of his neck. The last thing he had heard had been exactly this plot. "Blood and Loot" had contained these names— He revolted against the idea. Not Horace Hackett's story!

He had an image of Horace, girded about with a dirty bathrobe, surrounded by cigarette butts, unshaven and sweaty, hammering thunderously upon his typewriter, ripping off copy by the yard.

Mike cast his mind back over the events of the past two days. Two men he had killed on the beach and wounded another tonight. And he had bested them with a rapier—a weapon about which he knew nothing, but which, in his hands, became abrupt demise. And there was something else: his head felt quite all right, and the bandage about it had mysteriously vanished; further, his side felt as good as new, and there was no pull of tape there. What mad world was this in which a man became possessed of sudden talents and healed in minutes? And then his sword scabbard and cape and hat had appeared magically overnight.

His own conduct and his speech had not been Mike de Wolf. Could it be that he was actually taking on the character of one Miguel Saint Raoul de Lobo, lord high admiral of the Spanish fleet in the Caribbean? Certainly his memory was becoming padded with odd memories which had no identity with his own, Mike's, past.

He was recalling just now that a woman named Anne awaited at Nombre de Dios to call him "dear," and that a Carib slave girl, a princess among her savagely beautiful people, sat watching the sea from the window of a balconied casa. He was remembering the thin, rapacious evil called Father Mercy and the giant Trombo, so ready with a cat or a headsman ax and so devoted to his admiral.

He was remembering a yesterday of play amid orange blossoms at Valencia and a proud Spanish mother and father looking fondly upon him as a cadet of the king; a kiss stolen in Morocco; the thunder of his vessels' guns at Gonai; the shrieks of men dying in a mist of smoke; the whimper of wounded in the dark; the soft hands of a pope making him a Knight of the Cross; soft, sweet arms in the hot humidity of Panama; the dance of a buccaneer swinging from a gibbet; dispatches from the king—

His hands whipped to his doublet and parchment crackled there. He took out the packets with their broken seals, sea-stained and wrinkled, but proud with the arms of Castile and Leon. By the light of a guttering guard lantern he glanced at them. How familiar was that language! Spanish, but as clear as any English!

ALMIRANTE;

The English and French bore like evil worms into the glorious Empire of Spain beyond the seas, sacking cities and flaunting our troops and governors. You are given, as inclosed, commissions as Lord High Admiral of His Most Catholic Majesty's Navies in the New World, empowered to use all vessels and forces of defense to put down forever the English and French dogs. You are to take no cognizance of any letters or commissions but are to hang buccaneers as pirates wherever found. You are to wipe out the coastal villages of any Caribbean Indians found to be aiding the English and French. This is not official war and your discretion is solicited while your utmost endeavor is requested. May you again arise victorious above our enemies upon the sea and keep glorious the golden banner of your native land.

PHILIPPE
KING

Mike had the idea that he had read these before, but their import now was staggering. Dispatches such as these upon his person! And Braumley barking at the landing that a Spaniard was in the house of the governor. And from what he had heard of this Captain Bristol, he doubted not that the man would be thorough and demand that his Maroons be allowed to see the Spaniard. And these dispatches—they would mean his death! But he dared not destroy them and thus destroy his own authority. He swiftly replaced the papers in his doublet, glancing about to see that no one had seen.

56

He was barely in time, for a soft footfall sounded near him on the parapet. It was Lady Marion.

She had not seen him yet, for she was studying the harbor below, and Mike felt a sudden jealous pang.

"Milady," he said.

She started and then smiled uncertainly at him.

"The unfortunate lesson merited by Captain Braumley and administered by myself seems to have upset you. Forgive such actions on my part—"

Good lord! What was wrong with him that he had to talk such a stilted way? And— *Yes!* There was the sound of that typewriter again!

"They are already forgiven, sir."

"Again I thank you," and he bowed.

They stood there for a little time, looking down the steep hill at the fleet in the harbor, yellow jewels set sparkling into black satin. Mike looked at Lady Marion as much as he could without staring. She had drawn a thin white wrap about her shoulders against the cool wind, and the high collar of it put an outer halo about the halo of her hair. Mike thought about paintings of the masters and could find no face to compare with hers, no coloring to match the vibrant life of her own.

"Soon you will meet Captain Bristol," said Lady Marion at last. "I hope you will like him."

"My affections," said Mike, "are yours to command."

"He might ... hold your Spanish grandfather against you. I hope you will understand that he was once confined in a Spanish prison when storm drove him on the reefs of Spain, and was tried by the Inquisition and condemned to the auto-da-fé as an English heretic. With great skill and courage he managed his escape, but had to leave many of his crew to die or wear out their lives on the galleys. He is bitter."

"Is that why he seeks the Spaniard in these waters?"

57

"Aye, and other things. We have a right to this sea, and Captain Bristol believes it can be enforced."

"He is most optimistic, judging from what I have seen of the fleets of Spain."

"His men are wild devils," said Lady Marion. "The deadliest marksmen in the world are the buccaneers who made their living shooting cattle and other wild game in Hispaniola. They are the restless spirits who chafed under navy discipline and managed to desert, who flouted authority and order and came out to the New World in prison ships or merchantmen. Only Captain Bristol has been able to unite them into a fleet, and there is much hope that the power of Spain may be broken in these colonies."

"So Bristol dreams of the wealth of Peru," said Mike.

"Aye. And the power of the 'bloody flag,' " replied Lady Marion. "Some day the cross of St. George and not the cross of Spain will float above the Caribbean."

"You seem to share the ambitions of your men," said Mike.

"Of Lord Carstone, sir."

"From the way he talked about you this evening, he seems quite well pleased with the daughter he has raised. And with reason."

She looked musingly down across the harbor, and then, withdrawing from the battlement, wandered into the castle hall, Mike keeping beside her.

"There was a time, sir, when my father was not pleased," she said. "For a girl in the family of a great merchant is no asset—and he never had a son."

"But that is all forgotten. It must be, considering the light in which he holds you. Never have I seen a man so proud of a daughter—or a son, either, for that matter."

"Aye?"

They were in the drawing room now, and it seemed quite natural to Mike that, in the yellow glow of candles, the polished keys of a piano gleamed. She left him to pour wine at the sideboard, and he, magnetized to the instrument, seated himself on the bench. He blinked wonderingly at the gold letters: "Steinway, Chicago."

"They say," said Lady Marion, "that when I was born and he was told that I was a girl he went away and did not return for months, so great was his grief at the misfortune." There was sadness lurking in her voice, and she seemed to be speaking half to herself. She gave Mike a glass and clinked hers against his.

"To the Empire of England in the New World," she proposed.

"Nay," said Mike swiftly. "I drink only to your beauty."

Lady Marion smiled and lowered her glass, while Mike drank his to the bottom against the necessity to answer her toast. Putting it aside, his fingers strayed to the ivory keys.

"Your father did not strike me as being such a foolish man," said Mike.

"He was not being foolish," said Lady Marion, spreading out her skirts as she sank down into a chair. "Who could carry on his business? Who could direct his ships upon the seas when he was gone? Nay, I understand. But for many years I did not. I could not know why he was so careless of me. But when my mother died he changed."

Mike's fingers caressed a musing chord from the instrument, and it lingered in the room.

"He gave me presents after that. Funny presents like saddle horses and toy guns and a sailing boat. And because I was not yet nine I did not disagree, but played with them and enjoyed them. And when I would ride to hounds later on and take the brush before the first among the men, or when I would helm a boat to victory on the Thames in a race, or when I would down bags of birds with a fowling piece, he would be pleased. And because he was the only one I truly cared to please—for he's a

59

darling old brigand—I developed what are strange skills in a woman."

"I would rather you called it fascinating," said Mike, playing softly a few bars from Brahms as a background to her lovely golden voice.

"Aye, my gallant sir. You would turn it to account. But women are not happy when they are able to beat men at their own games. When they can slap the face of a cad and have at him at dawn upon the field of honor, and yea! walk away from his quivering corpse."

"You've done that?" said Mike, the piano suddenly still.

"And worse. I'm useless to myself and to the world, sir. What is a woman but a wife? And how happy is a wife who has a man weaker than she?"

Mike's fingers drew out melody from the keys. "I can understand. In a time when women are supposed to be all froth and faint, the masculine accomplishments must set ill upon one so lovely."

"It is funny, in a way," said Lady Marion. "I hope you forgive my statements and ha' no thought of my being an empty braggart, for these things to me are curses rather than accomplishments. Strange tastes for a lady. And how poor a sham am I. Tonight"—and her voice dropped a note and softened—"I almost was burst by my enthusiasm over your thrashing that vulgar hound, Braumley. I almost cheered my bravoes to you and shook your sword hand. But I tried to remember. I tried to be a lady. I turned and went away from men who would brawl before me. Of course, it was not your fault," she added hastily. "But, as I say, sir, I am a counterfeit. No men dance with me. They salute me. No men send me flowers for fear they'll be returned in a nest of white feathers—aye, and vixen that I am, I've done for, for I despise a coward. I am a lovely woman, you say, sir, but I am a sham as a lady. Ah," and she sighed, "would that I *had* been born the boy my father wanted."

60

Mike looked at Lady Marion and found her sweet in her melancholy. There was strength in this woman as there is strength in a hunting leopard, and there was also a straight-forward attitude, a fearless ability to look any man in the eye which a seeking gallant might find very disconcerting. This, then, was the riddle of this woman. The loveliness of a siren and the courage and accomplishments of a knight. She had looked with longing upon men and had found them wanting. What strength and what ability the man must have who would at last win her affection—for she seemed afraid of giving that affection to any.

Mike strayed into Mendelssohn and, for a little time, lost them in the ecstatic depths of music. But he grew conscious at last of her eyes upon him, and his playing softened so that he could speak above it.

"He that would hold you would have the rarest jewel on earth, milady. Sorrow about yourself is like an oyster feeling badly about his pearl."

"I am told," she said, "that pearls are caused by a grain of sand irritating the oyster." And then she smiled. "I have told you of my woes. You have a right to tell yours."

"Ah, but you would not believe mine," said Mike. "You could not understand the story of a man trapped into a world quite foreign to him, playing a role which he does not understand, distrusting the reality of all things on earth and above, seeing no reason and having his own outraged, believing that all will fade too soon, and grasping the fleeting instants of joy which, like gentle clouds hiding a scorching sun, too often and too swiftly blow away."

She was looking at him now, seeing him fully. And what a strange fellow she found him. A swordsman, better than an expert like Braumley, who could play better than anyone she had ever heard play, who could look like a king and talk like a poet. Ah, yes, he was a very strange fellow. A strangely fascinating fellow. Here was not the straightforward bravery of Bristol, but the ultimate in gentility. Fearing weakness in her eyes, no man had ever played to her or said such fragile things to her before. But, then, she sighed, there would be some flaw in him. There must be. There was in every other man. Some failing, perhaps a lack of courage in war or clearness in thought— With a start she realized that she had quite forgotten about Bristol, for a trumpet on the ramparts was even then beginning to bray of his approach.

Mike stopped playing and stood up. Far off they heard doors groan open and footsteps bang upon stone and iron and salutes from officers in the fort. And then they heard, at the other end of the hall, the hoarse boom of Carstone's welcome.

Mike fingered the hilt of his sword. Tom Bristol had come.

A coldly quiet voice was in conversation with Lord Carstone. Judging from the tones, the welcome speech had not been accepted, and there seemed to be deadly business afoot. Lady Marion stood straighter, seemingly comprehending the situation perfectly; she advanced to the door and threw it open to go up the hall and into the room with her father and Bristol.

"My intelligences," said the clear, cold voice, which evidently belonged to Bristol, "are quite different, sir."

"Aye, but damme, fellow, he's a guest!"

"Guest be damned, sir. I'll have a look at this don."

"He's no don," came Lady Marion's protest. "He's Irish."

"And perhaps, milady, a liar in the bargain," said Bristol steadily.

Mike could not see them, for they were in the dining salon. But he could see the guard, which had evidently come up with Bristol, and he liked the sight not at all. These brawny lads lounged in the corridor, whispering among themselves. They were sea-booted, and clad in gay but stained jackets and half breeches, and two of them wore headsilks, indicating that they were French. Swarthy and cruel of visage, they were quite obviously brethren of the coast, and the only thing which held their voices down was their presence here in the governor's fort and the fact that they were Bristol's escort. The eight of them in the corridor were complemented by five more in the balcony above the courtyard steps, five who guarded the offerings which Bristol had brought. Some twenty bearers, Maroons and Caribs, had eased down their heavy loads and now sat upon them awaiting further orders.

Mike did not know how it could be, but he recognized three of those Maroons. Tall, blade-faced fellows they were, not much darker than the English and French brethren, and certainly cleaner and taller. Their names, those three, were Catshy, Zuil and Suyda. Mike was so intent upon his own danger that he took these things as they came and did not question. There were three fellows which he had ordered flogged and thrown to the sharks, and yet—here they were. They knew him! Mike moved back from the door before he was seen. If he was clever about it, they'd never get a look at his face.

Meantime the argument raged and Captain Braumley's demands were added to Bristol's. "In the name of the crown, sir, we owe ourselves this much protection. If he is a Spanish officer and managed his escape, why, odd bodkins! he'll carry back a complete record of the disposition of our forces and know our harbor and the ships in our fleets, and he'll know where he can land his troops! I say it's only fair that Bristol has a look at him."

"Aye," said Bristol. "Better now than to see him victor above a field of battle he has won by means of his inspection of this place. This, sir, is war!"

"Damme if you don't paint a gruesome picture of it, lad," said Carstone. "Well, peel your peepers at him, as you sailors say. But mind you don't try to act the boor that Braumley did." Carstone chortled heavily. "Blind me, captain, but you *did* look the clown, rolling down those steps!"

"Very well," said Bristol, "Where is he?"

"In the drawing room," said the Lady Marion.

There was a sound of moving feet, and the buccaneers in the hall glanced at Bristol's face and loosened up their cutlasses in their bucklers and started to follow after.

"Stay!" said the Lady Marion. "Is this my home or a quarterdeck, sir?"

"Stand easy, lads," said Bristol. "The devil himself has never been known to fly."

The footsteps came on.

Mike stood beside the window, his face in dimness, his shadow painted gigantically upon an ancient tapestry by the guttering candles. His very first glimpse of Bristol told him that here was a man who would have to be removed if he himself was ever to be safe again.

Bristol was lean and hard. His handsome face was keen and strong. His eyes were as pale and cold as Arctic ice. He wore his own blond hair, and it came in a metallic sweep down to the shoulders of his flaring cloak collar. There was a hard steel quality about the fellow which Mike felt would, in itself, turn the edge of a battle-ax.

"Michael O'Brien," said Lady Marion, "Captain Thomas Bristol. Captain Bristol, Michael O'Brien."

Mike bowed stiffly. Bristol nodded. Their eyes, since they had first seen each other, had caught and held and did not relax now for an instant. There was war in the atmosphere.

"I'm told," said Bristol, "that you were cast up by the sea after the wreck of a galleon. A fortunate escape."

"Aye," said Mike. "And from your bearers out there I suppose you to have had a successful voyage."

"Passing," said Bristol. "Would you like to look at the loot?"

The question was a trap to get him into the sight of those Maroons, Mike knew. And yet it seemed a good bait to grab.

"Why, yes. I wouldn't mind," said Mike. "How many ships and prisoners did you take, if I might ask?"

"Sufficient," said Bristol.

"A glass of wine, gentlemen?" said Lady Marion, putting glasses into their hands and pouring.

They drank without relaxing their vigils over each other. Carstone was uncomfortable, and shuffled his feet and coughed. Braumley hovered just inside the door, ready for instant flight.

"The Spanish will weep when they hear of your success," said Mike.

"Aye. The English have wept too long," said Bristol.

"I might be persuaded to take one of your voyages with you," said Mike.

"I suppose you might," said Bristol. "And now, if you would like to look at the loot—" He turned to Carstone. "With your permission—"

But Carstone, while a good merchant, was not quick on his feet when it came to such subtle byplay. He mistook Bristol's design, or saw it not at all, for he said, "What? Look at it in the dark? Damme, Bristol, I thought you said that the presents—"

"Are yours, milord," said Bristol sharply in disappointment. "Have in the chests, Scudder!"

The word was passed, and the Maroons and Caribs again took up their burdens to bring them into the drawing room and strew them over it. Mike stood with his face out of the light, and Bristol had had no time to communicate his desire to the Maroons, and so they withdrew without noticing the guest.

Bristol flung open a few chests, and the candles made the jewels and gold pieces glitter and flame. He ran his hands through them and made them cascade back, letting some fall carelessly upon the carpet.

Carstone forgot all about this minor hostility and instantly began to open the rest of the chests and calculate their worth while Bristol stood back, still watching Mike. He seemed to find something deeper than a military menace in this stranger, for he was too brilliant, was Bristol, to fail to note that Lady Marion had sought to protect the fellow.

"And no prisoners for slaves?" said Carstone at last. "We've acres upon acres untilled for want of labor. And if you ran across galleys, certainly you brought their oarsmen with you."

"No galleys," said Bristol. "Only prisoners of war."

"Bah!" said Carstone. "There's no such thing existing as a state of war. Spain and England and France are all at peace. How can they be prisoners of war? There are fields lying fallow and cane to be planted. And the weaklings they empty out of English jails die like rats from this damned fever."

Bristol seized upon that. He faced the door and called. "Scudder! Have in Zuil for a message to the ships!"

Presently the tall Maroon came. He was loose of movement, very free, almost regal, for his father was a cacique. His lemon-colored body was proudly wound about with bloodstained calico to hide the marks of the Spanish lashes.

He did not bow to the company, but nodded to his captain.

"Zuil," said Bristol. "We've a few prisoners on the *Fleetfoot* which his lordship would like to see. Have them brought up."

"Aye, aye," said Zuil.

But Bristol did not let him go, and he cursed the man for not seeing the don there in the shadow. "Those on the *Fleetfoot,*" he repeated. "Dons. And we regret that Miguel Saint Raoul de Lobo is not among them."

"Aye, we regret it," said Zuil, a little puzzled by this loquacity in one so usually taciturn.

66

"Have them up right away," said Bristol, nearly swearing.

Zuil turned and went away. Bristol angrily drained off another glass of wine as a toast to eventual success.

"Been long in these waters?" said Bristol.

"No," said Mike.

"Wonderful place," said Bristol.

"Aye," said Mike. "Wonderful."

"Except for the fever," said Bristol. "That gets the best of them."

"Aye, it must," said Mike.

Conversation languished as though words perished in this highly electrified atmosphere. Several more glasses went the rounds and Carstone happily spent the time inspecting the spoils in detail. Bristol was getting madder by the minute, for a diamond necklace burned in his doublet to be clasped about the throat of Lady Marion. What a hellish homecoming! His eyes strayed to Mike continually and promised themselves compensation for this.

At last Zuil came back to say, "The prisoners are in the yard below, captain."

Bristol sighed with relief. "We'll go out and look at them. All of us," said he. "And you, too, O'Brien, for you must see how low these dons can be reduced."

There was no refusing that without arousing further suspicion, and so Mike trailed. He was somewhat startled to recognize his own hat, wide of brim and dark of plume, upon the piano as he passed, for he did not recall landing with a hat. He put it on and drew it down to mask his features, and so got through the buccaneers and then the three Maroons he knew. The light was too bad and their suspicions too sleepy in this fort for them to take heed.

The prisoners were a mixed lot, many of them common sailors, battered and dirty and despairing, a few were soldiers and marines, stiffer but no less wretched. Two of

67

them were officers, cloakless and swordless, but disdainful of their captors.

"Here they are, your lordship," said Bristol. "And a sorry lot they be."

"Aye, but slaves are scarce," said Carstone. And he started down at one end of the line, two boys bearing flambeaux beside him to light the yard, feeling muscles and looking at teeth, oblivious of the surly eyes of the captives. Carstone commented happily on each, calling off the faults.

The two Spanish officers were suddenly straighter and taller, but it was not they who betrayed Mike. He had lagged behind beside Lady Marion, listening to the chatter among the others.

And now, as they came to a mere child in the line, a ship's cadet from a gentle family, there was a sudden cry of gladness. Chains notwithstanding, the tiny cadet threw himself out of the line and at the feet of Mike.

"Almirante! Almirante! Save me!" And he gripped Mike's knees, weeping aloud, repeating: "Save me, almirante!"

Mike kicked the child out of the way as gently as he could, but with speed. For down from the landing came the brethren, led by the three Maroons, and out from the scabbard leaped Bristol's rapier.

Stunned by his own activity, gripped, it seemed, by a gigantic power, dancing back with blade shrieking, Mike got the edge on the first Maroon. The Indian's cutlass went flying from the suddenly agonized hand, and Catshy was rolling over and over, pierced from navel to spine. There was a commotion in the line of prisoners, and then one of the officers had the cutlass and was breasting the tide which swept down the stairs. The flambeaux in the yard made it light below and shined into the eyes of the brawny lads coming down.

Mike was quite certain he was lost, for he could never stand these devils off with the help of just one officer!

Clank!

The prisoners had all been chained together, but now there was a shift. Each one was miraculously chained independently in such a way that he would be wielding his fetters as a weapon!

Lady Marion screamed, and Mike whipped about to find himself faced by Bristol. Their weapons engaged with fury, and then Bristol was suddenly yanked down from behind by the Spaniards and Mike whirled back to the steps in time to help block the rush of buccaneers.

It was a seething maelstrom of blades and cloaks, but it was brief. Soldiers up on the battlements were streaming down to join the fray, and these, too, had the disadvantage of having to come down narrow stairs, for the slaves-to-be had heavy wrist chains which they used to deadly purpose, crushing skulls and limbs at every sweep.

Over a courtyard slippery with blood and brains, Mike rushed to the gates, crying the Spaniards after him in their tongue. The flambeaux bearers had been ground underfoot, and the only light came from a moonless sky and a faraway harbor, and then from flaming powder. The furious volley splashed the courtyard redder still, and the balls whined by or thudded into bodies.

"The gate!" bellowed Mike. *"La puerta!"*

The three chained gangs of Spaniards sought to follow; one of them, the farthest away, flayed the soldiers with such ferocity that even it won through. Another volley crashed, and along the chains could be felt dead weights. Dragging their wounded and corpses alike, married to them by iron links, the Spaniards came up to Mike.

Four soldiers had surged from the sentinel boxes to stop the escape. The only light here was a lantern's dim beams, and it showed them a tall demon with a naked, dripping rapier in a lace-cuffed hand. Two knelt to fire, two drew.

Mike faced those guns with horror. At point-blank

range even a muzzle-loading musket could not miss! And those two tunnels were lined upon his breast as true as though laid by a transit. And the linstocks were raised to the touchholes, and in a moment Mike would be torn to shreds!

Clank!

He had a steel corselet about him which he had not had before. He made a mental note to thank Hackett and, even as he acted, had a sudden chill of knowing that, so far, something had always happened to save him, but that he could not possibly continue to depend upon it. The hero, Bristol, might. But not Mike, the villain of the piece!

Mike's rapier tore out the throat of a soldier who had drawn and nearly in the same movement punctured the other where his belts crossed whitely.

And then another fighter blocked the way—Bristol! He threw himself at Mike with an icy fury and a strength which would have thrown down soldiers or sailors like empty bottles. But Mike caught the hilt of the other's blade with his own hilt and they stayed there, locked, pressing, faces but inches apart.

"You Spanish hellion!" snarled Bristol. "I'll never rest until I see you swing! In the eyes of the English, you'll be nothing but a spy from now until the day you're dead!"

"I'm not a pirate," said Mike through his teeth.

"God's blood, I'll have your heart for that!"

"And I," said Mike, "will probably have your Lady Marion. Out of the way, gutter sweepings!"

The gangs of Spaniards had halted for an instant, but now they swept over Bristol and battered him under and went racing through the gates.

Mike groped for a moment in the dark, for a ball had extinguished the lantern. He found the corpse of a soldier and grasped his powder horn. From another, a cannoneer who had rushed down from the walls, he snatched a burning linstock.

Then to the gang of Spaniards who waited for him he cried: "Shut the gates!"

Musketry was going from the inner fort, but most of the soldiers had leaped up the walls in an attempt to sweep the Spaniards from the road below. Balls snapped about Mike and thudded into the wood of the gate. A squad was making a rush for the portals, and Mike narrowly missed being cut off from his men. He got the gate closed with Spaniard help and then emptied the horn at the foot of it, trailing the powder after him as he leaped back. He dropped the linstock's spark into the chain. There was a puff and then a swift sweep of greenish flame which raced back to the pile and swooped upward along each edge of the nearly closed doors. These, being of wood and subjected to such terrific heat, caught and blazed.

Mike, balls thudding all about him, sped after his rescued troops. Not yet was the light behind bright enough to show up the whole road, and in an instant they had turned the bend and were on the steep part of the trail which led to the town.

Mike urged them on when he reached them. They were shadows against the lighter dark, and for a moment he could not understand the dragging sound which went with them, or what cut down their flight. And then he trod upon a wounded man being dragged along by the others attached to his chain.

"Alto!" said Mike. "Captain, your cutlass here, sir."

It was gruesome and bloody work, cutting the corpses out of that chain, severing limbs which were less resistant to a blade than iron. Only two of the wounded were able to stagger along with help. The others, knowing what lay behind them in English hands, begged for death, not abandonment.

And then Mike, about to order that death much to his

71

own horror, changed that order. "Pick them up, you hulks. Are we English?"

They burdened themselves with the wounded.

The sound of the typewriter faded to nothing.

The burning gate and the musket fire had attracted attention in the town, and now buccaneers and some of the soldiers of the customs house came struggling up the hill through the hot night to investigate, arming themselves about with swords and pistols as they came. But their hurry was too great for torches.

"Into the brush!" said Mike.

The Spaniards dodged under the bushes and crouched there while the men streamed up. But Mike stood on the side of the road, crying: "Hurry! It's been attacked by the Spanish from the hills! Hurry!"

They hurried. And after three or four minutes the road was wholly clear. Mike led them down, straight upon the town. Behind them on the hill could be heard shouts and further firing, for the English had evidently concluded that if they had not been upon the road, then they had taken the trail to the beach which flanked the castle.

The buccaneers, heavy with pay and lust, had been well begun upon the evening, and those who could still walk had hurried to the castle's "defense." It was easy to get through the town. Drunken songs rolled out of the taverns, inert men lay in the gutters. The Spaniards were armed when they reached the dock. They threw themselves into longboats and, despite their chains, managed to row. The lights of the tallest ship attracted them, making a yellow pathway to them. And when they neared it they were again entertained by loud and bawdy verses from "The Grave at Gaverley" and "The Mermaid." After the custom of the brethren, there was no discipline in port, and this, the ship guard itself, was slopping with brandy to the point that they did not decry a boat or offer it salute.

The longboats came in alongside the main ladder, and

72

Mike leaped up. The deck was badly lighted, but he could see men gaming and drinking on a tarpaulin over a hatch. They, in turn, did not see him against the blackness. Other men slept in the squat shadows of guns, empty pots beside them. Mike waved up his Spaniards, and it was not until their chains clanked upon the deck itself that they were seen.

The gamblers stared, round-mouthed, at these tatterdemalions and at the steadily held pistols in their hands.

Mike looked them over and said: "Ye'll make much better slaves alive than dead. Raise a voice and we'll let it out of the side of your throats. Captain Fernando, find the carpenter's chest and an anvil. Those chains are a mite too heavy for the rigging. Lieutenant Rescate, clap these beggars under hatches. And now, where's the cadet that gave it away."

"He's dead, almirante," said a soldier.

Mike walked over to the gunwale and looked steadily at the fort on the hill. He walked aft and up to the quarterdeck and still stared at it.

When the sails were shaking out in the light evening wind, Mike again gave his attention to the boat. He had the lights knocked out and, with his helmsmen alert, began the task of working quietly past the fort, tense with the knowledge that they might receive a withering cannonade from there, darkness or no darkness.

He stood back, detached from himself, and heard strange terms issue from his lips. Not only was he giving the proper nautical orders, but also he was giving them in Castilian!

He could not speak Spanish, but he was speaking Spanish! He knew nothing about boats, and yet, with masterful ease, he was sailing one of a type three centuries vanished from the deeps!

Could this be Mike, man about town, dilettante of the arts?

And how strange it was to find this all so common to himself! Here he had killed seven or eight men in twenty-four hours more or less, had engineered an escape from a fortress, had met the deadliest enemy he would ever have, was in command of a vessel of war, and . . . and—could it be, now that he thought of it?—fallen in love with the loveliest woman he had ever seen in any picture or any clime.

Could that have been Mike—Michael de Wolf—who doffed his hat so grandly and drew so wickedly and spoke with such gallantry and poise?

What strange power was this which decreed all these things?

They worked their way past the snoring fort and stood out from the island with the east trades sighing in the hemp and canvas aloft.

"Starboard a point," said Mike.

"Steady," said Mike.

Tall masts against the stars, cool wind against his cheek, the restive but soothing breast of the sea— What lay ahead of him now? He had heard himself set the course for Nombre de Dios. Did such a place exist?—though part of him seemed to know that it did and even recalled how it looked. And there—certainly they'd know him for a fraud.

Almirante Miguel Saint Raoul de Lobo, commanding his most Catholic majesty's fleets in the New World, commissioned to seek out and destroy the English and the French, pitted against buccaneers who fought like hop-headed wild cats and drank like barrels, pitted against Captain Tom Bristol, the coolest and toughest and cleverest of them all!

Mike shuddered and wrapped his beautiful cloak more tightly about him. The shadow of the helmsman showed up against the dully glowing binnacle. The soft hiss of sea came from under the *Fleetfoot's* stern. The long white wake faded into the dark behind and the path of a star reached out to them before.

"She's luffing her t'ps'ls," said Mike. "Bring the breeze farther astern."

Had he said that?

How did he know?

How— Why—

WHY?

And how would all this end?

CHAPTER SIX

Nombre de Dios was a sweat-soaked town, fried by sun, steamed by jungle, depopulated by fever, commanded by a martinet, shaken by earthquakes, worked by slaves and cluttered with great stacks of silver and gold.

Once there had been two-story houses here, but the earthquakes had taught the Spaniards better. Once there had been Maroons in the jungle behind, but those who were not dead and who had not been chained into the work gangs on the docks and in the forts had prudently taken themselves far back into the tangled hills. Once this had been a quiet curve of the shore; now it was the shipping point of all the gold which came by mule train across the Isthmus, and from here sailed the mighty plate fleet, carrying, ship by ship, a ransom which would have bought Cæsar.

There was yellowjack and malaria. There were scorpions and centipedes. There were bright parrots and chattering monkeys. There were masts in the shipyard and gay shawls upon the low balconies. There were Spanish soldiers in bright-yellow uniforms, Spanish sailors in tasseled caps and striped shirts, black slaves in hoarsely rattling chains, grand ladies in carriages, dogs in sunlight, potbellied Indian children snoozing in the shade, mules with silken-covered saddles or gay paniers, rowboats on blue water, fortress battlements against blue sky, and over it all the golden banner of Castile and Leon.

When the great gold trains came with their inconceivable wealth, merchants and Indians and gentlemen and ladies jammed the town's thin streets, but they did not linger, for lingering might be as expensive as one's life—such was the fever.

Mike sat in a long chair, cooling his hand with a drink. From this silk-canopied balcony stretched the town, swooping away down the hill to the harbor.

For the first month Mike had been fascinated by the intricacy of this place, by the brutality shown slaves, by the gagging reality of yellowjack, by the whole, mad colorful picture of Spanish life in the New World. But now Mike was bored. For another month he had languished. Little by little he had brought up seemingly concrete memories of his past. Without hesitation, he recognized people and called them by their right names and inquired properly after their children. But he had lived in a state of dread lest they suddenly discover that he was Mike de Wolf, not Miguel Saint Raoul de Lobo, lord and almirante. Now that dread had nearly vanished, for one and all they found him wholly credible and were most bowingly polite—all except one called Father Mercy and another, Lord Bagatela, governor of all this and captain of its forces.

Father Mercy was so repulsive that Mike had been at much trouble not to be found alone with him. And Lord Bagatela was such a dismal bore with his tales of the last war and how he had won it for his most Catholic majesty—practically single-handed—and so jealous of the sweeping authority Mike had from that most Catholic majesty's hand that Mike was made most uncomfortable by him.

Only one man seemed to be impossible to shake, and that was Trombo. He was a gigantic creature with a blankly relaxed face, a small pin-pointed head with no brow at all, and an arm which could crush the life out of a man with one squeeze. Trombo went about clad in dirty white pants, his bare chest agleam with greasy sweat. He

78

had no hair upon him and was a shade of bright yellow, as though he had been painted thickly. Trombo never, for one instant, let Mike out of his sight. And Mike had protested, but:

"Almirante señor, once I let you go and you were almost killed. When next the barbarian English touch you, Trombo shall be there and Trombo's great sword shall make the heads fly." Here came a dreamy expression, like a child lushing up an ice cream soda on a hot day. "Ah, yes, almirante señor, and the blood will spatter about like rain. Rain!" He laughed soundlessly and added: "And the other English will think maybe Mount Peele had exploded again! I, Trombo, shall teach them not to touch my almirante!"

That was that, and there he sat, knees drawn up to his chin, fondly regarding his admiral. It was enough to give a man screaming nightmares!

There were some divergencies from the usual in the scene which had at first made Mike's mind reel, but which he now accepted—being unable to do anything else. Monkeys chattered incessantly, night and day, and parrots screamed without rest. There were women in the streets who seemed to have no function but to parade endlessly, never stopping anywhere. The sea and the sky were never anything but blue—when seas are usually every shade in the spectrum at various times.

Mike had been able to come to a definite conclusion regarding his predicament. He had no doubt that this was "Blood and Loot," by Horace Hackett, and that the whole panorama was activated only by Horace Hackett's mind. And what Horace Hackett said was so, was so. And what Horace Hackett said people said, they said. And when Horace Hackett said that the almirante waited two months for the repair of his gale-battered fleet and the arrival of ships from Spain to augment it, then the almirante did nothing for two months but wait. And if

79

Horace Hackett forgot to complete a scenic effect, then it was incomplete. But if he generalized and said this was Nombre de Dios of 1640, then it *was* Nombre de Dios of 1640, with all the trimmings and the people. And if he said it was an ever-blue sea, then, b' God, the sea was bluish even at night. And if Horace Hackett stated that the parrots and monkeys screamed and chattered endlessly, so they did. And if women paraded continually, they paraded continually.

Mike understood now that the whole story ran in one limitless scene which continued in all places together. But the scene of the story in particular shifted from spot to spot, from character to character, so that men were become puppets of the pen and, realizing it not at all, were put through actions to suit the plot. Mike knew now that he must have been described early in "Blood and Loot" as an accomplished swordsman, a talented sailor, and a brilliant strategist, for it would be like Horace to make his villains good and strong, the more to baffle the hero. Under the invisible spotlight of Horace's genius, Mike had carried through the situations splendidly. But, it was somehow horrible to suddenly begin to talk in stilted English or Spanish, to become poised and gallant and deadly, and to be swept along by a force which was wholly invisible and untouchable.

Mike had found himself, upon his arrival at Nombre de Dios, spending a great deal of time thinking about the Lady Marion and sighing for her company. It was real and deep and hurtful, and it made his nights restless.

Then Mike, pondering, had brought himself to face the fact that this love for the Lady Marion was a part of the plot, and that if he succumbed to that feeling, why then he was inevitably doomed. He knew how Horace Hackett plotted. Lady Marion would attract him. He would raid an English island in an attempt to carry her off. Bristol would be infuriated beyond reason by the success of the attempt and would move hurricanes to get at him and have the lady back. And that would be the end of Mr. Almirante Miguel de Lobo, spitted like a chicken upon Tom Bristol's lightning blade.

This, for a space, nearly smothered his love for milady. But in his dreams he kept seeing her, and at times like this his boredom tricked him into thinking fondly of her. And the first thing he knew he was furious with Tom Bristol for being the hero of this tale, for eventually getting the lady, for eventually stabbing the almirante.

There was a bare chance that Horace might break down and make a tragedy out of this thing, and if so, then it would be Tom Bristol who would die, and the Lady Marion would be Mike's and all would be well. But that could not be depended upon.

Mike saw his fate laid out in the neat pattern of Horace's plot. Already he had seen men die in agony upon this scene. Already he had drunk the blood of human beings with his rapier. And he did not doubt, when he found at last that he did not return to his own world, that he would meet his complete end behind the pages of "Blood and Loot." Horace Hackett, all unwitting, would murder his friend. And Mike disliked the idea of dying, not only horribly, but completely defeated and disgraced. No, it was not probable that he would get out of this story. And the hell of it was that this story was real—figment of Horace's imagination or not.

Wouldn't he like to tell Horace a thing or two now! Batting him on the head, caving in his side—were those polite things to do to your best friend? He could imagine Horace sitting there—dirty bathrobe swathed about his rotundity, half-empty coffee cup full of dead butts—being wittily incredulous.

And the more Mike thought about it, the madder he got. And the more he tried to forget her, the more he loved the Lady Marion.

Nights he lay twisting about on sweat-soaked sheets, cursing his luck and fate. And just now, sitting on his shaded balcony, calm of face but mentally aboil, Mike de Wolf planned revolt.

He'd show this Horace Hackett a thing or two. He'd take this story into his own hands!

He knew how it went, or could guess at it. How much time he had he did not know, for he understood that time in the world and time here were two different things—for here Horace merely had to say "three months went by," and so they did, day dragging after day, whereas it only took a second or two to hammer out those four words on the typewriter. It was possible then for him to get together a fleet that would really be a fleet and wipe the English and French out of these islands by an attack nothing could stop. It was also possible for him to refuse to take the field against Tom Bristol at all, but he knew that if he remained inert, then Bristol would come for him.

"You bothered," said Trombo with the air of one announcing the solution to months of high-gear mental effort.

"Why?" said Mike.

"You no see Zuilerma at all. She cry and not leave her room and say she is grown too old for her almirante. She not yet eighteen. Why you not like her?"

Mike gave a slight shudder. Usually Trombo talked decent Spanish, but now he spoke bad English. Evidently Horace Hackett had shifted his spotlight for a moment to Nombre de Dios. All right, let him shift it. To hell with Horace Hackett. He, Mike de Wolf, wouldn't talk!

"Letters come from Panama," said Trombo stubbornly. "Anne write and write and write and say why the almirante no send escort for her? She say she is not afraid of the fever here if it means she can see her almirante. She say she dead with worry about you, and why you not write her."

Still no answer from Mike. He felt a small thrill of triumph. He could keep from talking! Even though this was an obviously posed scene.

"You in love," said Trombo with finality.

"What?" cried Mike. "Nonsense!" And he was instantly sorry, for he doubted then his ability to run this scene.

"You in love. Fifty-'leven most beautiful women in New World die for sight of you and you in love. Why not whistle? Almirante whistle, any woman on earth run to him. He is the *almirante!* He is beautiful!"

"I want no women," said Mike.

"You in love," said Trombo. "You think I blind? You say what woman and Trombo take ship and get her and bring her back. Not good for you to love woman. You take her, you forget about her."

"You're treading on swampy ground, Trombo."

"You walking into fever if you not perk up. If you not think Trombo better go get this woman, then let Trombo go get Anne. Or send for Zuilerma. Or buy twenty-thirty slave girl. Or make love to governor's wife. She almost die whenever she look on you, and she plenty young and a great lady, too. Who you want you can have. You are the almirante! You are beautiful!"

"Stop it," said Mike. "Do you think if I actually wanted a woman I would not take her?"

"Well? Then why not take this one?"

"She ... she is a long way away. And ... she is English."

"English!" cried Trombo, leaping up in horror.

"Aye," said Mike quietly. "She is the Lady Marion Carstone, the sweetheart of Captain Bristol."

"The ... the sweetheart of a pirate!" cried Trombo. "Oh, oh, oh, the almirante has been too much in the sun. The fever has him!" He held his head in his hands and rocked as though in pain.

"And," said Mike quietly, "I intend to have her, as a prisoner of war."

83

Trombo stopped. The despair went slowly from his face, to be replaced by pleasure. "This Captain Bristol, he is a terrible name on the Main now. He has a big fleet, but the almirante will stop him. Ah, ah, ah! To defeat him, to yard-haul him! To cut out his guts before his eyes and feed them to a dog! And to take his woman— Ah, that is revenge great enough even for the almirante! Ah, ah, my almirante, forgive me. I am blind. You are quiet because you plan this!"

"Aye," said Mike, aghast at feeling pleasure from such a gruesomely stated picture.

"Why . . . why, even Zuilerma can see sense in that!" cried Trombo. "When you have become bored with the English woman, you can give her to Zuilerma and Zuilerma will be pleased. She is clever with a knife, is Zuilerma—"

"No!" cried Mile. "I really love the Lady Marion, Trombo."

"Ah, love, pah! I saw you in love with fifty-'leven women. You take 'em, you get bored, you forgot 'em. There is Zuilerma. You heard of her beauty and fought and killed full two hundred Indians to capture her. And now you bored. You spend nights risking fever with a guitar under Anne's window, and now she begs you let her come to you and you not answer letters."

"This is different," said Mike severely.

There was rebuke in the tone, and so Trombo became silent. But the certainty of knowledge did not die from his face. He knew his almirante, and he felt much better about the whole thing. All that had to be done would be done.

But a gray shadow drifted over the shining hardwood floor and it was not to be as simple as that. Father Mercy had come in like a pallbearer, even more grizzly than ever. He had, quite obviously, been eavesdropping.

"My son," said Father Mercy, "I have come to pay a call."

"Delighted, father," said Mike. "Sit down."

"What I have to say I would rather say standing up, my son." And his corpse face remained still, lips unmoving though he spoke. "I have dissuaded the sale of English captives ever since you have known me, my son."

Mike looked at him insolently and sipped his drink. He felt a strong repulsion for this horror of a man, one that was not born out of Hackett. And so strong was it that Mike momentarily slipped away from the grip upon him.

"You soul-scavenging buzzard," said Mike. "When I pulled into this harbor you damned near had the town upside down, telling people that I ought to give you the captives I took. Well, to hell with you. They're English, and they're men, and if you crave autos-da-fé every day, use up Indians and leave white men alone. They're at the fort now, working. And I have them counted every day. And the first one that is missing will find me shelling that hell hole you call a religious prison! Now get out of here!"

Father Mercy gaped. "My son—they are heretics! The rack and the Iron Maiden alone can extract their sins. It is the only way to get them to believe and save their souls."

"Kill a man to save his soul. What's so damned valuable about a soul, you crow? Why tear a man's body to bits and send him to his God in chunks? I've a packet of orders in that strong box there which empower me above church and state, and if I so decree it, they empower me above God as well so far as you are concerned. You and your sadistic lechery ought to be wiped out of this town like I'd squash a centipede."

"Have a care, my son. I am a man of God, and as such I am more powerful in my influence than you in yours. These statements which you have made can, perhaps, be overlooked, though I have never had to listen to such blasphemy before." And, indeed, Father Mercy was shivering under emotional stress. "Just now I happened to overhear your designs upon an English girl. I came in to again demand the souls of those English you captured and I stay to demand that all English heretics landed here shall become the charges of our church. And this girl, too, must be delivered like the rest. The governor, Lord Bagatela, has just now said that he cannot give them up without your permission, and I have just told Lord Bagatela that I am about to report the matter to Spain via the first advice boat—and you cannot touch religious mails. Unless you promise this thing, I shall use every power of the church to have you removed from command and given over to our care, for now your blasphemy tempts me to report above all else. However, if you give me these captives, and if you promise me this"—he swallowed hard—"English woman, you are safe."

"Feed white flesh to your damned racks?" cried Mike. "I'll blow this town off the map first, and I've got the ships and guns to do it."

"You cannot force the hand of God; sir."

"God?" said Mike, suddenly thinking upon the true identity of this priest's god and vividly envisioning Horace Hackett. "God, did you say? Your god, sir priest, is as lecherous as thou. Now go and cease to drag your dirt on my floor!"

"Blasphemy!" chattered the priest. "You ... you are mad!" And he expected the heavens to cave in on him. "B-b-blasphemy!" And he fled with skirts streaming behind him from out of this ghastly presence.

Mike laughed and Trombo shuddered.

"Love," muttered Trombo, *"has* driven you mad, almirante. Father Mercy—will have you racked! And his report to Spain cannot be touched. You are *mad.*" And he wept.

CHAPTER SEVEN

Mad or not, Almirante Miguel Staint Raoul de Lobo set sail from Nombre de Dios with bands playing, pennons streaming, and the gilded hulls of his galleons and round ships majestically reflected in the water. He was escorting the plate fleet past the leeward islands and the hands of his cannoneers itched to apply the linstock to the touchhole with English buccaneers as a target.

Mike, for all his outward decision, was fighting a mighty battle within himself. How he ached to attack St. Kitts as soon as this plate fleet was safely into the Atlantic! And why shouldn't he? He knew the defenses and the channel. He knew the positions of the forts and the disposition of the troops and very nearly could guess the number of vessels which would be on hand. To attack and take, and, if Buccaneer Bristol was not among the slain or the captives, then to hold the Lady Marion as hostage against future behavior—that was the indicated plan, and one in which he was certain he could succeed.

But Mike had slightly the edge of these other denizens of Never-never Land. While they were quite human and much alive, and while they supposed themselves in a world quite as concrete as the world from which Mike had come, they were not on talking terms with their deity. And Mike knew every plot twist of which Horace Hackett was capable. And he knew that even though this looked so neat, there must be something wrong with it. His captains had already mentioned its feasibility and had advised

87

its operation. Even Father Mercy, with the prospect of putting a fair English lass upon the rack, argued austerely that it was good colonial policy. Aye, Mike told himself, there was something damned wrong with it if the others had all thought of it.

Sailing six points from the wind to beat through Mona Passage and ride the Gulf Stream to the Old World, the transports waddled along, bellies deep in the sea with riches. Striding the twenty paces up and down his quarter-deck on the *Josef y Maria,* Mike recalled, one by one, Horace Hackett's previous tales. Porpoises rolled along beside the ship, flying fish flashed in fright away from the white-toothed bows, sails to port, starboard and astern blazed white and red and gold against the achingly hot sky. Mike turned and turned again, soft white boots making little sound above the sigh of wind.

This world was so *real* to those who lived in it. They lived and were born and they got sick and felt pain and died. And they looked up into the blue, wholly unconscious that they might well hear the rattling of a typewriter's keys and smell the horrible pipe which Horace Hackett clenched in yellow teeth. From whence had this world come, whither would it go? These people all thought they remembered long pasts and ancestors. They were convinced that their progeny would continue up the ages. They believed in their ingenuity and trusted their calculations. And yet—

Mike could never remember a story in which Horace Hackett had refrained from killing his villain. The hero triumphed, got the girl and slaughtered the evil one. Well, Mike was the "evil one," but he did not care about being slaughtered.

"If I could only figure it out," muttered Mike. "If I could turn this plot and get Bristol—" Yes, there was a chance, for Horace Hackett was not always concerned with each scene simultaneously. Right now, sailing along, Mike knew that he was free from Hackett's direction.

And, being free, he could talk as he pleased and act as he pleased and—

Supposing . . . supposing he did not wind up at St. Kitts. Supposing he went somewhere else, and when Horace had the attack all figured out for St. Kitts, the Spanish fleet was some hundreds of miles hence!

Mike grinned.

The ships swept grandly onward.

He would control this strange love for the Lady Marion. He would refuse to fall into such an obvious trap. He would wipe the English from the Main and leave Tom Bristol much alone. Aye!

Hell, now he was doing it by himself.

Aye.

Accordingly, some days later, the naval vessel hauled yards, and while their brilliant canvas fluttered from luff to leech, dipped their flags in salute to the onward-surging round ships. The long Atlantic swell made their gun tackles creak and jumped pans off the galley stoves, but they lay in the trough for an hour to make certain that the plate fleet was out on the broad highway, unpursued by buccaneers, headed for Spain with the Caribbean far behind. They wore ship then and, forming a long line, braced and steadied for Mona Passage.

"It might be easier," said Fernando in the chart room, "to stand out and come down on St. Kitts with the wind a-quarter."

Mike's compass poised over the crudely drawn parchment chart which showed things as though the view was from above the horizon and not the zenith. He looked at Fernando.

"Perhaps," said Mike, "we'll not attack St. Kitts."

"But . . . but I thought your orders, sire—"

"My orders are most general, captain. I am supposed to wipe out the English, and there is more than one English settlement in the New World."

"But I had heard— That is, the rumor had it—"

"That a woman was involved?"

"Something like that, sire."

"Mike grinned. "Fernando, have you ever thought much on destiny?"

"Why—no, sire. The church—"

"Destiny is a marvelous thing. Circumventing destiny is possible only by refusing to do the obvious."

This seemed like blasphemy to Fernando, and he remained silent.

"Strategy is of the same stuff," said Mike. "Men are lifted into key positions, they know not why. They strive and fail or succeed, still not knowing why. They have the breaks or they have not the breaks. But, in a limited scope, they can determine their own futures."

It certainly did sound like blasphemy, but Fernando, in obedience to his almirante, nodded.

"And so," said Mike, "you will issue orders to officers commanding the rest of the fleet to the effect that we are proceeding not to St. Kitts, but a place much nearer to us. Tortuga."

"But—why?"

"There is an English and French settlement there. There will be vessels there which could ultimately aid Bristol in attacking our towns and colonies. It is the buccaneering hotbed of the Caribbean—and if we have any luck, the buccan hunters will all be out leveling their sights upon wild steers while we level ours upon their settlement. We will land and destroy the place—with all due humanity, of course—and we'll burn what ships we find there, thus weakening Bristol's future fleet. Then if Bristol attacks, what men he would normally get from Tortuga will be safely inside our prisons or quietly dead."

"Why—that's brilliant!" said Fernando. "And that woman—I mean in St. Kitts— Father Mercy was wrong in saying that you—"

"There are spies. All Indians are spies. Perhaps, cap-

90

tain, that was a remark calculated to disturb the peace of mind on St. Kitts and make our attack on Tortuga simple. Perhaps."

Fernando beamed with admiration. And then: "The course, sire?"

"West sou'west, b' half south," said Mike. "Locate a sea artist in our fleet who has been in there and have him come aboard the flagship here as pilot."

"Si, si, almirante," said Fernando, and hurried away from the cabin.

Mike sat contemplating the chart before him. He was not particularly amazed any more by these sudden abilities of his. First as a swordsman, then as a linguist. And now out of the clear he found himself a naval strategist. But he wasn't giving it much thought. He was too pleased with himself for having bested his own desires and having turned the tables on one Horace Hackett.

Tortuga, so named because, as now, it looked like a gigantic turtle's back awash in the sea, hove up with the dawn. A silent fleet was coasting along Haiti's north at two knots, banners but half seen from ship to ship in the mist.

Mike stood in the great cabin of the *Josef y Maria* and addressed his captains, who had gathered from the ships for his orders. They sat quietly drinking their morning coffee, their aristocratic faces without trace of concern for the forthcoming battle. Mike, booted and cloaked for action, paced up and down the great stained-glass stern ports as he spoke, the sun coming up to silhouette him in the scarlet flame of dawn.

"The ships will attack as outlined," concluded Mike. "The landing parties will get away as soon as the harbor vessels are smashed, and these will take the forts as I have outlined. But I wish to make one thing clear to you, gentlemen. We are captains and sailors of his most Catholic majesty's navy, and we will conduct ourselves as such. There will be no ravishing of this town. There will be no useless slaughter. We are here on a military objective and civilians are not fair game. I will enforce this order with all the authority at my command."

The captains looked wonderingly at one another, for, after all, weren't these people of Tortuga English and French? But orders were orders, and they nodded politely, drained their coffee and went on deck to call for their boats. In a short time they were aboard their own vessels. In an hour the *Josef y Maria's* prow was thrusting past the earthworks of eastern Tortuga, while the lead ship of the other line readied to blast out the fortresses of the Haitian shores.

The battle flag on Mike's flagship dipped.

A rolling broadside shook the very sea. White smoke whirled out to darken the mists. The trumpeters of the fleet knifed the morning with their calls and signals. The marines rapped out a hysterical background to the cannon with their muskets. The forts on either side of the channel were churned vales of flying masonry from which scrambled men who sometimes almost got away.

The Spanish raid on Tortuga had begun.

Six hours later the battle was over.

The anchorage had been but sparsely populated with ships, except for fifteen merchantmen which had put in there for food and stores and some twelve buccaneer craft which were undergoing, for the most part, overhaul. The merchantmen had gaped at the Spanish fleet in all its flaming glory and had struck almost to a man, but the buccaneer vessel, even though careened and in no position whatever to give resistance, knew that even a small fight was better than no fight and an end on a Spanish gibbet. These latter ships had fought furiously if unavailingly to oppose the landing on the island. They were now blazing wrecks filled with roasting corpses.

Tortuga had been attacked at an unfortunate time—for Tortuga. Its inhabitants combined the trade of hunting and curing meat with raiding on the Main, and at this season nearly the entire male population was deep into Spanish Haiti, drumming up the wild beef which had, over the years, retreated to higher ground away from the coast. Accordingly, there were very few in the forts—only those who had been hurriedly rushed there to man the cannon upon the first appearance of the Spanish. Shot and powder had been fed the guns in some cases by women and children, and these were now dead in the rubble.

A few of the houses on the island offered the appearance of fortresses, and these were shelled heartily by the Spanish ships before Mike could pass the order.

A company not more than a hundred strong had drawn a battle line upon the sand to oppose the landing of five hundred Spanish marines. And now the sand was a dark, thick red. Onward had swept the landing party, to cut off the retreat of men from the forts, and shortly after, the golden banner of Castile and Leon was flowing over Tortuga.

Six hours and the battle was over.

Mike had recall sounded. But in the din ashore it might as well have been whispered. Mike had the other vessels signaled, but no signalmen answered. The anchorage lived with longboats filled with Spaniards. The jungle behind the town moved with yellow-jacketed marines. A signal gun bidding them return to their ships went unnoticed.

Too long had these Spaniards lost to the buccaneer to show mercy now. And the sky began to blacken with the smoke of burning buildings, mingling with the smoke of charring ships. With cutlass and crossbow, musket and lance, the population of Tortuga was being slaughtered to the last child.

As soon as he realized what was happening, Mike rallied the crew of the *Josef y Maria* which was still aboard, poured them and his marines into the boats and drew them up on the beach. At their head he set out to quell this madness. But a hundred yards into the town his men thinned, dribbling away one by one, hungry after loot and wine and death, and Mike was left upon the smoking street, alone save for Trombo.

With the flat of his sword and the might of Trombo's arm, Mike sought to stop the massacre. Women fled from doorways to be seized or struck down before they could cry out. The drunken marines flung all possessions from the homes and ripped them apart, searching for valuables. They could not hear Mike's voice. Old men and priests were being tortured to discover the hiding of money in the hills.

The place was a howling shambles with walls caving in, smoke everywhere, screams of agony and wails for quarter on all sides. Dead and wounded sprawled in the dust. And sailors and marines rushed on in search of more loot, more women, more brandy and rum. Five thousand devils in yellow and blue gutting the heart from Tortuga's twenty thousand women, children and old men.

Mike, sweating and furious, laid about him with his rapier, powerless to bring any men to recognize him and failing, in his anger, spitted them and slashed them down. But it was for nothing that Trombo strove so mightily with him, and by midafternoon Mike gave it up, sinking down upon a stone step of a house not yet burned, holding his head in his hands, sick with the horror of it and the realization of what he had loosed.

"They mad and drunk," said Trombo, trying vainly to understand why the thing had to be stopped. "Tomorrow they listen to you."

"Tomorrow!" cried Mike. "Tomorrow there won't be a thing alive on Tortuga."

"They all English and French," shrugged Trombo.

"I'll court-martial the whole fleet!" vowed Mike. "I'll have them under hatch all the way to Nombre de Dios. I'll string them up by their thumbs and yard haul them and . . . and—" He relapsed into apathy.

Trombo suspected sunstroke as the cause of this strange mental quirk, and he sought about for something to quench his almirante's thirst and take his mind from the crew's disobedience. Of course, a man is always angry, thought Trombo, when his men refuse to obey him. He looked up at the white walls of this so-far-spared home. It was bigger than most, and it ought to be richer. Gold and good wine whetted Trombo's appetite. He made sure his almirante was all right, and then, throwing his shoulder against the door with all his mighty strength, caved the portal as though it had been built of sand.

Mike lifted his head from his hands and wondered where Trombo had gone. He shouted for him once or twice, but he could not hear his own voice in the bedlam of the town. He turned and saw that the door of the place was open and, suspecting, got up to look in. Almost immediately he found Trombo. The giant was carrying a flagon of brandy, which he proudly set down and from which he poured a drink for his almirante.

Past them, from the street, dashed several sailors, who instantly went about the work of ransacking the place for money and jewels, paying no heed in their drunken eagerness to Mike. And a moment later the place was jammed with men. Upstairs there were screams and a pistol shot. Trombo picked up Mike for fear of what Mike would do and carried him into the road.

The smoke was getting thicker, until it was almost impossible to find anything but black in the sky. Red flames leaped high here and there to increase the terrible heat. Panting Spaniards fought among themselves over booty and, collecting it, threw it away and dashed on in the hope of better.

From another large house the steady bang of firing proceeded. Three groups of Spaniards had gathered there to storm the place, but they had little organization and rushed forward, only to stumble and fall grotesquely under the hammer of slugs from the roof of the flat-topped structure.

Now and then a gay headsilk was seen to ripple up there and perhaps eight or nine buccaneers were making a last stand of it. The heap of bodies around the place grew slowly, and then from the beach came fully thirty gunners with a cannon at the end of ropes. They swiveled the weapon around and crammed its mouth with round shot. It roared and bucked and a hole was in the wall. The sharpshooters on the roof got the gunner and then his successor. The men changed the angle of sight and poured a bucketful of musket balls into the smoking muzzle. Chips and splinters flew from the raised edge about the roof. The next load was round again, and another section of the wall was smashed in. With a cheer, the sailors and marines poured through the breech and swarmed up to the roof, though several were dropped down the stairs with shots from above, impeding the progress of the rest.

Trombo gave Mike another drink of brandy, and Mike sat in the shade, looking somberly at the futile action in the house.

Screams and curses sounded on the roof amid the clang of steel on steel and, shortly, down came the successful stormers, lugging a few guns, which they threw away in the street. One of them was buckling on a sword belt, but decided he didn't like it and cast it aside. Nine Spaniards were employed in a quarrel over booty which Mike could not see. They came closer to the doorway, hauling something.

Mike suddenly leaped into the house and snatched the pistols from his sash. They were dragging a woman with them and still fighting to get a cutlass away from her. Her face was bruised and darkened with powder grime. Her dress of fine silk was ripped from shoulder to waist. And even now she got free and cut at one of them. They bore her down to the floor, and, by stamping on her fingers, got the cutlass away from her. Trombo had been much amused until he saw the expression on his almirante's face as Mike stalked forward.

"Almirante!" cried Trombo in fear. "They are too mad to know you! They will kill you!"

But Mike was deaf, for the woman beneath those battle stains was the Lady Marion!

At point-blank he let a sergeant have a ball in the stomach and a sailor the other in the face. And then his rapier was out and shimmering greedily.

"Let her go, you illegitmate sons," snarled Mike.

They leered drunkenly at him and recognized him not at all, for he, too, was blackened and his lace was torn. They let go the Lady Marion and sought to bring up weapons against him. The rapier licked the life from two as swiftly as two seconds fled, and then Mike was smothered in their rush.

A mighty roar was above the pile, and the men were yanked away to have their heads bashed in against the walls. Shortly Trombo had the last one at squirming arm's length while Mike retrieved his sword and staggered forward toward the Lady Marion. This was the only egress from this room, and so, trapped, armed again with a cutlass, she waited for him.

"Miguel Saint Raoul de Lobo," said Mike bitterly. "Admiral of this rabble. Your arm, milady, so that I can escort you to the safety of my flagship."

She started to object, and then understood the folly of staying here. She straightened up and, with a slight curtsy, took his arm.

CHAPTER EIGHT

The fleet was afraid of Mike, but behind his back even the officers raised a knowing brow. Mike had changed these past few months, and perhaps some of the steel of his character was truly entering into him, for he had punished the rape of Tortuga with such thoroughness and attention to detail that half the men bore the mark of the bastinado and the other half wore the scars of Mike's withering beration. All ships were on half rations, despite the gigantic mound of stores which had been carried away from Tortuga. Marines, staring court-martial in the teeth, stalked outside storerooms and by the water casks.

"Sire," said long-faced Fernando, "you breed mutiny. These crews live like rats and die like mice under fever. Was it so terrible that they loosed their passions upon the English and French. After all, sire, think upon what the English and French have done to us!"

"Wrath begets wrath," said Mike.

"But we are armed to meet it."

"The Spanish colonies are not. One by one they'll be sacked. We've given Bristol and his hellions the excuse they need to sweep the Spanish from the Main."

"We can destroy them."

"If three pirate vessels had run into Tortuga last week while this fleet was unmanned, we would have been sunk to a ship."

"But they did not," said Fernando brightly.

"And now every criminal and thief in the jails of

France and Spain will be launched into the Caribbean to mauger the King of Spain's beard. You're a pack of fools, Fernando."

Fernando flinched, for he was too high born to bear insult. "I repeat, sire, that you breed mutiny."

"Then, sir, I'll deal with the fleet as one deals with mutineers." He felt a shadow fall upon the room and looked up to see Father Mercy. "What gives you permission to come in here?" demanded Mike.

Father Mercy bowed and smiled until it seemed his face would crack.

"Why so pleased?" demanded Mike.

"The English captives, my son, are all safe under hatch, waiting for the church in Nombre de Dios."

"And that tickles your fancy," said Mike. "They are my prisoners, padre."

"Would you profit at the hands of God?"

"No," said Mike, "but you would. I repeat that they are mine, to do with as I like. Forget them."

"For a price," said Father Mercy, rubbing his hands, which gave out the sound of sandpaper.

"You bargain with me now," said Mike.

"You have in your cabins, my son, a heretic of . . . ah . . . especial interest to me. I will trade you your other prisoners for her."

Mike stood up, angry. "Listen, you stinking fraud, if you say one more word about captives or about Lady Marion, I'll . . . I'll have you torn over your own rack! Now out before I change my mind and drill you where you stand." He reached for a pistol, and Father Mercy almost fell over himself getting out of there. But he had the temerity to thrust his scaly head back in and say: "Think upon it. Your prisoners and your commission for one silly English heretic. Is it a fair trade, my son?"

Mike threw the pistol at the face and it vanished.

Fernando was grave. "Almirante, there is something strange about you. That was a father of the church, and yet— Don't you know it is madness to try to oppose such as he?"

"I have a fleet and he has a rosary," said Mike. "I leave it to you to discover which one fires the heaviest broadside."

"I think," said Fernando, leaving, "that you'll discover that it's the rosary."

Mike slumped down in his chair and stared at the door, which was now closed. He could hear the hiss of water from the open stern ports of his cabin and the ornate lamp swung rhythmically to and fro from the beams. He sat there for quite a while and then, with a shrug, poured out a drink.

There was a footfall at his side and he saw Lady Marion there. She had repaired her gown and removed the stains, and after much rest looked herself again.

"I could not help but hear," said Lady Marion. "I am causing you a great deal of trouble."

"They pillaged against my orders," said Mike. "I am either almirante or I am not."

"If I know aught of sailors, such treatment is liable to be fatal."

"You know buccaneers," said Mike. "These are soldiers and sailors of Spain, not gutter sweepings and criminals."

"You imply an insult, I think."

"Think as you please," said Mike.

"I do," said the Lady Marion. "I know quite well that all this punishment, for instance, is to impress me with your own haloed innocence in the matter. Perhaps you count on my taking back word to St. Kitts that you aren't the demon you are painted. Well, sir, I know you now."

"Know me, do you?" said Mike.

"For a very clever and forceful gentleman," said the Lady Marion, "whom, in other circumstances, I might

101

come to admire, if not for his mercy, at least for his audacity."

"Your praise is somewhat cold," said Mike.

"Aye, perhaps it is. I owe you my life, you think, forgetting that your fleet put my life in jeopardy. You are clever, but not quite clever enough, sir."

"You are conceited," said Mike, "to believe that I attacked Tortuga because I had heard you had gone there. I had not heard anything of the sort. You were sent away from St. Kitts because your father expected an attack on that place. I attacked Tortuga for the same reason—and to destroy possible pirate vessels and to weaken the defense of St. Kitts."

Her face was crimson. "You imply, sir, that I think so well of myself that your desire of me could cause what you have done!"

"That," said Mike, "is what I imply."

"The only answer you have, sir, to make that a lie is to send me by advice boat and have me set down on St. Kitts."

"And that," said Mike, "is something I will not do."

She smiled, again at ease. "And why not?"

"Because," said Mike, "as much as I detest blowing away your cloud of self-esteem, I must hold you only because you are hostage against the behavior of Tom Bristol."

She stood. "If you for a moment think that Bristol will be stayed by such a thin threat, you are mad. He knows better than to trust any Spaniard, and would expect to find me dead, whether he behaved or not. No, milord, you won't stop Tom Bristol. And you'll not succeed against him when he comes!"

"You," said Mike, "are more a fool than I thought you at first. To deny that I love you is folly. To deny your beauty is foolishness. But your charm is quite safe in my care, milady, for I've no taste for playing the part of a bungling buccaneer."

102

She crimsoned again and, turning, slammed her cabin door behind her.

A few seconds later Mike was again appalled at himself. Why had he talked that way? It would have been so simple to have smoothed it all out. What was wrong with him? Here he was divorcing himself from fleet and church and from this woman as well— But his words could not be recalled. He—

His words. *His* words. HIS WORDS!

Suddenly he shook an angry fist in the direction of the sky. "Damn you, Horace Hackett! So I'm to wreck my fleet, am I? So I'm to fall in love like a puppy with this English girl, am I? I'm to bowl myself over by opposing the church, and then I'm to be murdered by your bucko-boy Bristol. Well, to hell with you and your damned typewriter! You're going to get something more than you expected before this thing is done!"

It was an empty boast, and Hackett's attention was now elsewhere—that he knew.

But God! He couldn't just sit here and walk straight to his death! Death was such a terribly permanent affair!

No typewriter whirred above Nombre de Dios now. The ever-blue sea, the ever-wandering women, the ever-working slaves in the dockyards went on in their unvarying functions. The fever took its victims and, still hungry, took more. The merchants assembled for the transshipment of bullion and jewels and, as ever, swiftly dispersed as soon as a fleet had sailed.

And Mike brooded in his great, shadowy house as the weeks went by. Events were happening elsewhere. Nombre de Dios was in a lull before the storm began to blast it. And if Mike knew the plots of Horace Hackett, the later quarter of the book had been entered upon and the latter quarter of Horace Hackett's books always dealt strictly with the victory and his savage surge to final victory. Horace Hackett had abandoned Nombre de Dios as a Spanish scene. Mike knew that when next it came under the invisible spotlight of Horace's questionable genius it would be with an English attack. No more pulling of Mike's puppet strings. No more painting the villain. That was all done and the villain was strictly upon his own, awaiting, despite anything he could do, his "just desserts."

In a way Mike was thankful, for it meant freedom of motion and speech. He would not again find his own mind betrayed into stupid actions and stilted speeches. He had a huge fleet, he had the guns of the fort to protect it. Behind him lay the Isthmus and the countless ambuscades into which the buccaneers must fall before they could come up to final grips. And if Horace Hackett thought he was going to push Tom Bristol through to the defeat of the Spaniards, the recovery of Lady Marion and the death of one Mike de Wolf without terrific opposition, then Horace Hackett had better go buy a plot jinni.

Left alone, Mike felt better. While it had been fine winning sword fights and forts with the help of the author, it had so irked Mike's sense of individuality that it was now almost with relief that he faced the final scenes, strictly on his own. He could say what he wanted and do what he wanted.

Knowing Hackett, he knew this. That he could run away from the scene and responsibility had several times occurred to him, but he did not trust his apparent ability to escape. He had a feeling that if he sailed out it would be to captivity in the hands of the buccaneers. And if he ran away into the Isthmus either Father Mercy or the Indians would attend to his finish. No, he had to remain at his post and ready himself for the final onslaught.

He sent out pinnaces to flit up and down the coast with orders to scud back to Nombre de Dios with any intelligence of the English. He sent letters to the governors of other Spanish colonies advising them that the English would soon retaliate. He inspected his fleet, or some portion of it, almost daily and held many conferences with his captains.

But all was not well. That speech he had made to Father Mercy had undermined his influence. The near-mutiny which Horace—he now realized—had made him talk himself into was still in the atmosphere, making it even more sultry.

As Mike came up the walk to his house one afternoon he found Fernando waiting for him. The captain was spurred and mud-spattered after a hard ride from Panama across the mountains. His long face was haggard.

"Buenas," said Mike.

Fernando bowed, a little stiffly. "I come to seek you, sire, with dispatches from the governor at Panama."

Mike tossed his hat to a chair and let Trombo pull off the cloak. He took the packet. "Well? You can tell me what's in them as well as though you'd read them."

Fernando crimsoned. "Yes, sire. The letter on top informs you that the panic you are spreading because of the English must be stopped because our blow at Tortuga will settle them for years to come. The next letter is from the bishop of Panama, telling you that you are to turn over the Lady Marion to Father Mercy for escort to Panama and examination by the bishop himself. The letter under that is from Anne, telling you that if you show so much preference for the English she will demonstrate the power of influence she has with the governor of Panama and that unless you give your Lady Marion over to the bishop, you may regret it. Forgive me for knowing these things but all Panama is sizzling with gossip about it."

"And you," said Mike, "let them sizzle."

Fernando shrugged.

"Perhaps you agree with them," said Mike.

Again Fernando shrugged. "Sire, I have already tried to make you understand the gravity of your action."

"Perhaps," said Mike, "you went to Panama just to make me see it further."

Fernando avoided his eyes.

"And perhaps," said Mike, "you'd like to have me show the white feather to Bristol by sending this woman back to him. If I did that, the English would have no high opinion of our ability to defend ourselves. It would be a tacit surrender. If I give over the Lady Marion to the bishop or Father Mercy, the results would be so horrible that no power on earth could stop this Bristol in his vengeance."

"And if you hold her here," said Fernando, "you destroy your own authority, your own career."

"Because of the stupidity of fools like you," said Mike, beginning to get mad. "Come into the house and ask the Lady Marion, if you like, what treatment she has received at my hands. Yes, of course that shocks you. But come anyway." And he forced Fernando inside.

The great hall stretched its shadowy depths before them for the blinds were drawn against the heat of the day. Massive furniture gleamed dully and the breeze rippled the tapestries.

"Trombo," said Mike, "inform the Lady Marion that we would like to see her here."

Trombo, like some hulking, hairless bear, waddled away. In the distance sounded a slammed door and a heavy thud and then Trombo came back feeling a new bruise upon his arm, looking guiltily at Mike. "She say 'no'."

Mike turned to Fernando. "She is my prisoner and nothing more. Now do you understand my position?"

Fernando looked at the bruise on Trombo's arm. "Well—"

Mike took the packet of letters and tore them in half all at once. He handed the fragments, with seals intact, back to Fernando. "You had a hard ride, captain. You've still a long ways to go. Perhaps you had better be on your way."

"On my way? Whither?"

"To the governor of Panama, to the bishop, to Anne. Tell them what I have told you and give them back these. Tell them that they are the best allies that Tom Bristol ever had. Now go."

Fernando sighed and got up. He wanted badly to object for it is a long, long ways from Nombre de Dios to Panama City and the Isthmus was acrawl with revolting Maroons. He tightened his sword belt and put on his cloak and, spurs rasping sullenly, went away.

"Trouble, my almirante?" said Trombo.

"Maybe."

"Almirante, I, Trombo, do not understand just how it is that this English woman can continue to disobey you. Why, no other woman ever hated the almirante. Maybe a good length of belt, neatly applied, might bring her—"

"I don't need your advice," said Mike. "Mutiny, religion, insubordination and now you tell me how to handle women. Go take a jump in the first lake you meet!"

Trombo sorrowfully went away from there and left Mike to his woes. And for an hour or two Mike nursed them with feeling language. They were all so convinced of Spanish superiority! All so sold on a man's duty to the church!

He paced back and forth, back and forth, passing each time a baby-grand piano in the corner, reading, despite himself, the gold letters on it, "Steinway, Chicago."

What a fraud all this was! What a mixed-up mess! He'd seen "Pittsburgh" on the steel cutlasses of the buccaneers. "C. I. O." stamped upon the lumber which was going into those galleons. Damn Horace Hackett for a blundering fool, unable to visualize a period completely. Why, it wouldn't be surprising to see Bristol hove into sight firing Lewis machine guns! Oh! By all that was unholy, why hadn't he, Mike, ever paid any attention to such crafts! Lewis machine guns against Bristol! But he knew he couldn't even fire one, much less make one. No amount of knowledge of a true world could correct anything in this.

To hell with that damned piano! And he banged both hands down on the keys. The instrument yelped in protest and Mike did it again. And then, because it was natural for him, he sank down on the bench and began to roll out a savage, melancholy concerto. But, little by little, the music soothed him and he began to play more softly.

For an hour and more his fingers roamed over the keys and he grew quieter until he had almost forgotten his troubles, aware only of music. It was with a start that he realized someone was standing against the window ledge looking at him. It was Lady Marion.

In her amber gown—for by author-magic she had landed here fully equipped—she looked even more heart-arresting than she had when he had seen her in St. Kitts.

"Don't stop," she said quietly.

Mike did not stop but played on, softly, looking at her, wondering why she had been so violent to Trombo and himself before but chose now to come out of her fortress. He guessed that she was about to plead for her own release and, when that was refused, would begin to storm anew. But music evidently had its effect upon her and he was careful to maintain it.

"A little while ago," she said, "I saw one of your officers come here. With dispatches."

"Yes," said Mike noncommittally.

"And when you sent for me and I refused to come—I opened the door again and heard what you said. In the many weeks—or is it months?—that I have been here I have learned some Spanish."

Mike cocked an ear at the ceiling and ceased playing for a moment. No slightest sign of a typewriter. "Yes?" he urged, continuing his playing.

"You refused to turn me over to the church no matter how they threatened you. What would they do to me?"

"Burn you as a heretic."

"Yes . . . yes, I thought that was it."

"But you see no helmeted guards out there, with crosses on their chests, waiting, do you? You have nothing to fear."

"No . . . I don't think that I have. But I was not thinking of myself . . . so much. Your men think it strange that you keep me here. That Fernando has argued with you before to send me away."

"Yes. I refuse to pamper Bristol. And with you as hostage he might not attack."

"He won't believe you. He'll think me dead. You have a glib tongue, Michael; you proved that on St. Kitts. It would be much safer for you to send me away."

"So you ask for that again? Am I to trust the crew with which I would send you? Am I to risk a trap by trying to land you on St. Kitts?"

It occurred to Mike that instant that he was taking all this far too seriously and that, in addition, he was lying. He had moldered here for months, dreaming about her, thinking about her, aching for her, and now here she stood, the object of all that misery, the only true happiness for which he could hope before he perished as perish he most certainly might at the hands of the soon-to-attack buccaneers.

His playing became dreamy. "You have a very bad opinion of me, milady, having seen me enact a role at St. Kitts to save my own neck and having witnessed the sack of Tortuga. And I have only to say that I did not order anything but a battle there and am now in trouble because I punished my men so much for running amuck."

"I . . . realize that now."

"There is something which I have wanted to tell you for some time," continued Mike, looking only at the keys.

"It has to do with why I am here, where I came from, where we are going." He lowered the music to somberness. "You do not know it but you are only the character in a story. A lovely, devastating character, it is true, and one who is, I find, really alive." He waited for her to question that, but she was still. "We, he continued, "are all characters in a story, nothing more. But once I was in another world, the world which will some day read this story and be somewhat amused. There I know the author. And I know other stories by him and know how he thinks and writes so that here I also know. Bristol is going to storm this place. You will ultimately be returned to Bristol and I shall be killed. That is the way this story is scheduled to run. And I am trapped here. I came without being asked and was made to play this part of villain no matter how I opposed it. I am doubtful if I will ever return to that other world."

She was studying him. "Forsooth, sir, you carry that simile far. That playwright Shakespeare wrote in a play I saw in London that all the world is a stage and that we are merely the actors. But by what strange necromancy can you attempt the blasphemy of knowing God, knowing how He thinks and what He will do?"

"Your god, milady," said Mike, "is not the god you suppose him. You have lived your life in this world and this is only a world of fantasy. You remember far back and know that you were born, have people; you have seen pain and misery and happiness. You yourself are a warm, living flesh and blood. I give up the effort of trying to make you understand from whence I came and why I am here."

"No one ever asked to be born, few ever ask for the parts they have to play," said Lady Marion. "And all men, in all their actions, think they are doing exactly right. But, milord admiral, this is not settling the problem of my disposition."

"Yes," said Mike, "I think it is. Whatever I do and

however I do it, the end will, of course, be the same. Bristol will win, will take you back and I will be killed."

"No one man can change destiny, milord, if you speak of that. I am afraid that it is only melancholy which leads you to such direful prophecy for yourself."

"You are here now," said Mike. "Why should I completely drown myself in misery by sending you away again? Let Bristol take you away—if he can. Let this plot run its course—if it will. But there is one thing, milady, which cannot change, and that—" He stood up, facing her.

She looked into his face with sudden awareness and her breathing quickened. Her hands were slightly raised as though to fend him off, but not so high as to actually do so. "Milord—" she said tremulously.

"Milady," said Mike, gathering her to him and holding her tightly against him. "I love you," he whispered.

She thrust at him and tried to get free, but his arms were strong and his lips, seeking hers, were gentle. And then her arms ceased their flailing and her hands crept up across his flat, straight back and locked there.

"Oh—my darling," she whispered.

CHAPTER NINE

For a month direful news came to Nombre de Dios by a seemingly endless stream of messengers. The pirates had sacked Robelo. They had gutted a merchantman and put her crew to the plank. Bristol himself had led an attack upon Santa Ysabel and not a Spaniard in the fortress had been left alive. Everywhere the buccaneer fleet ranged in search of the Spanish fleet, but ships were slow and, at this season, winds were few. The advice boats and scouts of Miguel Saint Raoul de Lobo failed utterly to locate the elusive pinnaces and carracks under the bloody banner of England. Refugees—those few who got through the wilderness and past the Indians—came crawling into Nombre de Dios with tales of horror which set Spanish teeth on edge.

"You must attack! You must find them and wipe them from the seas!" howled Governor Bagatela, banging his cane down on the walk and turning purple.

"Aye, and leave this harbor with only your forts to hold it," said Mike. "To leave completely open the road to Panama. If I contact them for certain, I'll attack. But to wander out upon the Main with every Indian on the shore passing information on to the English, would be to do just what Bristol wants us to do. Here we stay until they are seen."

And Fernando, commanding a galleon out on scout, came back without word of the buccaneers save that he

113

had found Terra Nueva a charred patch of black strewn with what bodies the Caribs had considered inedible.

"They've loosed the Indians upon us," said Fernando. "They've given them guns and knives and hatchets and it's said the English are paying a bounty of a pound for every Spanish head that is brought to them."

"That last is a lie," said Mike. "Bristol is in command of that fleet somewhere out there and Bristol only wants one thing. He probably seeks to draw us away from this place by attacking small, unfortified spots. Then, by a list of successes he continually strengthens his fleet. Bristol wants the Lady Marion back, for he must know from spies here that she is still alive. His men want gold. They don't give a damn about king and empire. They're buccaneers, already scarred with the bastinadoes and cats of his majesty's royal navy. Calm down. Eventually Bristol will have to make his brag good and attack Nombre de Dios. When he does we'll roll him up like a sheet of paper and throw him away."

It was a definite stand to take, but he could take it with the powers he had. Messages from the governor of Panama he answered all in one phrase, "Are you so eager to be gobbled by the buccaneer that you'll remove me?" Sheer bravado but it had a slight effect.

Father Mercy, white-hot for English blood, came storming to the house on the hill. "They're murdering priests! They're killing every Spaniard that wears the cross. They're exalting the blasphemous Protestant creed! Out after them, you coward! Why do you sit here shivering in port while they sweep Spain from the Main? Does that English—"

Mike struck him to his knees and Father Mercy, in real terror, his rage quite cooled, looked up at the tall, beautiful devil whose rapier point licked avidly before the priestly nose.

"Down that hill and into your church," said Mike.

"Pray for the souls of the people killed by the buccaneers and add a prayer for yourself, thanking your God that He put me in between the buccaneer fleet and the shore here at Nombre de Dios. They'll string you up fast enough as it is if they catch you."

Father Mercy went down the hill.

Another month passed with more alarms and wild guesses and sacked villages and vanished cargo vessels, and Mike waited patiently, knowing very well that he could do no good ranging the Main, and understanding clearly Bristol's real goal. Bristol would have to come to Nombre de Dios.

A short message went out from Mike via an Indian who was suspected of being a spy:

SIR PIRATE:

Your fate is already determined. I object seriously to being considered so thick-witted as to mistake your true intentions. Butchering Spaniards from Cartagena to Florida may keep your men amused, but, personally, the uproar you've created bores me. The Lady Marion is well and safe as the bearer, who is probably in your pay, will attest. Kindly fall upon Nombre de Dios so that we can have done with you.

Your obedient servant,

MIGUEL ST. DE LOBO,

Almirante.

P.S.: The Lady Marion wishes to send her love.

The note was answered a few weeks later:

SIR SPY:

Please tell the Lady Marion that we are coming after her immediately and please have her bags packed.

BRISTOL.

"I hope," said Mike at the supper table that night, "that Bristol is as good a commander as he is made out to be. Or perhaps that the god in the case is witty enough to see the import behind this."

"You make me uncomfortable with your talk of 'god,' Mike."

The candlelight caught in her hair, flame answering flame. And the goblet of wine which she held matched her beautiful eyes. Mike grinned happily. Why shouldn't he be happy for a little while?

"Shall I order your bags packed, my dear?" said Mike.

"That little horse you gave me today is a darling," said the Lady Marion.

And so the matter stood.

Mike was not in error about Hackett this time, for such an obvious bit of strategy could not go past without notice. No admiral with any sense at all would hurl a fleet at a port which was expecting him. Rather, he would hold off, prepare himself, lie quiet for a space and so convince the enemy that he does not wish to accept the challenge.

And so Mike won a little more time—which proved his own undoing.

CHAPTER TEN

The gold train came from Panama. Little mules gay with bells, musketeers brave in yellow and scarlet and steel, merchants who had waddled over the rough trail in slave-borne sedan chairs, and gold, emeralds, silver and silver and emeralds and gold came streaming into Nombre de Dios. And with them came Lord Entristecer, governor of Panama.

Nombre de Dios glittered and hummed and the surface of the harbor was laced by the wakes of boats and barges dashing to and fro. The ships from Spain stood salt-stained in the roads awaiting their precious cargoes and the Spanish fleet swung dazzlingly from cables, looking dangerous. All day and all night the town teemed with people and resounded with music and quarreling.

The governor of Panama and the governor of Nombre de Dios—the latter being much junior—dined in state with all the nobles present. Great platters of meat and high bottles of wine and dishes of gold and a slave behind each chair. It was a gala dinner, entirely too gay to foreshadow disaster. And yet, when it was done, Lord Entristecer withdrew into the coolness of the drawing room, indicating that he wanted only three men to accompany him—Lord Bagatela, Mike and Captain Fernando.

"Gentlemen," said the melancholy lord of the New World, "I have news."

"And I also have news," said Mike.

"Yours first, then," said the sad governor.

"It is probable that the fleet will be attacked on the high seas by Bristol and the English," said Mike, "for all this gold is high bait. It is my plan, which I may tell you in detail later, to send only a small escort with the plate fleet and to keep the main body to windward in such a way as to catch the English napping. For I've a notion that when Bristol sees how few are guarding the plate fleet he will detach but few to take it. Then Bristol will send the bulk of his ships to attack Nombre de Dios. Up will come our fleet, crush the portion of Bristol's and then, turning, come down on Nombre de Dios and crush him against the guns of the forts. This plan is based on my knowledge of the psychology of . . . of Bristol. If—"

"Your news is not news," said the melancholy old man from Panama. "It is strategy which looks very slim. And, Sir Miguel, it is not likely to be put to use."

"How's this?" said Mike. "Am I not admiral of—"

"You are not," said the governor from Panama. "To-day, with the coming of the ships from Spain, I received this dispatch from his most Catholic majesty the king." He took it out and unrolled it. "As you can see for yourself, Sir Miguel, it removes you from command. I had asked for more, but this is all the reply. You will notice that it places Captain Fernando in complete charge of naval operations on the Main."

Mike steadied himself and gave Fernando a contemptuous glare and then, before they could say more, he stalked from the room.

Much later that night, sitting in the moonlight window of his room, Mike imparted the news to the Lady Marion.

"Then . . . then," she said, "you no longer can command anything?"

"Neither afloat nor ashore," said Mike.

"Who did this?"

"Several people."

"And I . . . I have been the cause of it all!"

"No," lied Mike. "Oh, no!"

"Oh, yes," she wept.

"Have you no thought of what might happen to you?" said Mike.

Evidently she had not yet considered that, but she looked up at him proudly. "You would not let them touch me."

"No," said Mike. "No, of course not."

And in the morning, when Father Mercy came armed with stacks of documents and accompanied by two squads of church troops, he found the entrance to the admiral's home barricaded.

"Open up!" cried Father Mercy. "Open up in the name of God!"

A bullet clipped the hairs of his head and he hastily went down the hill again, his soldiers tumbling after.

Five days later a ship stood into the roadstead of Nombre de Dios. She moved sluggishly for her belly was full of sea water and her masts had been mowed as though by a scythe. But, limping under jury rig, wanly flying her battle flag from a splintered truck, she managed to brace about for the last mile up the channel and get her anchor down. There was something sorrowful about the way she swung into the wind.

The town went down to cluster on the quay and wait silently for news. A barge went out, carrying Lord Bagatela.

"Make way," whispered the people in the back of the crowd. And people moved to one side and the tall, ominous figure of Mike made its way to the stone steps where the barge must land upon its return.

A priest squeaked in excitement and dashed off to find some church troops, but Mike did not even deign to notice his going. Hand on hilt, cloak stirring a little in the wind, he waited for the slowly rowed barge.

When Lord Bagatela came alongside the quay his face was chalky. And in the cockpit beside him lay a blenched gentleman in blood-soaked silk who already had the gray of death upon his aristocratic face. Captain Fernando was handed up. He saw Mike standing there and reached out feebly and pleadingly toward him.

"Almirante," whispered Fernando. "They ... attacked in full force ... thousand of them. Only ... only my flagship got away ... after it could do nothing more. Of the fleet ... there are not thirty men left alive for there was no quarter. It's ... all gone ... almirante. Your fleet ... I should never have helped take it from you. I wanted to be forgiven ... please, almirante. I am dying."

"Aye," said Mike sadly. "You're forgiven. May whatever place you go to have a kinder god than this. Good luck, Fernando."

Mike turned aside as they bore the captain away. No typewriter in the sky here. Nothing but real, agonizing death. Those streaks down from the scuppers of the *Josef y Maria,* real blood had made those.

"There he is!" cried a priest excitedly. "There he is!" And some thirty church troops rushed in to close on Mike—and found Lord Bagatela between their quarry and themselves.

"Stay!" cried Bagatela. "Stay, or my guard will fire!" And his guard leaped to man the bow chaser of the small barge.

"He's infidel!" cried Father Mercy. "He disobeys the church!"

"You've no authority to touch one of my staff, church or no church!" roared Bagatela.

"He is not one of your staff!" howled Father Mercy.

"If he had commanded that fleet, the buccaneers would be dead to a man!" countered Bagatela. "I see it now. He had a plan and that plan would have worked. And now, just when we may be attacked, you wish to throw him on a rack. Think of your own filthy necks, you hell-hounds!"

Father Mercy stopped, for the populace was beginning to take it up and it is never good policy for a member of

120

the church to show such thirst for vengeance against such protest.

Father Mercy and the other priests backed up and with them went their troops. And Mike forgot about them. He was already looking to the sea.

"How's that, eh?" said Lord Bagatela. "How's that?"

"Thanks," said Mike indifferently. "Do you think your forts can withstand a bombardment from a fleet?"

"Maybe," said Bagatela. "But a fleet that size, such as Fernando reported—"

"I'm thinking so myself. Governor, have the guns off the *Josef y Maria,* for she's no use to us now. Have them mounted here on the shore to oppose landing. If they get past your forts, they'll try to sweep ashore and we'll meet them here with grape."

"You have authority," said Bagatela eagerly, sweating at the picture Mike had so indifferently painted. "Do anything you like, sir. Anything!"

"It will be little enough now," said Mike. "Oh, well— Get a runner off to Panama City. If we fall here, they'll come across the Isthmus and attack there. Get reinforcements if you can, but I don't think we'll have time before the devils stop binding up their wounds."

"Immediately," said Bagatela, hurrying off.

Mike smiled a little. It had its points, this business of being branded, so offhandedly, a military genius and, by that token alone becoming one. Well! There was little hope now, but he'd try what he could. In one respect he *had* changed the plot and so he had a very faint hope that he might change it further. With fury, then, he went about the task of trying to make that faint hope bloom.

"And so," said Horace Hackett, grandly laying aside his latest chapter, "that is how it goes to date. Now Bristol—"

Jules shook his head sorrowfully. "I don't like it."

Horace looked around the chromium-plated office as

though searching for a witness to this blasphemy. He found one in René LaFayette, who, manuscripts on his lap, was dozing comfortably awaiting his turn with the publisher.

"You hear that?" said Horace. "You hear that, René? He says he doesn't like it. He says he doesn't like the greatest sea battle ever written!"

"I didn't either," said René helpfully.

"See?" said Jules. "He didn't either. And from the way you are protesting I think you don't like it neither, Horace."

"Me? Why I sweat blood writing that sea fight! Can't you just see Bristol, swooping at the head of his hellish crew down upon the Spaniards? Can't you hear the roar of cannon and the screams of maimed and mangled men? Can't—"

"Nope," said Jules, "and you can't neither." He looked accusingly at Horace. "That's what you writers always do. You take some point in your yarn that you don't like and so you figure an editor won't like it so you come in and tell the editor just how swell that point is. You writers are a lot of fakes!"

Mortally wounded, judging from the appearance of his round, somewhat oily face, Horace sank back and was silent.

"Nope," said Jules, "I don't like it. Where was this Spanish admiral, huh? You don't say a word about this Spanish admiral in this whole fight. Bristol comes up and there's the Spanish fleet. So Bristol tackles them and the Spanish fleet sinks. That ain't tough enough, see? You got to have it a lot tougher on Bristol. Now what's he got to fight but a few shore batteries? And do you think them Spaniards would be so stupid as to send out a lot of gold when there was a pirate fleet waiting to take it? And—"

"All right," said Horace, peeved. "All right, I didn't think it was so good either."

122

"Well, your strong man in this story is this Spanish admiral and where was he?"

"I dunno," said Horace. "You got to understand that sometimes, when you're writing, a story just takes care of itself."

"Well, that one didn't. Here you are at the climax, and yet you ain't got any Spanish admiral in charge of that fleet or anything. This is a sea story, not a land story, and if Bristol is going to get this Spanish admiral to rights and recover Lady Marion, why it's got to be done on the sea. They gotta have a fight on the quarterdeck of the admiral's flagship."

"That's been done!" said Horace.

"So what? It was good, wasn't it?" Jules, having won his point, looked smug. "Now you get up a fight that won't look like two kids swatting at each other with straws. This has got to be powerful, see? It's the whole story!"

"You mean I've got to tear up perfectly good copy?" said Horace.

"Why not?" said Jules unsympathetically. "It ain't good anyway."

"You hear that, René? He says to tear up pages and pages!"

"You're lucky he didn't make you tear up the book if it's all as lousy as that," said René.

"Nuts," said Horace. "Just because a guy can write good you expect him to write good all the time! All right, I'll tear up that chapter and to hell with your deadline."

"You tear it up *and* rewrite it *and* get it in here in time to go to press Monday or I'll ... I'll let Tritewell illustrate it!"

Horace shuddered. "All right," he surrendered. He got up and gathered the manuscript into its envelope and slouched away. When he passed René LaFayette he muttered, "And after all the drinks I've bought *you*."

René grinned.

CHAPTER ELEVEN

All was serene in the town of Nombre de Dios. The monotonously blue sea spread without a ripple beyond the channel and the empty bay was undisturbed save for two barges hauling cannon out of the wreck of the *Josef y Maria*.

The shore battery, protected by logs and screened by brush behind the quay, was growing with the sweat of several hundred Indian slaves. Up and down through the works strode Mike, making suggestions, ordering changes, attending to the best disposition of the guns. He was weighed upon by the impossibility of holding this place against such a fleet as he knew was coming. Now and again before sudden reinforcements of one character or another had magically appeared, but, so far, nothing untoward had happened. And for three toilsome days he had flayed this battery into existence, working three shifts through the hot days and nights until he himself was worn to gauntness. In addition he had sent out small vessels with orders to return instantly with any word of the buccaneers, and these reports awakened him each time he tried to rest.

The Lady Marion had been very sweet, but she had not mentioned that he should rest for fear he might take this adversely, believing her still anxious to be rescued—which she most certainly was not, even to the point of writing a note to Bristol and sending it by a known spy.

At three o'clock that afternoon, Lord Bagatela came

waddling down to see what went on and within another half-hour Mike had laid his last gun.

Mike, mopping at his face with a linen kerchief given him by Trombo, paused to wave it in the direction of the long battery.

"Well, there she is," said Mike. "And now we'll have up the powder and balls and grape and we can at least make it uncomfortable for them when they arrive."

"Uncomfortable?" gaped Bagatela. "My dear almirante, I do hope that you can promise more than that!"

"I'm too tired to be optimsitic," said Mike.

Bagatela looked along the battery and sighed. "I do hope something comes of this. You've worked these men to rags, and when I think of that, it reminds me that you haven't slept a great deal either. Shouldn't you take a rest after all this labor? So that your thoughts will be clear if they come on the morrow?"

"I suppose I should," said Mike. "Well, I'll be off. If anything happens, call me immediately."

"Indeed I will!" said Bagatela.

Mike started up the curving road through the town toward his house. And then it happened!

There was a ripping sound somewhere high overhead. The whole coast trembled! There was a repetition of splashes in the harbor and a shaking roar along the beach! All went dark!

Mike was no longer on the path; he was on the quarter-deck of the *Josef y Maria!*

Dazedly he gazed around him through the night, surprised that all was so calm again and that the few sailors who worked at a deadeye did not seem aware of anything having taken place. There was a full moon in the sky and, if Mike remembered properly, "last night" had seen the moon in its last quarter. By the brilliance of it he had a clear view of the beach and another shock.

No shore battery!

126

Days and days of work and now no sign!

Anxiously he scanned the forts which, before, had been wholly on the north side of the channel. Now there were not only twice as many ramparts and embrasures on the north side, but also a massive fortress directly across from it on the south side!

The character of the town seemed but slightly altered save that it was bigger, better lighted and appeared to have more people in it, judging from the amount of music and laughter which came out across the water.

Mike took a turn around the deck. He was not even jolted to find the harbor filled with ships. Yes, filled. Nearly the entire Spanish naval fleet as well as the plate ships were there in force, lighted like churches and just as rugged.

"Almirante!"

Mike turned to find Captain Fernando, in the best of health, at his side.

"Almirante, I have just received word from an advice-boat captain that the buccaneer fleet is now but a few leagues from Nombre de Dios and coming up a strong wind astern!"

Mike heard Fernando and he also heard something else—the faint rattle of keys high in the sky.

"Very good," Mike heard himself say. "You may fire recall guns and have trumpeters sound quarters. How much does it lack until dawn?"

"Five hours, almirante."

"Aye, five hours. And within seven those English dogs will be shark bait. Pass the word for a captains' conference."

"Aye, aye, sir," said Fernando.

When Fernando had gone away an ominous gray shape drifted across the quarter-deck toward Mike. "Almirante," simpered Father Mercy, "I would like now to make claim for the English captives. The rack starves for heretics."

Mike was about to make violent retort when from his

lips came the words: "Aye, the rack must be fed and the stake as well. You'll have fodder for your religious zeal before the night and day are done, Father Mercy."

"Thank you, almirante. And the fellow Bristol?"

"Ah, Bristol," Mike heard himself say. "Father, if there's anything left of Bristol, ye're welcome."

"The English girl," said Father Mercy. "What about her now?"

"The Lady Marion," said Mike, angry at being a puppet but helpless, "is my particular own—if I can tame her."

Father Mercy grinned evilly and drifted away.

While trumpets blared and drums rolled and recall cannon thundered, Mike leaned on the taffrail of the *Josef y Maria* and looked on. Barges came flying back to the ships aglitter with the helms, corselets and pikes of the soldiery. The vessels teemed with confident activity and orders flew swiftly back and forth.

And then the typewriter in the sky faded away and left the activity continuing.

Mike was worried. Quarter moons which become full moons instantly and a fleet which sprang back up out of Davy Jones' locker and dead men walking again were no worry to him. But those words he had said about the Lady Marion, about the English captives— Things had changed. And Marion—

He leaped down to the waist from the stern castle and bawled for his barge. When it was laid alongside the stage he jumped into the stern sheets and gripped the tiller. Trombo dropped into the bow and Trombo's bastinado cracked out to give energy to the oarsmen.

The barge fairly leaped through the water under Mike's urging and swerved in alongside the quay. With the command to wait, Mike sprang to the dock and started up the hill toward his house. But Lord Bagatela was there to make him pause.

"All is ready ashore, almirante. Your trap is laid for them and we cannot help but win. How goes the sea?"

"All's well," said Mike. And edging away, "Did you notice anything strange a while ago?"

"Strange?" said Bagatela. "No, can't say that I did."

"And the full moon?" said Mike. "It was at its last quarter last night."

"Oh, I've seen those things happen before," said Bagatela. "The will of God."

"And the fleet out there?" said Mike. "It's there again."

"Why, it's been there all along, hasn't it? Why? What should have happened to it?"

Mike departed, fearing the worst. He was greeted with huzzahs as he hastened through the streets and several times had to refuse to stop and drink to victory.

On the veranda of his house he paused, wondering if he could take what was coming, and he knew now that come it must. A servant threw open the door for him and he strode in.

"The Lady Marion?"

"Is in her room, under guard, as usual," said the servant.

Mike motioned away the guards and thrust open her door. He stopped.

Tall and regal, her face wreathed with disdain, she faced him. "Well, now, Sir Admiral! You did not expect Bristol to come, and yet come he has! And he'll pick your rotten bones before night."

"Aye, so even you think he's a vulture!" said Mike. He had tried to stop that, but now again he was aware of the clicking sound on high.

"Now go to your defeat!" said the Lady Marion. "My curse shall follow you!"

Mike got mad. Unaccountably mad. He slammed the door and rushed away, down the hill toward his ships, and he went, to the sound of bugles blaring, the clicking again faded. Mike ceased to be angry and was only hurt. He stopped and faced about, irresolute.

Marion! His darling Marion! Marion whose sweet head upon his shoulder had solaced these long months of waiting, whose lips had drawn away the bitterness of his being trapped. And now—

There was no use. Desolated, he went on down the hill. Bristol. All this had to be fixed for Bristol! Bristol, a damned puppet!

Well, he'd see about that. He had a huge fleet and the harbor was now so strong that anything short of a miracle would find it stanch. He must not allow himself to be betrayed now. He'd do for Bristol and then, coming back, he'd awake the love which Marion had had for him.

"Damn you!" said Mike, shaking his fist at the sky. "I'll show you! Do you hear me? I'll knock your fair-haired son of a witch into the briny and then we'll see what you'll do about it! I'm going to *win!*"

And back aboard the *Josef y Maria* he stalked up and down the table, past the swinging lanthorns, past the eager faces of his captains, and gave them their orders.

"Gerrero," said Mike. "Your squadron will act as a decoy. You will draw away from the battle line as though fleeing and when the pirates come through that hole you will ware ship and knife his column in two. Then you, Bolando, with your three vessels, will come up into the action and crush Bristol's spearhead against our battle line's rear. And you, Sorenzo, will swing your squadron on our left wing in a half-moon so as to engulf the half of Bristol's fleet which will not pass through the break. We will then maneuver to do all possible damage and, finally, draw off to seaward. The wind will force Bristol down upon the forts and, while we hold off on a broad reach, both our vessels and the forts will hammer him to fragments. Above all things, gentlemen, watch the flagship for your signals. And do not allow yourself to be boarded, for the soul of this strategy is to split up Bristol, wreak havoc

130

to his ships and then throw him into a position where destruction to his fleet is inevitable. That is all. We sail in a half-hour. His most Catholic majesty expects every man to die rather than surrender."

Glowing with confidence the captains trooped out. And Mike stared after them until they had gone, still resolute.

CHAPTER TWELVE

Dawn cracked like the firing of a pistol and there was the sun, just up over the eastern horizon, a great scarlet ball which sent ribbons of flame quivering across the zenith. The sea was smooth, and though this hour in these waters should have had no wind, there was wind, about twenty miles of it, quite sufficient to send prows knifing and foaming. But no ships were moving.

In this moment all was still. There was the buccaneer fleet, a long line of small, fast vessels drawn in battle order from north to south. Here was the Spanish fleet, huge and ponderous and brilliantly gilded, drawn in a parallel line. There was a mile and a half of open water between them and the black silhouettes of the English against the sun.

Mike, cloaked against the dawn chill, leaned his telescope against the deck house to steady it and focused it upon the English fleet, but he could see nothing for he was nearly blinded by the sun. He lowered the brass and shook his head.

As nearly as he could tell, they had two-to-one superiority over these English, broadside for broadside, but Mike was no longer a trusting sort. The lead ship, opposite his own, he supposed to be Bristol's, for it resembled the *Fleetwood*, the vessel he, Mike, had stolen from St. Kitts. Just how it had gotten back into Bristol's command he was not sure, but there it was. Behind the

Fleetwood ranged thirty-six vessels of varying sizes, but all rigged square without a lateen showing on any stick.

The ships were sailing now and water hissed under the stern of the *Josef y Maria* while braces creaked in the strain of swift air, driving the vessel harder. Behind her plowed nearly fifty Spanish ships of line. This heartened Mike in one respect, but in another made him nervous, for he had left port with but twenty. A rake of his telescope showed him that all bore the ensign of the Caribbean command and so were his vessels, and that the men on their decks were numerously standing to quarters with linstocks lighted. Marines were in their tops, matches poised until they came within musket distance. Gun captains checked the lay of their pieces and all went on in a quite usual manner.

The two battle lines were forging toward a point where they would range.

"Fire me a serpentine, extreme range," said Mike to Fernando. "We'll gauge by it."

The word was passed and a serpentine crew on the main deck elevated the weapon's muzzle with handskipe and slid quoins out until the base of the cannon was resting on the last bed of the carriage.

"Clear!" said the gun captain.

The gunners leaped aside and put a strain on the beeching which limited the recoil. The gun captain ran a line of powder with his belt horn down from the touchhole, along the gun to the base ring. He smartly applied his smoking linstock, snapping his hand out of the way. There was a huff and a spit and a thin line of hot smoke soared from the touchhole.

Bam!

The cannon leaped upward about three feet and back about six, the crew straining at the beechings. The white smoke engulfed the port and the side of the ship and the crew.

The fifty-three-and-a-half-pound ball skittered over the

sea and plunked into a swell two thousand paces from the ship, about five hundred short of the closing *Fleetfoot*.

"Toss a basilisk into him just to show him we can," said Mike.

The word was passed forward to the fo'c's'le where the long-range five-inch cannon usually acted as bow chasers. The crew there slued the short carriage about, blocking the wheels against the roll. Ten pounds of powder in a parchment cartridge went down the muzzle, followed by the wadding and the fifteen-pound shot. The muzzle was elevated and the gun captain applied his powder horn and then cried, "Clear!" The linstock drew a huff of flame.

Bam!

Mike lost track of the ball against the sun, but in a moment saw a spar come tumbling down from the *Fleetfoot's* foremast.

"All basilisks," said Mike. "At will."

Pennons went rushing up the signal hoist and, a moment later, the Spanish fleet had its light long-rangers in action.

The English could not yet reply to this sparse fire. Up and down the Spanish battle line, at long intervals, puffs of smoke and thunder indicated the loss of more English rigging.

"We're closing in," said Mike. "Stand ready with cannon royal on the gun deck."

The signal hoist was alive again and word went down to fifty gun decks. Battery captains poised themselves at the forward end of their long batteries and waited. Gun captains waited on the battery captains.

The range narrowed down to eighteen hundred paces.

"Fire!" said Mike.

On fifty ships battery captains loped from fore bulkhead to aft, chopping down a hand as each gun was passed. If they had all been fired at once, the gunwales would not have stood the strain. And so their flame and

135

fury lasted down the length of the vessel for half a minute, lasting over the fleet for nearly three minutes and hiding all the gilt and all the flags completely in a fog.

"Ware ship," said Mike.

The signal could not be seen, but it was a usual maneuver. Presenting a stern to the enemy while smoke hid much of the vessel, the ship of line could go downwind as it turned, thus staying with the smoke a little longer and coming out of it with the fully loaded banks bearing.

"Fire," said Mike.

Thunder again engulfed the Spanish fleet and once more the water and air, bulkheads and spars around the English received a murderous drubbing. While only twenty percent of the broadsides began to take any effect, there was weight enough in those sixty-six-pound cannon royals to blast the heart out of any enemy.

Again and again the maneuver was repeated, perfectly timed, the loading going on with haste while the loaded batteries were presented and fired. But now the English with their demicannon were getting to work. The third-of-a-hundredweight balls plunked noisily into the sea and sprayed the decks, plucked spars down and knocked great gouges in the bulkheads, sending violent and jagged splinters flying everywhere, deadlier than shrapnel.

The guns were getting hot and had to be swabbed, which slowed the Spanish firing. Now, when they recoiled, they very often leaped violently to crash against the beams overhead or knocked themselves on their sides or, getting free, wiped out their gun crews in a breath and went thundering on across the gun decks to batter havoc everywhere until at last caught and overturned.

Mike paced back and forth, splinters plucking at him, feeling the acrid powder smoke in his lungs, already deaf from the cannonading and almost blind. The sun, though the engagement had already lasted an hour, was not one inch higher above the horizon than it had been at the beginning!

Until now Mike had taken this thing as a matter of course, for there lurked in his mind a carelessness born of the fact he was a puppet and that all this was stage scenery. But now happened a thing which hurled him into reality with soul-shocking force.

The buccaneer fleet had worked in within six hundred paces, pouring in a continuous cannonade and taking fearsome punishment. And now, by double-charging their few mammoth cannon royal and shotting them with chain-connected balls, they commenced upon the clear of the galleon quarter-decks and the severance of shrouds. One such shot came tumbling like a loose dumbbell from the *Fleetfoot,* swinging around and around, traveling slowly enough to be visible. It swung ponderously one last time as it passed over the quarter-deck of the *Josef y Maria.* Captain Fernando did not even give it pause, for it mangled him into two chunks and his feet still stepped back to brace as shoulders and head were squashed against the helm, spattering the quartermasters.

Mike had flinched and now, staring, he felt himself turn green-white. From there his glance, shocked to acuteness, swept to the waist of the vessel and saw how red the scuppers ran into the sea, how the sand laid down to prevent slipperiness from just this cause had been washed away. Tangles of spars and lines, splinters, the smoking ruins of cannon, the smashed gunwales, the heaps of slain from which came tributaries to feed the scuppers' flowing, made him shiver. Above the ceaseless roar of guns and the shrill cracking of musketry sounded the agonized screams of the wounded and dying.

He fought to get back his hold on his nerves, to cultivate again that contemptuous air of detachment, to remind himself that all this was in the hands of one Horace Hackett. He regained his nerve in a few moments, but not for any of these reasons. It was Bristol that was doing this to him, Bristol who would soon defeat him, Bristol who would soon take back forever the woman Mike loved.

Angry now, Mike commanded the hoist once more and up leaped the gay flags from out the white smoke and into the sunlit sky beside the topmasts.

Whether the order was obeyed or not, Mike could not tell. But within a very few minutes the line of English ships bent in the center, making a V which speared into the break and must have appeared at the far end of the Spanish battle line.

Mike cupped his hands and bawled the order to his sailing master which sent the wounded *Josef y Maria* about on a tack to beat eastward across the stern of the *Fleetfoot,* thus crossing the English T. The plainly done stern-castle of the buccaneer vessel loomed through the choking mist, prey to the higher guns of the great galleon.

With the chop of his hand Mike sent his battery captains rushing aft, causing each cannon of the starboard broadside to batter murderously into the *Fleetfoot.* Balls from snipers in the buccaneer's rigging tore up wood about Mike's feet as the stern of the *Fleetfoot* came abeam and then abaft of the *Josef y Maria.* Not a port light or a plank was left in the *Fleetfoot's* stern and so close had been the gun mouths that fire now jabbed greedily among the ruin. Fore and aft the *Fleetfoot's* decks had been swept by splinter and ball and now her main began to tilt slowly to starboard while the topmen either dived widely into the sea or sought to scramble down. The *Fleetfoot* was a shuddering ruin.

The ship next in line behind Mike took the buccaneer next the *Fleetfoot,* passing between it and the wreck and blowing it, like its mate, into fragments. No. 3 Spanish ship crossed the T the third English ship down and again made a quivering horror out of a once-saucy bark. No. 4 Spanish took No. 4 English again, and so went the succession of penetrations, like a multifingered hand penetrating the gaps of its multifingered mate.

That the English were still able to move at all was a shock to Mike, for when he looked back he saw that the *Fleetfoot*, splinters, corpses and flames, still proceeded toward the break in the Spanish line, even though the *Josef y Maria's* sister which had been at the other end had begun the same awful toll of that side of the English V. And, even though the squadron which had pulled out to make the trap came about, cutting through the English, that still did not stop the infiltration of the buccaneers through the Spanish formation.

Punished until it was incredible that it could still float, the buccaneer fleet finally gained the leeward of the Spanish fleet and went coursing down toward Nombre de Dios.

Mike made a hasty survey of his vessels. Fully twenty were in sinking condition, their crews fighting off sharks in the water, the screams of the wounded cut off and turned on gruesomely by the slap of the waves. With signals, Mike caused several of the Spanish vessels to swerve out of line to pick up survivors and then, with the *Josef y Maria* making the final cut of the figure-eight maneuver which his fleet had executed to so rake the buccaneers, steered for the stragglers of the buccaneers and began to chop them to chunks with calculatingly murderous fire as he passed them close aboard.

There was elation struggling to surge up from Mike's heart, but he kept it down until this was done. Now he would ride the English up against the channel batteries at Nombre de Dios, and if a man escaped it would only be because the Spanish had willed to pick him up as a prisoner. And the buccaneers seemed unaware of the two-sided press which was about to crush them. This and this alone worried Mike now. It did not seem possible that Bristol, the vaunted Captain Bristol, could so foolishly allow himself to be smashed in such a trap. Still— there were the buccaneers, sailing handsomely, even eagerly, into the jaws of destruction.

Mike paced the quarter-deck. Now and again, as the *Josef y Maria* gybed to cross a wounded English quarter and blast him completely out of action, he looked uneasily along the wrecked decks for Bristol. That he had not seen Bristol when the *Fleetfoot* had been raked worried him. That he was succeeding worried him. That he had not heard any clattering on high worried him further still.

There was decidedly something very spooky about this action. He was winning it!

Behind him the sun still hung its inches above the horizon and the sky was still bathed in its scarlet light, which made blood out of the sea and tinted the sails a deceptively charming pink. Mike knew that Horace had forgotten to move his time. He spoke of it to his sailing master in a lull, but this fellow found nothing strange about it!

And then, suddenly, the sun leaped up the sky and in the blink of an eye was on the zenith!

The sailing master didn't think that was odd either.

When Mike pointed out to Trombo that there were nearly as many English ships left in action as there had been at the beginning, even though half the English fleet had been sunk, Trombo shrugged and muttered something about the will of God.

Ranging back and forth and nipping at the heels of the English, driving them downwind to Nombre de Dios, the Spaniards seemed to be enjoying themselves. There seemed to be only one thought in the buccaneering fleet and that was to get away from the horrible punishment which kept searching their decks. They seemed to be quite blind that they were coursing down upon a mighty shore battery.

At last the coast lost its blue cast and became green and filled with definite markings, and the harbor of Nombre de Dios opened its mouth to them. And like a host of shepherds running sheep, the Spanish forced in the wings and made the English spear toward that harbor.

And like quaking sheep the English let themselves be herded.

Mike kept telling himself that there was something wrong with this victory. But maybe Horace had had a stroke—he hoped.

And then the foremost buccaneer, astonishingly enough the *Fleetfoot,* came into range of the Spanish forts. And swiftly narrowed the mile of blue waves to a gap a quarter of that.

And nothing happened.

Mike bawled to his signalmen and up rushed flags to break angrily, commanding the shore batteries to wake up and fire. Half the buccaneer fleet was in range now and, as the seconds raced by, finally was all within.

And still the forts did not fire.

"Treason!" howled Mike. "Trombo! Run that hoist again!"

Evidently the commander of the fort was not at all interested in Mike's signals.

Still, Mike told himself to cool himself down; it was not such a task to cut these English up, anyway, with just his fleet. They were so badly wrecked that they could not do much in return. He shouted for hoists to order his fleet to close in.

Not until then did Mike get an inkling of what had happened to them. They were speeding up on the English which were in the shoals just off the forts. And the forts opened fire! But not on the English.

A hurricane of smoking hot iron crashed out at the Spanish fleet, and in one blast sent masts tottering and magazines exploding and men falling by the regiment!

Stunned inactivity descended upon the Spanish. Half a dozen ships broached to and lay there broadside, perfect targets as their sails shivered helplessly.

The forts thundered again and again.

The Spaniards struggled to beat up out of the shoal

waters where the lighter-draft Englishmen had run. On every side the flaming ruins of tall galleons struck rocks. The sea was alive with the swimming men and aglitter with the metal of scattered spars.

Suddenly the wind increased in force, and those which had struggled free on their six-point tacks now made so much leeway that they were again within range of the butchering forts.

Orders were nothing. The *Josef y Maria* clawed to windward while English ships, sailing, incredibly, much closer and faster, rushed out like wolfhounds to hang on her and rake her decks with flame. In seconds she was a smoking shambles, and a buccaneer to either side was casting grapnels over her gunwales to lay her aboard.

Cutlasses were making quick work of her boarding bets and now came to her decks a howling flood of half-clothed demons to sweep her shattered defenders forward and, thence, over her bows into the sea.

Across a deck carpeted with the blood of Spaniards and decorated with dismembered corpses came a hurricane of a man—Bristol!

Rapier in fist, battle lust distorting his face, the English captain leaped up the stern-castle gangway, shouting his battle cry.

Mike stood amid the ruins of his quarter-deck and toppled mizzle and beheld the devil swoop upon him. This, then, was the end. This was the part where Bristol ran him through for a dirty spick and fed his corpse to the sharks. And this was not cardboard scenery or puppet men. Pain and death were real!

Knowing well that he was doomed without trial, Mike acted without a glance at the rules. He sprang back without drawing his rapier, for he knew destiny meant death with that. A small serpentine which had been swiveled about to sweep the waist, but whose crew had died in the act without firing it, was pointed at Bristol. The linstock lay sizzling upon the planking. Mike scooped it up and slapped the touchhole. The huff singed his hand and then there was a white-hot flash!

Bristol was wreathed in smoke, untouched even by powder sparks.

Mike was struggling in the sea, swept away toward the shore by the spar which he had grasped. And in his battered ears rang the English cheer which meant victory, and the whir of a contented typewriter in the sky.

CHAPTER THIRTEEN

It was nearly midnight when Mike, cast up again by the sea but only because of his own endeavor, gained the wooded heights above Nombre de Dios. He had struggled across the battlefield behind the forts, thus answering the riddle of the treachery. Bristol had landed a force to take them from the unfortified rear while the Spanish fleet was sucked into the trap from the sea.

There was no typewriter clattering now. There was nothing but the hot, sultry wind in the palms to remind him of it. The sullen sky was low upon Nombre de Dios and the smoldering ruins of the sacked city added their greasy thickness to the night.

It was the end, that was certain.

It was all over, though the English vessels still stood there in the roadstead, swinging at their cables while their crews debauched themselves. The story for Mike was done!

But Mike, weary and wounded, with no magic words to heal his hurts or his exhaustion, was not content. He had for one space changed that plot. And now there was no typewriter in the sky.

He had been created a swordsman without peer, a military genius, a clever and even treacherous gentleman. That had not been taken away.

Trombo was dead. They were all dead. But here was Mike, dragging himself through the tangle of wood

145

toward the night-shrouded house which had so long been his home.

The windows showed lights behind their blinds as he crept by them, but he had not come here to peep through cracks and skulk. His rapier was at his side and no matter how tired was his arm—

He stepped up to the porch and found a buccaneer sentry sprawled there, left to guard but now very drunk. Mike pulled a pistol from the fellow's sash and, holding the weapon in his left hand and keeping his sword in his right, kicked open the front door.

The table was very beautiful, lit by tall yellow candles whose soft beams fell upon Mike's crystal and gold. At one end sat the Lady Marion, painfully beautiful, smiling still though now she looked toward the door.

Bristol, silk-shirted and gold-sashed, started to his feet, the candlelight still in his eyes.

"Gog's wounds! Who's this?"

"I'm Mike de Wolf. The fellow you call Miguel St. Raoul de Lobo. Can it be," he added with sarcasm which had become habitual, "that I am not welcome in my own house?"

"Damme!" said Bristol. "Ye're a ghost!"

"No m'lad," said Mike. "It's you that are a ghost!"

Lady Marion was white as she looked from Mike to Bristol.

"But ye're dead!" cried Bristol. "With my own eyes I saw it!"

"You've got the same eyes now," said Mike.

"But why . . . have you come back?" said Bristol.

"To kill you," said Mike.

It had no great effect upon Bristol. He had led a charmed life for so long that he was afraid of nothing. He reached toward his rapier which lay on the arms of a chair beside the wall.

Mike ached to drill him with the pistol, but he knew

the effect it would have upon the Lady Marion. He was too weary and starved to duel and he did not intend to give Bristol, who had had all the breaks, any others.

"Maybe you English fight before your women," said Mike. "I don't. There's light on the porch."

Bristol snorted in derision. "Marion, please pardon me while I kill this gentleman once and for all." And he strode past Mike, through the door and to the porch.

Mike shut the door behind himself and stood there for a moment looking at the English hero.

"You found her very glad to see you I've no doubt," said Mike, humanly prey to jealousy.

"Aye," said Bristol. "And I've a debt to pay you, you hound, for sullying her fair name."

"It's not so sullied but what you asked her to marry you," said Mike.

"So I did," said Bristol.

"And she accepted," said Mike, "and then, amid a very touching scene, she said she could see you marching in triumph through the streets of London with your name on every lip and that at last she had found a man brave enough to command her humbleness and that she would be content to spend the remainder of her life worshiping you. And then she kissed you."

"Of course," said Bristol. "But . . . how did you know?"

"There's a lot I know."

"I hope you know I do you favor to fight you. I've a town full of my men—"

"All drunk," said Mike, glancing down the hill at the burning, raped wreck of the city. "And it's no favor."

Bristol shrugged. He had been pulling off his boots the better to grip the floor with his feet.

"I fear," said Mike, "that you'll never live to spend the millions in bullion you found here today. For, Tom Bristol, I intend to run you through."

"Garde!" cried Bristol.

Their blades crossed and, with furious attack and defense, they went at each other.

Mike thought the fury of Bristol's attack was the cause of the floor's shaking. He thought the way the lantern jiggled was done by a wild thrust. And he thought the roaring in his ears was in his head, an aftermath of cannon fire.

But it wasn't.

The shaking was soon so violent that it threw both of them down. Bristol, cursing, struggled up and was again thrown. Mike saw the porch roof start to come down and scurried back.

Lightning flashed down the sky, bluely lighting the woods where trees were falling. Thunder, by its very sound, seemed capable of tearing Mike apart. The porch came down and Bristol and the sleeping buccaneer were devoured in its shambles.

A frightened voice was crying from within the house, and then the Lady Marion was at the door, striving to force away the beam which blocked her egress. Again the lightning flared and the rain slashed furiously down.

Mike seized the Lady Marion's wrist and pulled her through the opening.

"What's happening?" she wept in terror.

"Come with me," said Mike, running down the path.

Again the lightning wiped out the blackness for a space and again the thunder rolled angrily over the sky. The wind was swiftly increasing in force and the rain was hammering painfully upon Mike's bare face. The earth shook and cast them down.

Through the water Mike reached for the Lady Marion and clutched her to him. It was impossible to stand. The flaring in the sky showed her scared face close to his.

"What is it?" she cried out to him.

"An earthquake and a storm," said Mike. "Nothing more."

"Where is Bristol?"

"He's dead," said Mike. "I didn't kill him. He was hit by the beams and buried when the porch fell."

"He's dead!"

"Yes. Marion, look at me. Have you no memory of loving me? Have you no thought of all the months we were together. You were happy with me—"

"Mike! Hold me! Hold me, Mike! I'm frightened!"

He held her close to him.

Lightning flashed so close by that Mike felt its concussion. And then, looking up against the whitened sky, he saw the huge black limbs and trunk of a tree come hurtling down at them.

He clutched Marion, trying to protect her body with his own. The earth shook and then vanished. The lightning cracked and snarled and then rain and earth and sky and wind, all these were gone.

And Mike's arms were empty.

CHAPTER FOURTEEN

"You O. K., buddy?" said the taxi driver. "You better let me take you home."

Mike looked wonderingly at the fellow, at the cab, at the dark street, quiet at this hour.

"If it's dough, you c'n pay me when you got it. But you shouldn't be lying here. Somebody'll clip you."

Mike got up with help. "I'm all right," he muttered.

"You don't smell like ye're loopy," said the cabby. "You been sick or something?"

"Yeah," said Mike. "Yeah, I been sick." He steadied himself against the lamp-post. "I'll be all right in a minute." He looked dazedly at the cab's license plates and finally it came home to him that they were those of the same year he had departed. It took him some little time to get it through his mind that he was back, alive and evidently safe.

"What's the name of this town?" said Mike.

"N'Yawk," said the cabby.

Mike felt relieved. He had come back, then.

"You sure you'll be all right?"

"Yeah. I feel fine now," said Mike.

"And you won't lemme take you home?"

"No. I'll walk a little ways if you don't mind."

"O. K., you're the boss," said the cabby, getting into his hack and driving away.

Mike stood there for a long time, getting himself adjusted to the strangeness of being home again. In a way it was swell to be back. He'd get his fingers in shape and take another crack at the Philharmonic. And he'd see René and Kurt and Win Colt and Horace—

It would be so funny seeing Horace Hackett. Would it be possible, he wondered, to ever tell Horace about all this? In a way he should, just so he'd never be put into a story again—but again he shouldn't because then Horace Hackett's already gigantic opinion of himself would probably expand beyond endurable limits. Horace was always talking about the powers of an author.

Mike essayed a walk and found that his faintness was gone. He slouched along the street, hands in the pockets of his sport jacket, chin on chest.

He had tried not to think about it and he tried now once more. But he knew. He had lost her. He would never see her again, for she was not of this world, and the other—maybe it did not even exist now. He had lost her, the only woman he would ever love. And though he tried not to he could still feel her sobbing against him, knowing somehow that it was all over and done and that she was dead. He would never forget that— He stopped and braced himself against a wall.

"Move along, buddy," said a cop.

Mike moved along.

To find her—in a story. And now she would never be again.

He threw it off with bitterness. He was angry now. Angry with Horace Hackett, angry with this world and that other. Angry with the fate which had been handed him—

Ah, yes. The fate. It was his luck to meet somebody in a story and then return without her. It was his luck. But you couldn't expect the breaks all the time. You couldn't ask luck to run your way forever. He had had her for a little while, in a land ruled by a typewriter in the clouds. And now he was out of that and there was no type—

Abruptly Mike de Wolf stopped. His jaw slacked a trifle and his hand went up to his mouth to cover it. His

152

eyes were fixed upon the fleecy clouds which scurried across the moon.

Up there—
God?
In a dirty bathrobe?

FEAR

Author's Note

There is one thing which I wish the reader could keep in mind throughout, and that is: this story is wholly logical, for all that will appear to the contrary. It is not a very nice story, nor should it be read alone at midnight—for it is true that any man might have the following happen to him. Even you, today, might lose four hours from your life and follow, then, in the course of James Lowry.—*L. Ron Hubbard.*

CHAPTER ONE

Lurking, that lovely spring day, in the office of Dr. Chalmers, Atworthy College Medical Clinic, there might have been two small spirits of the air, pressed back into the dark shadow behind the door, avoiding as far as possible the warm sunlight which fell gently upon the rug.

Professor Lowry, buttoning his shirt said, "So I am good for another year, am I?"

"For another thirty-eight years," smiled Dr. Chalmers. "A fellow with a rugged build like yours doesn't have to worry much about a thing like malaria. Not even the best variety of bug Yucatan could offer. You'll have a few chills, of course, but nothing to worry about. By the way, when are you going back to Mexico?"

"If I go when my wife gives me leave, that'll be never."

"And if I had a woman as lovely as your wife Mary," said Chalmers, "Yucatan could go give its malaria to somebody else. Oh, well"—and he tried to make himself believe he was not, after all, envious of Atworthy's wandering ethnologist— "I never could see what you fellows saw in strange lands and places."

"Facts," said Lowry.

"Yes, I suppose. Facts about primitive sacrifice and demons and devils— Say, by the way, that was a very nice article you had in the *Newspaper Weekly* last Sunday."

The door moved slightly, though it might have been

caused by the cool breath of verdure which came in the window.

"Demons and devils, my brother? Who talks about us in these ignorant times?"

"When you have been here longer, my sister, you will find that a college can be expected to talk about anything."

"Thank you," said Lowry, trying not to look too pleased.

"Of course," said young Chalmers, "you were rather sticking out your neck. You had your friend Tommy frothing about such insolence. He's very fond of his demons and devils, you know."

"He likes to pose," said Lowry. "But how do you mean, 'sticking out my neck'?"

"Who is this Tommy, my brother?"

"Professor Lowry's best friend. Now hush."

"You haven't been here much under Jebson," said Chalmers. "He nearly crucified a young mathematician for using Atworthy's name in a scientific magazine. But then, maybe our beloved president didn't see it. Can't imagine the old stuffed shirt reading the *Newspaper Weekly,* anyway."

"Oh," said Lowry. "I thought you meant about my denying the existence of such things. Tommy—"

"Well, maybe I meant that, too," said Chalmers. "I guess we're all superstitious savages at heart. And when you come out in bold-face type and ridicule ancient belief that demons caused sickness and woe and when you throw dirt, so to speak, in the faces of luck and fate, you must be very, very sure of yourself."

"Demons? Devils? Dirt in the faces of luck and fate? My brother, tell me about that man Lowry."

"In a moment. Now hush."

"Why shouldn't I be sure of myself?" said Lowry, smiling. "Did anyone ever meet a spirit of any sort face to

158

face? I mean, of course, that there aren't any authenticated cases on record anywhere."

"Not even," said Chalmers, "the visions of saints?"

"Anyone who starves himself long enough can see visions."

"Still," said Chalmers, "when you offer so wildly to present your head in a basket to the man who can show you a sure-enough demon—"

"Did he write that?"

"Hush, sister."

"And my head in a basket he shall have," said Lowry. "For a man of science, you talk very weirdly, old fellow."

"I have been in a psychiatric ward often enough," said Chalmers. "At first I used to think it was the patient and then, after a while, I began to wonder. You know, demons are supposed to come out with the full moon. Ever watch a whole psychopathic ward go stark raving mad during the three days that a moon is full?"

"Nonsense."

"Perhaps."

"That doctor, my brother, is a man who sees too much."

"Let him see. Who would believe?"

"Chalmers, I tried, in that article, to show how people began to believe in supernatural agencies and how scientific explanation has at last superseded vague terror. Now don't come along and tell me that you can cast some doubt on those findings."

"Does the fellow believe nothing at all, my brother?"

"Oh"—and Chalmers began to laugh—"we both know that 'truth' is an abstract quantity that probably doesn't exist. Go crusading against your devils and your demons, Professor Lowry. And if they get mad at you, argue them out of existence. I myself don't say they exist. It merely strikes me strangely that man's lot could be so consistently unhappy without something somewhere aiding in that misery. And if it is because electrons vibrate at certain speeds, or if it is because the spirits of air and earth and water are jealous of any comfort and happiness that man might have, I neither know nor care. But how comforting it is to knock on wood when one has made a brag."

"And so," said Lowry, slipping into his topcoat, "the goblins are gonna get me if I don't watch out."

"They'll get you all right if Jebson saw that article," said Chalmers.

"Listen, my sister. You know where to find a Superior One. Go bring him to me swiftly."

"You are amused, my brother."

"And will be more amused very soon."

"Where will you be, my brother?"

"Following Professor Lowry. Make haste, my sister. I have been bored today."

"Have you any plan?"

"As yet, nothing sufficiently horrible. But make haste, my sister. I must catch up with him."

The door moved ever so little—but then, perhaps it was just the cool, sweet breath of spring whispering through the window.

Lowry, swinging his stick, went out into the sunlight. It felt good to be home. The place looked and smelled good, too. For beyond the change of the seasons, there was never any difference in this town, never any real difference in the students; and when the college built a new building, why, it always looked somehow old and mellow before it was half completed. There was a sleepy sameness to the place which was soothing to one whose eyes had been so long tortured by the searing glare of spinning sun on brassy sand.

As he walked along toward his office he asked himself why he ever left this place at all. These great elms, putting forth their buds, yawning students stretched out upon the fresh green of grass, colorful jackets, a mild blue sky, ancient stone and budding ivy—

For the briefest flicker he half recalled the birth of his own wanderlust. A theft in his dorm, accusation, expulsion and disgrace; and three years later—three years too late to completely remove the scar—they had finally reached him to tell him that the guilty one had been found within a week after his running away. Remembering, he again felt that seep of shame through him and the shy idea that he should apologize to the first one he met.

But it passed. It passed and the air was full of spring and hope and the smell of moist earth. Clouds, hard driven high up, occasionally flashed shadows over the pavement and lawns; the breeze close to earth frisked with the remnants of autumn, chasing leaves out of corners and across lawns and against trees, bidding them vanish and make way for a new harvest later on.

No, little ever changed in this quiet and contented mecca of education. Twenty-five years ago Franklin Lowry, his father, strolled down this same street; twenty-five years before that Ezekiel Lowry had done so. And each had done so not once but on almost every day of his mature life and then, dead, had been carried in a hearse along this way. Only James Lowry had varied such a tradition and that only slightly, but then James Lowry, in his quiet but often stubborn way, had varied many traditions. He had been the first Lowry to even start to stain that scholastic name, and he was certainly the first Lowry with the wanderlust. But then he had been a strange child; not difficult, but strange none the less.

Reared up in a great tomb of a house where no word was less than three syllables long and where the main attention paid to him was, "Hush!" James Lowry had, perforce, built a universe of his own from the delicate stuff of dreams. If he cared to look in that old dean of a mansion, he knew he could find his boyhood companions tucked out of sight below the planks which covered the attic floor with indifference: Swift, Tennyson, Carroll, Verne, Dumas, Gibbon, Colonel Ingram, Shakespeare, Homer, Khayyam and the unknown creators of myth and legend of all lands had been his advisers and companions and playmates, taking him off among discards and dust and whispering strange thoughts to him, a wide-eyed child, smear-faced with jam and attic cobwebs. But, he supposed, walking down in the warmth of the new sun, he, too, would keep on walking down this street, past these stores with pennants in the windows, past these students in bright jackets, past these old elms and ancient walls; and he, too, would probably be carried in a hearse over this pavement to a resting place beside his letter-burdened forefathers.

He was fortunate, he told himself. He had a lovely lady for a wife; he had an honest and wise gentleman for a friend; he had a respected position and some small reputation as an ethnologist. What of a slight touch of malaria? That would pass. What if men did not understand so long as they were respectful and even kind? Life was good and worth the living. What more could one ask?

A group of students passed him and two, athletes from the bars on their sweater arms, touched their caps and called him "sir." A professor's wife, followed at a respectful distance by her bundle-laden maid, nodded to him with a friendly smile. A girl from the library followed him with her glance a little way and without knowing it he walked the straighter. Indeed life was good.

"Professor Lowry, sir." It was an anæmic book-delver, assistant to an assistant in some department.

"Yes?"

The young man was a little out of breath and he took a moment or two, standing there and wringing a wretched cap in his hands, the better to talk clearly. "Sir, Mr. Jebson saw you pass by and sent me after you. He wants to see you, sir."

"Thank you," said Lowry, turning and retracing his

steps until he came to the curving pathway which led up to the offices. He did not wonder very greatly at being summoned for he was not particularly afraid of Jebson. Presidents had come and gone at Atworthy and some of them had had peculiar ideas; that Jebson was somewhat on the stuffy side was nothing to worry about.

The girl in the outer office jumped up and opened the door for him with a muttered, "He will see you right now, sir," and Lowry went in.

Once or twice a new president had brought some furniture here and had even tried to change the appearance of this office. But the walls were older than paint and the floor had seen too many carpets pass away to shift itself much on the account of a new one. Dead men stared frostily out of frames. An eyeless bust of Cicero stood guard over a case of books which no one ever read. The chairs were so deep and so ancient that they might have been suspected of holding many a corpse that they had drowned.

Jebson was looking out of the window as though his inattention there might result in a collapse of the entire scene visible from it. He did not look around, but said, "Be seated, Lowry."

Lowry sat, regarding the president. The man was very thin and white and old, so stiff he looked more like plaster than flesh. And each passing year had dug a little deeper in the austere lines which furrowed his rather unkindly face. Jebson was motionless, for it was his pride that he had no nervous habits. Lowry waited.

Jebson, at last, opened a drawer and took out a newspaper which was partly printed in color; this he laid out before him with great care, moving his pen stand so that it would lie smoothly.

Lowry, until then, had felt peaceful. He had forgotten, completely and utterly, that article in the *Newspaper*

Weekly. But even so he relaxed again, for certainly there was nothing wrong in that.

"Lowry," said Jebson, taking a sip of water which must have been white vinegar from the face he made, and then holding the glass before his face he as he continued: "Lowry, we have stood a great deal from you."

Lowry sat straighter. He retreated to the far depths of himself and regarded Jebson from out the great shadows of his eyes.

"You have been needed here," said Jebson, "and yet you chose to wander in some lost and irretrievable land, consorting with the ungodly and scratching for knicknacks like a dog looking for a bone he has buried and forgotten." Jebson was a little astonished at his own fluent flight of simile and paused. But he went on in a moment. "Atworthy has financed you when Atworthy should not have financed anything but new buildings. Atworthy was not built on nonsense."

"I have found more than enough to pay for my own expeditions," ventured Lowry. "Those money grants were refunded three years ago—"

"No mind. We are here to develop the intelligence and youth of a great nation, not to exhume the moldering bones of a heathen civilization. I am no ethnologist. I have little sympathy with ethnology. I can understand that a man might utilize such play as a hobby, but, holding as I do that man is wholly a product of his own environment, I cannot see that a study of pagan customs can furnish any true light by which to understand mankind. Very well. You know my opinions in this matter. We teach ethnology and you are the chair in anthropology and ethnology. I have no quarrel with learning of any kind, but I do quarrel with a fixation!"

"I am sorry," said Lowry.

"And I am sorry," said Jebson in the tone a master inquisitor of the Inquisition might have used condemning a prisoner to an auto-da-fé. "I refer, of course, to this article. By what leave, may I ask, was it written?"

"Why," floundered poor Lowry, "I had no idea that I was doing wrong. It seemed to me that the function of the scholar is to give his learning to those who might use it—"

"The function of the scholar has nothing to do with this, Lowry. Nothing whatever to do with this! Why, this wretched rag is a brand! It is trash and humbug! It is stuffed with lies under the name of scientific fact and has done more harm for the cause of truth than Fascism itself! And," he stated, ominously lowering his tone, "this morning I was confronted with the name of Atworthy in such a place! If a student had not brought it to me I might never have seen it at all. There it is, 'By Professor James Lowry, Ethnologist, Atworthy College.'"

"I saw no reason to sign anything else—"

"You had no right to inscribe it originally, 'Professor Lowry of Atworthy College.' It is cheap. It is a wretched attempt at notoriety. It demeans the very name and purpose of education. But then," he added with a sniff, "I suppose one cannot expect anything else from a man whose whole life has been highly irregular."

"I beg your pardon?" said Lowry.

"Oh, I have been here long enough to know the record of every man on our staffs. I know you were expelled—"

"That matter was all cleared!" cried Lowry, blushing scarlet and twisted with the pain of the memory.

"Perhaps. Perhaps. But that is beside the point. This article is cheap and idiotic and by being cheap and idiotic it has demeaned the name of Atworthy." Jebson bent over it and adjusted his glasses upon the thin bridge of his nose. " 'Mankind's mental ills might in part be due to the phantoms of the witch doctors of yesterday!' Humph! 'By Professor James Lowry, Ethnologist, Atworthy College.' You will be writing about demonology next as something which one and all should believe! This is disgraceful. The entire town will be talking about it——"

Lowry had managed to control his shaking hands and now erased the quiver from his throat which sought to block his voice. "That is not an article about demonology, sir. It is an attempt to show people that their superstitions and many of their fears grew out of yesterday's erroneous beliefs. I have sought to show that demons and devils were invented to allow some cunning member of the tribe to gain control of his fellows by the process of inventing something for them to fear and then offering to act as interpreter——"

"I have read it," said Jebson. "I have read it and I can see more in it than you would like me to see. Prating of demons and devils and the placating of gods of fear—— By your very inference, sir, I suddenly conceive you to mean religion itself! Next, I suppose, you will attack Christianity as an invention to overthrow the Roman capitalistic state!"

"But——" began Lowry and then, turning red again, held his tongue and retreated even further into himself.

"This wild beration of demons and devils," said Jebson, "reads like a protest of your own mind against a belief which association with the ungodly and unwashed of far lands might have instilled in you yourself. You have made yourself ludicrous. You have brought mockery upon Atworthy. I am afraid I cannot readily forgive this, Lowry. In view of circumstances, I can find no saving excuse for you except that you desired money and gained it at the expense of the honor and esteem in which this institution is held. There are just two months left of this school year. We cannot dispense with you until the year is done. But after that," said Jebson, crumpling up the paper and tossing it into the wastebasket, "I am afraid you will have to look for other employment."

Lowry started up. "But——"

"With a better record, I might have forgiven. But your

record has never been good, Lowry. Go back to the forgotten parts of the world, Lowry, and resume your commune with the ungodly. Good day."

Lowry walked out, not even seeing the girl who opened the doors for him; he forgot to replace his hat until he was on the walk; he had wandered several blocks before he came to himself. Dully he wondered if he had a class and then recalled that it was Saturday and that he had no Saturday classes. Vaguely he remembered having been on his way to attend a meeting or to have luncheon—no, it could not be luncheon, for it was evidently about two, according to the sun. And then the nudge of thought itself was swallowed in the wave of recollection.

He was shivering and it brought him around to thinking about himself for a moment. He mustn't shiver just because this world, for him, had come to an abrupt end; there were other colleges which might be glad to have him; there were millionaires who had offered to finance him, seeing that his traveling returned the investment and more. No, he should not feel so badly. And yet he shivered as though stripped naked to a winter's blast.

The racing clouds above darkened the street for whole seconds at a time; but there was something dead now in the sound of last year's leaves getting chased out of corners and there was something ugly in the nakedness of these elms. He strove to locate the source of his chill.

It was Mary.

Poor Mary. She loved this world of teas and respect; she had been brought up in this town and all her memories and friendships were here. It was enough that he would be talked about. It was too much that she leave everything that was life to her. Her friends would shake their heads barely in her sight.

No, she wouldn't want to stay here, where everyone would speculate on why he was busted, where everyone would have no more reason to ask her to teas.

167

And the big scholarly mansion—she loved that old place.

He failed to understand Jebson, for he was too generous to be able to run the gamut of Jebson's thought process, starting with a little man's desire to injure a big one, and envy for Lowry's rather romantic and mysterious aspect, passing through indirect insult to the college, and, finally, coming to light as a challenge to Christianity itself in some weird and half-understood way. Lowry was left floundering with only one fact on which to work: this was the culmination of a disgrace for which he had suffered acutely and innocently nearly twenty-one years before. And that pain and this pain were all entangled in his mind and driven hard home with the ache which was all through him, an ache he had forgotten was malaria.

Poor Mary.

Poor, beautiful, sweet Mary.

He had always wanted to appear grand to her, to make up somehow for being so many years older than she. And now he had brought her disgrace and separation from that which she knew best. She would take it well; she would follow him; she would be sorry and never once mention that she felt badly on her own account. Yes. Yes, she would do that, he knew. And he would not be able to prevent, nor even be able to tell her how badly he felt for her.

Again he had the recollection of having an appointment somewhere, but again he could not remember. The wind was chill now and tugged at his hat, and the clouds which swept their shadows over the pavement were darker still.

"Here is the Superior One, my brother. Have you begun?"

"Just begun, my sister. Welcome, sir."

"You have plans, little one? Have you set the problem?"

"Ai, sir. If you will enter that house just ahead and—"

He looked about him and found that he was within

sight of an old house with iron deer before it, the home of Professor Tommy Williams, who, for all his bachelorhood, maintained his family place alone.

Feeling strangely as though all had not yet happened to him and experiencing the need of shelter and company, he walked swiftly to the place and turned up the walk. The mansion seemed to repel him as he stared at it, for the two gable windows were uncommonly like a pince-nez sitting upon the nose of a moldering judge; for an instant he hesitated, almost turned around and went away.

And then he had a mental image of Tommy, the one man in this world to whom he could talk, having been the one kid with whom he had associated as a boy. But if he had come out of his boyhood with a shy reticence, Tommy had chosen another lane, for Tommy Williams was the joy of his students and the campus; he had traveled much in the old countries and therefore brought to this place an air of the cosmopolitan, a gay disregard for convention and frumpy thought. Tommy Williams loved to dabble with the exotic and fringe the forbidden, to drink special teas with weird foreign names and read cabalistic books; he told fortunes out of crystal balls at the charity affairs and loved to eye his client afterward with a sly, sideways look as though outwardly this must all be in fun, but inwardly—inwardly, mightn't it be true? Tommy was all laughter, froth and lightness, with London styles and Parisian wit, a man too clever to have any enemies—or very many friends.

No. He need not pause here on the threshold of Tommy's home. It would do him good to talk to Tommy. Tommy would cheer him and tell him that old Jebson was, at his finest, a pompous old ass. He mounted the steps and let the knocker drop.

Some dead leaves on the porch were going around in a harassed dance, making a dry and crackly music of their own; and then inanely they sped out across the lawn as though trying to catch up with a cloud shadow and so save themselves from an eventual bonfire. Nervous leaves, running away from inevitable decay, unable to cope with the rival buds which were pushing tenderly forth all unknowing that those things which fled had once been bright and green, coyly flirting with the wind. This was Lowry's thought and he did not like it, for it make him feel ancient and decayed, abandoned in favor of the fresh and green that had no flaws, who were too young to be anything but innocent; how many days would it be before another had his job? Some youthful other, preaching, perhaps, from Lowry's own books?

He dropped the knocker again, more anxious than before to be admitted to the warmths of fire and friendship; his teeth were beginning to chatter and he had a sick, allgone sensation where his stomach should have been. Malaria?—he asked himself. Yes, he had just come from Chalmers, who had called these chills malaria. He had not two hours ago peered into a microscope where his basically stained blood was spread out so that they could see the little globes inside some of the red corpuscles. Malaria wasn't dangerous, merely uncomfortable. Yes, this must be a malarial chill and shortly it would pass.

Again he dropped the knocker and felt the sound go booming through the high-ceilinged rooms within; he wanted to go away from there again, but he would not bring himself to leave just as Tommy came to the door. He shivered and turned up his collar. Very soon he would begin to burn; not unlike a leaf, he told himself. He peered through the side windows which flanked the door.

He had once more the idea that he had an engagement somewhere and pondered for an instant, trying to pull forth the reluctant fact from a stubborn recess.

No, he wouldn't keep standing here. Houses were never locked in this town, and Tommy, even if he was not home, would welcome him eagerly when he did return; he pushed open the door and closed it behind him.

It was dim in the hall; dim with collected years and forgotten events, with crêpe long crumbled and bridal bouquets withered to dust and smoky with childish shouts and the coughing of old men. Somewhere there was a scurrying sound as though a scholarly rat had been annoyed at his gnawing upon some learned tome. To the right the double doors opened portentously upon the living room, and Lowry, sensing a fire there, approached, hat in hand.

He was astonished.

Tommy Williams lay upon the sofa, one arm dangling, one foot higher than the other and both feet higher than his head; his shirt was open and he wore neither tie nor coat. For an instant Lowry thought he must be dead.

And then Tommy yawned and started a stretch; but in the middle of the action he sensed his visitor and came groggily to his feet, blinking and massaging his eyes and looking again.

"Heavens, man," said Tommy, "you gave me a start for a moment. I was sound asleep."

"I'm sorry," said Lowry, feeling unnecessary. "I thought you were gone and that I might wait until you—"

"Of course!" said Tommy. "I've slept too long anyway. What time is it?"

Lowry glanced at the great hall clock. "Five minutes after two."

"Well! That shows you what all play and no sleep will do to a fellow. Here, give me your hat and get warm by the fire. Lord, I've never seen a man look quite so blue. Is it as cold as that out?"

"I seem to be a little cold," said Lowry. "Malaria, I guess." He felt a little better—Tommy seemed so glad to see him—and he moved across the room to where two logs smoldered upon the grate. Tommy came by him and stirred them into a cheerful glow and then busied himself by the liquor cabinet, putting a drink together.

"You've got to take better care of yourself, old fellow,"

said Tommy. "We've only one Professor Lowry at Atworthy and we can't run the risk of losing him. Here, take this and you'll feel better."

Lowry took the drink in his hand, but he did not immediately partake of it; he was looking around the room at the old glass-fronted cases and the china figures on the stand in the corner. When he had been little he and Tommy had never been allowed to come into this place except when there was company and they were to be presented; and then, scour-faced and feeling guilty of some crime, they had been allowed to sit stiffly in a stiffer chair and gradually relapse into suffering stupidity.

How different was that Tommy from this one! Still, there was the same winning grin, the same shining head of black hair, always slightly awry in an artistically careless way, the same classic face, startling pale against the blackness of the hair, the same graceful slenderness and the quick dancer movements with which he had always done things. Tommy, thought Lowry with a sudden clarity, was pretty; maybe that was what Lowry saw in him, something which complemented his own blunt ruggedness. Lowry sipped at the drink and felt the warmth of it spread pleasingly out to meet the glow from the brightly snapping flames.

Tommy was sitting on the edge of the sofa now; he always sat as though expecting to arise in another instant. He was lighting a cigarette, but he stared so long at Lowry that the match burned his fingers and he dropped it and placed the tip in his mouth. Presently he forgot about the sting and succeeded in applying the fire.

"Something is wrong, Jim."

Lowry looked at him and drank again. "It's Jebson. He found an article of mine in the *Newspaper Weekly* and he's raving mad about it."

"He'll recover," said Tommy with a rather loud laugh.

"He'll recover," said Lowry, "but just now I'm wondering if I will."

"What's this?"

"I'm being ousted at the end of the term."

"Why ... why, the old fool! Jim, he can't mean that. It will take an order from the board—"

"He controls the board and he can do that. I've got to find another job."

"Jim! You've got to straighten this thing out. Jebson has never liked you, true, and he has muttered a great deal about you behind your back; you are too blunt, Jim. But he can't let you go this way. Why, everyone will be furious!"

They discussed the matter for a little while and then, at last, a sort of hopelessness began to enter their tones and their sentences became desultory to finally drop into a silence marked only by the occasional pop of the wood.

Tommy walked around the room with a restive grace, pausing by the whatnot stand to pick up a china elephant; tossing the fragile beast with a quick, nervous motion, he turned back to Lowry; there was a queer, strained grin on Tommy's lips but bleakness in his eyes.

"It would seem," said Tommy, "that your article has begun to catch up with you."

"That is rather obvious."

"No, no. Don't ever accuse me of being obvious, Jim. I meant the article was about demons and devils and tended to mock them as having any power—"

"Tommy," said Lowry with one of his occasional smiles, "they should put you to teaching demonology. You almost believe in it."

"When creeds fail, one must turn somewhere," said Tommy jokingly—or was it jokingly? "You say that the gods of luck are false; you wrote that it is silly to seek the aid of gods beyond the aid of the one supreme God; you said that demons and devils were the manufacture of Machiavellian witch doctors and that men could only be herded by the fear of those things they could not see; you

173

said that men thought they found a truly good world to be an evil world in their blindness and so built a hideous structure of phantoms to people their nightmares."

"And what if I did?" said Lowry. "It is true. The world is not evil; the air and water and earth are not peopled with jealous beings anxious to undermine the happiness of man."

Tommy put the elephant back and perched himself on the edge of the couch; he was visibly agitated and kept his eyes down, pretending to inspect his immaculate nails. "No man *knows*, Jim."

Lowry rumbled out a short laugh and said. "Tell me now that you are so studied in those things that you actually credit a possibility of their existence."

"Jim, the world to you has always been a good place; that's a sort of mechanical reaction by which you like to forget all the ghastly things the world has done to you. You should be more like me, Jim. I *know* the world is an evil, capricious place and that men are basically bad and so, knowing that, I am always pleased to find some atom of goodness and only bored to see something evil. You, on the other hand, march forward relentlessly into sorrow and disappointment; to you all things are good, and when you find something which is mean and black and slimy you are revolted—and you've come to me today shivering as with the ague, racked by a treacherous turn done you by a man you should initially have thought good. That view of yours, Jim, will never bring you anything but misery and tears. Phantoms or not, that man is the safest who knows that all is really evil and that the air and earth and water are peopled by fantastic demons and devils who lurk to grin and increase the sad state of man."

"And so," said Lowry, "I am to bow low to superstition and reinherit all the gloomy thoughts of my benighted ancestors. Devil take your devils, Tommy Williams, for I'll have nothing of them."

"But it would appear," said Tommy in a quiet, even, ominous way, "that they will have something of you."

"How can you arrive at that?"

"It would appear," said Tommy, "that the devils and demons have won their first round."

"Bah," said Lowry, but a chill coursed through him.

"You said they do not exist, in an article in the *Newspaper Weekly*. That same article arouses the rage of a vindictive fool and thereby causes your scheduled dismissal from Atworthy."

"Nonsense," said Lowry, but less briskly.

"Be nice and say the world is an evil place, filled with evil spirits. Be nice and forget your knightly manner. And now be nice and go home and fill yourself with quinine and rest."

"And I came to you," said Lowry with a smile, "for solace."

"To solace is to lie," said Tommy. "I gave you something better than that."

"Devils and demons?"

"Wisdom."

Lowry walked slowly into the hall, the chill making it difficult for him to speak clearly. Confound it, he was certain that he had an appointment somewhere this afternoon. He could almost recall the time as a quarter to three and the old clock was chiming that now. He reached toward the rack where his hat lay in a thick mass of coats and canes.

"Now, little one?"

"Now."

CHAPTER TWO

It was dusk, at the twilight's end; all along the street windows were lighted and people could be seen through some of them, people with talk and food in their mouths; the wind had picked up along the earth and brought a great gout of white scurrying out of the dark—a newspaper. High above, a cool moon looked out now and then through rifts of anxiously fleeing clouds, and now and again a star blinked briefly beyond the torn masses of blue and black and silver.

Where was he?

The street sign said Elm and Locust Avenues, which meant that he was only half a block from Tommy's house and about a block from his own. He looked worriedly at his watch by the sphere of yellow in the middle of the street and found that it was a quarter to seven.

A quarter to seven!

The chill took him and his teeth castaneted briefly until he made his jaw relax. He felt for his hat, but it was gone; he felt panicky about the loss of his hat and cast anxiously about to see if it lay anywhere near.

A group of students strolled by, a girl flattered by the teasing of the three boys about her; one of them nodded respectfully to Lowry.

A quarter to three.

A quarter to seven.

Four hours!

Where had he been?

Tommy's. That was it. Tommy's. But he had left there at a quarter to three. And it was now a quarter to seven.

Four hours!

He had never been really drunk in his whole life, but he knew that when one drank indiscreetly there usually followed a thick head and a raw stomach; and as nearly as he could remember he had had only that one drink at Tommy's. And certainly one drink was not enough to blank his mind.

It was horrible, having lost four hours; but just why it was horrible he could not understand.

Where had he gone?

Had he seen anyone?

Would somebody come up to him on the morrow and say, "That was a fine talk you gave at the club, Professor Lowry"?

It wasn't malaria. Malaria in its original state might knock a man out, but even in delirium a man knew where he was, and he certainly had no symptoms of having been delirious. No, he hadn't been drunk and it wasn't malaria.

He began to walk rapidly toward his home. He had a gnawing ache inside him which he could not define, and he carried along that miserable sensation of near-memory which goes with words which refuse to come but halfway into consciousness; if he only tried a little harder he would know where he had been.

The night was ominous to him and it was all that he could do to keep his pace sane; every tree and bush was a lurking shape which might at any moment materialize into—into— In the name of God, what was wrong with him? Could it be that he was afraid of the dark?

Eagerly he turned into his own walk. For all that he could see, the ancient mansion slept, holding deep shadows close to it like its memories of a lost youth.

He halted for a moment at the foot of the steps, wondering a little that he saw no light in the front of the house; but then perhaps Mary had grown alarmed at his failure to come home and had gone to his office—no, she would have phoned. A clamoring alarm began to go within him.

Abruptly a shriek stabbed from the blackness:

"Jim! Oh, my God! Jim!"

He vaulted the steps and nearly broke down the door as he entered; for a moment he paused, irresolute, in the hall, casting madly about him, straining to catch the sound of Mary's voice again.

There was nothing but silence and memory in this house.

He leaped up the wide stairway to the second floor, throwing on lights with hungry fingers as he went. He glanced into all the rooms on the second floor without result and sprang up the narrow débris-strewn stairs to the attic. It was dismal here and the wind was moaning about the old tower and trunks crouched like black beasts in the gloom; he lighted a match and the old familiar shapes leaped up to reassure him. She was not here!

Trembling he made his way down, to again examine the rooms of the second floor. He was beginning to feel sick at his stomach and his blood was two sledge hammers knocking out his temples from within. He had lighted everything as he had come up, and the light itself seemed harsh to him, harsh and unkindly in that it revealed an empty house.

Could she have gone next door?

Was there a dinner somewhere that she had had to attend without him? Yes, that must be it. A note somewhere, probably beside his chair, telling him to hurry and dress and stop disgracing them.

On the first floor again he searched avidly for the note, beside his chair, on the dining-room table, in the kitchen, on his study desk, on the mantelpiece— No, there wasn't any note.

He sank down on the couch in his study and cupped his face in his hands; he tried to order himself and stop quivering; he tried to fight down the nausea which was, he knew, all terror. Why was he allowing himself to become so upset? She must not have gone very far, and if she had not left a note, why then she intended to be back shortly.

Nothing could happen to anyone in this lazy, monotonous town.

Her absence made him feel acutely what life would mean without her. He had been a beast, leaving her and running away to far lands, leaving her to this lonely old place and the questionable kindness of faculty friends. Life without her would be an endless succession of purposeless days lived with a heavy hopelessness.

For minutes he sat there, trying to calm himself, trying to tell himself that there was nothing wrong, and after a little he did succeed in inducing a state of mind which, if not comfortable, at least allowed him to stop shivering.

The outer door slammed and quick footsteps sounded in the hall. Lowry leaped up and ran to the door.

She was hanging up her new fur wrap.

"Mary!"

She looked at him in surprise, so much had he put into the word.

"There you are, Jim Lowry! You vagabond! Where were you all this time?"

But he wasn't listening to her; his arms were almost crushing her and he was laughing with happiness. She laughed with him, even though he was completely ruining the set of her hair and crumpling the snowy collar of her dress.

"You're beautiful," said Lowry. "You're lovely and wonderful and grand and if I didn't have you I would walk right out and step over a cliff."

"You better not."

"You're the only woman in the world. You're sweet and loyal and good!"

Mary's face was glowing and her eyes, when she pushed him back a little to look up at him, were gentle. "You're an old bear, Jim. Now account for yourself. Where have you been?"

"Why—" and he stopped, feeling very uneasy. "I don't know, Mary."

"Let me smell your breath."

"I wasn't drunk."

"But you're shivering. Jim! Have you gotten malaria again? And here you are walking around when you should be in bed—"

"No. I'm all right. Really, I'm all right, Mary. Where were you?"

"Out looking for you."

"I'm sorry I worried you."

She shrugged. "Worry me a little now and then and I'll know how much I worship you. But here we are gabbing and you haven't had anything to eat. I'll get something immediately."

"No! I'll get it. Look. You just sit down there by the fire and I'll light it and—"

"Nonsense."

"You do as I tell you. You sit there where I can look at you and be your most beautiful and I'll rustle up my chow. Now don't argue with me."

She smiled as he forced her down into the chair and giggled at him when he dropped the sticks he had picked up from the basket. "Clumsy old bear."

He got the fire going and then, putting out his hand as a protest against her moving, he sped through the dining room and into the kitchen, where he hurriedly threw together a sandwich from yesterday's roast beef and poured himself a glass of milk. He was so frightened that she would be gone before he could get back that he resisted all impulse to make coffee.

181

Presently he was again in the living room, sighing in relief that she was still there. He sat down on the lounge opposite from her and held the sandwich in front of his face for a full minute, just looking at her.

"Go on and eat," said Mary. "I'm no good at all to let you sup on cold food."

"No, no! I won't have you do a thing. Just sit there and be beautiful." He ate slowly, relaxing little by little until he was half sprawled on the lounge. And then a thought brought him upright again. "When I came in here I heard screams."

"Screams?"

"Certainly. You sounded like you were calling to me."

"Must be the Allison radio. Those kids can find the most awful programs and they haven't the least idea of tuning them down. The whole family must be deaf."

"Yes, I guess you are right. But it gave me an awful scare." He relaxed again and just looked at her.

She had very provocative eyes, dark and languorous, so that when she gave him a slow look he could feel little tingles of pleasure go through him. What a fool he was to go away from her. She was so young and so lovely— He wondered what she had ever seen in an old fool like himself. Of course, there were only about ten years between them and he had lived outdoors so much that he didn't look so very much over thirty-one or thirty-two. Still, when he sat like this, studying her sweet face and the delicate rondures of her body and seeing the play of firelight in her dark hair and feeling the caress of her eyes, he could not wholly understand why she had ever begun to love him at all; Mary, who could have had her choice from fifty men, who had even been courted by Tommy Williams— What did she see in a burly, clumsy, granite-being like himself? For a moment he was panicky at the thought that some day she might grow tired of his silences, his usual lack of demonstrativeness, his long absences—

"Mary—"

"Yes, Jim?"

"Mary, do you love me a little bit?"

"A lot more than a little bit, Jim Lowry."

"Mary—"

"Yes?"

"Tommy once asked you to marry him, didn't he?"

A slight displeasure crossed her face. "Any man that could carry on an affair with a student and still ask me to marry him— Jim, don't be jealous again; I thought we had put all that away long ago."

"But you married me instead."

"You're strong and powerful and everything a woman wants in a man, Jim. Women find beauty in men only when they find strength; there's something wrong with a woman, Jim, when she falls in love with a fellow because he is pretty."

"Thank you, Mary."

"And now, Mr. Lowry, I think you had better get yourself to bed before you fall asleep on that couch."

"Just a little longer."

"No!" She got up and pulled him to his feet. "You're half on fire and half frozen, and when you get these hangovers the best thing for you is bed. I couldn't ever see what pleasure a man could get out of wandering off to some land just so he could roast in the sun and let a bug bite him. To bed with you, Mr. Lowry."

He let her force him up the stairs and into his room and then he gave her a long kiss and a hug sufficient to break her ribs before he let her return to the living room.

He felt very comfortable inside as he undressed and was almost on the verge of singing something as he hung up his suit when he noticed a large tear on the collar. He inspected it more closely. Yes, there were other tears and the cloth was all wrinkled and stiff in spots as if from mud. Why, good grief! The suit was ruined! He puzzled over it and then, in disgust for having destroyed good En-

183

glish tweeds, he crammed jacket and trousers into the bottom of a clothes hamper.

As he got into his pajamas he mused over what a lovely person Mary really was. She hadn't called his attention to it and yet he must have looked a perfect wreck.

He washed his hands and face in an absent sort of way, musing over how he could have wrecked his suit. He dried himself upon a large bath towel and was about to slip on his pajama coat when he was shocked to see something which looked like a brand upon his forearm.

It was not very large and there was no pain in it; interested, he held his arm closer to the light. The thing was scarlet! A scarlet mark not unlike a tattoo. And what a strange shape it had, like the footpads of a small dog; one, two, three, four—four little pads, as though a small animal had walked there. But there were few dogs that small. More like a rabbit—

"Strange," he told himself.

He went into his room and turned out the light. "Strange." He eased in between the covers and plumped up his pillow. A mark like the footprint of a rabbit. How could he have torn his suit and stained it with mud? What could have put this stamp upon his arm? A chill came over him and he found it difficult to stop his jaw muscles from contracting.

The cool moon, blanked out for seconds by the racing clouds, laid a window pattern across the foot of his bed. He flung the covers back, annoyed that he had forgotten to open the window, and raised the sash. An icy belt was thrown about him by the wind and he threw himself hurriedly back between the covers.

Well, tomorrow was quite another day, and when the sun came he would feel better; still, malaria had never given him this sick feeling in his stomach.

The cool moon's light was blue and the wind found a crack under the door and began to moan a dismal dirge;

the sound was not constant, but built slowly from a whisper into a round groan and then into a shriek, finally dying again into a sigh. And lying there Jim Lowry thought there was a voice in it; he twisted about and attempted to cover up his right ear, burrowing his left in the pillow.

The wind was whimpering and every few seconds it would weep, "Where?" And then it would mutter out and grumble and come up again as though tiptoeing to his bedside to cry, "Why?"

Jim Lowry turned over and again pulled the covers down tight against his ear.

"Where?"

A whimpering complaint.

"Why?"

The window rattled furiously as though something was trying to get in; with tingling skin, Lowry came up on his elbow and stared at the pattern of light. But the cool moon's light was only marred by the speeding clouds. Again the window was beaten and again there was only moonlight.

"I'm a fool," said Lowry, pulling up the covers again.

A sigh.

"Why?"

A whimpering complaint.

"Where?"

The curtain began to beat against the glass and Lowry flung out to raise it all the way so that it could not move. But the string and disk kept striking against the pane and he had to locate a pin so that he could secure them.

"I'm a fool," said Lowry.

He had listened to drums off somewhere in the black. He had slid into dark caverns to feel tarantulas and snakes running over or striking his boots; he had once awakened with a moccasin slithering out from under his top blanket; he had mocked at curses; he had once taken a cane knife away from an infuriated and drunken native—

A sigh.

"Why?"

A whimpering complaint.

"Where?"

Fear's sadistic fingers reached in and found his heart and aped its regular rhythm to send his blood coursing in his throat. Just the moan of the wind under a door and the protest of the curtains and the rattle of the sash and the moon's cold blue light upon the bottom of his bed—

The door opened slowly and the curtain streamed straight out as the wind leaped into the room from the window. The door banged and the wall shivered. And a white shape was moving slowly toward him on soundless feet and a white face gleamed dully above a glittering knife. Nearer and nearer—

Lowry sprang savagely at it and knocked the knife away.

But it was Mary.

Mary stood there, looking at him in hurt amazement, her hand empty but still upheld. "Jim!"

He was shaking with horror at the thought he might have hurt her; weakly he sank upon the edge of the bed, and yet there was relief in him, too. A broken glass lay upon the rug when she turned on the light and a white pool of warm milk steamed in the cold air. She held her hand behind her and, with sudden suspicion, he dragged it forth. He had struck the glass so hard that it had cut her.

He pulled her small hand to the light and anxiously extracted a broken fragment from the cut and then applied his lips to it to make it bleed more freely. He opened a drawer and took out his expedition first-aid kit and found some antiseptic and bandages. She seemed to be far more anxious about him than about her hand.

"Mary."

"Yes?"

186

He pulled her down to the edge of the bed and threw part of the spread about her shoulders.

"Mary, something awful has happened to me. I didn't tell you. There are two things I didn't tell you. Jebson found that *Newspaper Weekly* article and at the end of this term I am going to be dismissed. We . . . we'll have to leave Atworthy."

"Is that all, Jim! You know that I don't care about this place; anywhere you go, I'll go." She was almost laughing. "I guess you'll have to drag me along, no matter how deep the jungles are, Jim."

"Yes. You can go with me, Mary. I was a fool never to have allowed it before. You must have been terribly lonely here."

"I am always lonely without you, Jim."

He kissed her and felt that this must be the way a priest might feel touching the foot of his goddess.

"And the other thing, Jim?"

"I . . . I don't know, Mary. I have no idea where I was between a quarter of three and a quarter of seven. Four hours gone out of my life. I wasn't drunk. I wasn't delirious. Four hours, Mary."

"Maybe you fell and struck something."

"But there is no bruise."

"Maybe you don't know all there is to know about malaria."

"If it blanks out a mind, then it is so serious that the patient isn't going to feel as well as I do now. No, Mary. It . . . it was something else. Tommy and I were talking about demons and devils and . . . and he said that maybe I should not have attacked them in that article. He said they might be trying . . . well— The world *is* a good place, Mary. It isn't filled with evil things. Man has no reason to walk in the shadow of dread because of phantoms."

"Of course he hasn't, Jim. Tomorrow you may find out

187

what happened. It might be something perfectly innocent."

"You think so, Mary?"

"Certainly. Now you lie down there and get some sleep."

"But—"

"Yes, Jim?"

"I feel . . . well . . . I feel as though something horrible had happened to me and that . . . that something even more horrible is going to happen soon. I don't know what it is. If I could only find out!"

"Lie down and sleep, Jim."

"No. No, I can't sleep. I am going out and walk and maybe the exercise will clear my head and I'll remember—"

"But you are ill!"

"I can't lie here any longer. I can't stay still!"

He put down the window and began to dress. She watched him resignedly as he slipped into a jacket.

"You won't be gone very long?"

"Only half an hour or so. I feel I must walk or explode. But don't disturb yourself on my account. Go to sleep."

"It's nearly midnight."

"I feel—" He stopped, beginning again with a different tone. "This afternoon I felt I had an appointment somewhere at a quarter to three. Maybe I went somewhere— No. I don't know where I went or what I did. No. I don't know! Mary."

"Yes, Jim."

"You're all right?"

"Of course I'm all right."

He buttoned up his topcoat and bent over and kissed her. "I'll be back in half an hour. I feel I . . . well, I've just got to walk, that's all. Good night."

"Good night, Jim."

CHAPTER THREE

The night was clean and clear and, as he poised for a moment on top of the steps, the smell of fresh earth and growing things came to him and reawakened his memories. It was the kind of night that makes a child want to run and run forever out across the field, to feel the earth fly from beneath his feet, driven by the incomprehensible joy of just being alive. On such a night he and Tommy had once visited a cave a mile out of town which was supposed to be haunted and had succeeded in frightening themselves out of their wits by beholding a white shape which had turned out to be an old and lonely horse. The memory of it revived Lowry: Tommy's fantastic imagination and his glib tongue!

And how Tommy loved to devil his slower and more practical friend; that had just been devilment today. Witches and spooks and old wives' tales, devils and demons and black magic. How Tommy, who believed in nothing, liked to pretend to beliefs which would shock people! How he adored practically knocking his students out of their seats by leaning over his desk and saying, in a mysterious voice, "To be polite, we call this psychology, but, in reality, you know and I know that we are studying the black goblins and fiendish ghouls which lie in pretended slumber just ouf of sight of our conscious minds." How he loved such simile! Of course, what he said was true, absolutely true, but Tommy had to choose that way of putting it; it was such a dull world, so drab; why not enliven it a little and stick pins into people's imaginations? Indeed, dear Tommy, why not?

The top of his head was cold and he reached up to discover that he had forgotten his hat, and, discovering that, remembered that he had lost it. Because his gear was mainly tropical he had only one felt hat, and one did not walk around Atworthy in a solar topi; not Atworthy! The loss of it troubled him. And his best tweed ruined beyond repair! But then his hat had his name in the band, being a good hat, and some student would find it where the wind had taken it and return it to the dean's office— Still, there was something wrong in that; there was a deeper significance to having lost his hat, something actually symbolic of his lost four hours. Part of him was gone; four hours had been snatched ruthlessly from his life and with them had gone a felt hat. It struck him that if he could find the hat he could also find the four hours. Strange indeed that anything should so perplex him, the man whom little had perplexed.

Four hours gone.

His hat gone.

He had the uneasy feeling that he ought to walk along the street toward Tommy's and see if the hat was there under a bush; it seemed a shame to leave a good hat on some lawn; it might rain.

Yes, most certainly, he had better find that hat.

He started down the steps to the walk, glancing up at the hurrying fleece between earth and the moon. He had been down these steps thousands of times; when he reached the "bottom" he almost broke his leg on an *extra step.*

He stared at his feet and hastily backed up, swiftly to discover that he could *not* retreat. He almost fell over backward into space! There were no steps above him, only a descent of them below him. Glassy-eyed he looked down the flight, trying to take in such a length of steps. Now and then they faded a little as they went through a dark mist, but there was no clue whatever of what might lie waiting at the bottom.

He looked anxiously overhead and was relieved to find that the moon was still there; he was standing so that his eyes were above the level of the yard and he felt that he could reach over to the indefinite rim and somehow pull himself out. He reached, but the rim jerked away from him and he almost fell. Breathless he stared down the flight to mystery. The moon, the steps, and no connection between himself and the porch.

Somewhere he thought he heard a tinkle of laughter and glared about, but it was evidently nothing more than a set of Japanese wind chimes on the porch. Somehow he knew that he dared not reach the bottom, that he had not sanity enough to face the awful thing which waited there. But then, all he had to do was descend two more steps and he would be able to reach up to the rim and haul himself forth. He descended; the rim retreated. That was no way to go about it, he told himself, glancing at his empty hands. He would back up—

Again he almost went over backward into a void! The two steps he had descended had vanished away from his very heels.

There was that laughter again—no, just the sweet chording of the wind chimes.

He peered down the angle of the flight, through the strata of dark mist, into a well of ink. Wait. Yes, there was a door down there, on the side of the flight, not thirty steps below him. That door must lead out and up again; the very least he could do would be to chance it. He went down, pausing once and glancing over his shoulder. How odd that these steps should cease to exist as soon as he passed along them! For there was now nothing but a void between himself and the front of his house; he could still see the lights shining up there. What would Mary think—

"Jim! Jim, you forgot your hat!"

He whirled and stared up. There was Mary on the porch, staring down into the cavity which had been a walk.

"Jim!" She had seen the hole now.

"I'm down here, Mary. Don't come down. I'll be up in a moment. It's all right."

The moonlight was too dim for him to see the expression on her face. Poor thing, she was probably scared to death.

"Jim! Oh, my God! Jim!"

Wasn't his voice reaching her? "I'm all right, Mary! I'll be back as soon as I reach this door!" Poor kid.

She was starting down the steps, and he cupped his hands to shout a warning at her. She could do nothing more than step out into space! "Stop, Mary! *Stop!*"

There was a peal of thunder and the earth rolled together over his head, vanishing the moonlight, throwing the whole flight into complete blackness.

He stood there trembling, gripping the rough, earthy wall.

From far, far off he heard the cry, dwindling into nothing, "Jim! Oh, my God! Jim!" Then it came again as the merest whisper. And finally once more, as soundless as a memory.

She was all right, he told himself with fury. She was all right. The hole had closed before she had come down to it, and now the trap up there was thickening and making it impossible for her voice to get through. But he felt, somehow, that it was all wrong. That she wasn't up there now. He began to quiver and feel sick, and his head spun until he was certain that he would pitch forward and go tumbling forever into the mystery which reached up from the bottom—the bottom he dared not approach.

Well, there was a door ahead of him. He couldn't stand here whimpering like a kid and expect to get out of this place. He'd seen the door and he'd find it. He groped down, feeling for each step with a cautious foot and discovering that their spacing was not even, some of them dropping a yard and others only an inch. The wall, too, had changed character under his hands, for now it was slimy and cold, as though water had seeped down from above for ages, wearing the stone smooth and glossing it with moss. Somewhere water was dripping slowly, one drop at a time, frighteningly loud in the corpse-quietness of this place.

He'd been in worse, he told himself. But it was funny, living in that house all those years without ever suspecting the existence of such a flight at the very bottom of his front steps.

What was he doing here, anyhow? He'd told himself that he had to find something—

Four hours in his life.

A felt hat.

Where the devil was that door? He had come thirty steps and his questing hands had yet to find it. Maybe he could back up now, but when he tried that he found that the steps had kept on vanishing as he went over them. If he had passed the door he could never get back to it now! A panic shook him for a moment. Maybe the door had been on the other side of the stairs! Maybe he had gone by it altogether! Maybe he would have to go down—all the way down to— To what?

Something sticky and warm drifted by his cheek and he recognized it as probably being a stratum of mist; but what strange mist it was! Warm and fibrous, and even vibrant, as though it was alive! He strung several strands of it with his hands, and then, as though he had caught a snake, it wriggled and was gone.

He rubbed his palms against his coat, trying to rid them of the tingling feeling. He stepped lower, and now the mist was clinging to him like cobwebs, sticking to his cheeks and tangling about his shoulders.

Somewhere he heard a faint call. "Jim! Jim Lowry!"

He tried to surge toward it, but the mist held him with invisible, sticky fingers.

"Jim Lowry!"

What an empty voice!

With all his strength he tore at the mist, expecting it to string out and tear away; but instead, it was like being released all at once, and he nearly fell down the steps he could not see. Again he sought the wall and felt his way along, now and again hopeful that the steps above had not vanished, but finding always that they had. There must be a door somewhere!

The shock of light blinded him.

He was standing on what seemed to be solid earth, but there was no sun—only light, blinding and harsh. Seared earth, all red and raw, stretched away for a little distance on every side; great gashes had been washed out of gratey stone.

A small boy sat unconcernedly upon a small rock and dug his initials out of the stony earth. He was whistling a nonsensical air, badly off key, with *whooshes* now and then creeping out with his whistle. He pulled his straw hat sideways and glanced at Lowry.

"Hello."

" Hello," said Lowry.

"You ain't got any hat on," said the boy.

"No. So I haven't."

"And your hands are dirty," said the boy, returning to his aimless talk.

"What's your name?" said Lowry.

"What's yours?" said the boy.

"Mine's Jim."

"That's funny. Mine's Jim, too. Only it's really James, you know. Looking for something?"

"Well—yes. My hat."

"I saw a hat."

"Did you? Where?"

Solemnly the boy said, "On my father's head." He gave

vent to a wild peal of laughter at his joke. Then he reached into his pocket. "Want to see something?"

"Why, I suppose so. If it's worth seeing."

The boy took out a rabbit's foot and held it admiringly toward Lowry. Then there was just a rabbit's foot hanging there, and darkness reached in from the outskirts of the land and swallowed even that. Lowry took a step and again almost fell down the stairs. He inched his way along; water was dripping somewhere; the steps were more and more worn with age; from the moss on them it was doubtful if many had passed this way.

Below he saw a dull gleam which seemed to emanate from a side entrance. Well! There was a door down there, after all! Why hadn't he walked off into the harsh red land and so found his way back to the top again! But, never mind, here was a door ahead of him, and a door meant egress from these stairs. Thank God he did not have to go to the bottom!

Mist swirled briefly and the door was faded out, but in a moment it had again appeared, clearer than before except that it was now closed and the light came from an indefinable source on the stairs themselves. He was not particularly frightened now, for he was intent upon a certain thing: he knew that somewhere he would find his hat and the four hours. He felt he should have asked the boy.

When he stood before the door he breathed heavily with relief. Once away from these steps he knew he would feel better. He tried the handle, but the portal was locked from within, and there was no sign of a knocker. He bent over to squint through the keyhole, but there was no keyhole. He straightened up and was not surprised to discover that a knocker had appeared before him; the thing was a verdigris-stained head of a woman out of whose head grew snakes, the Medusa. He dropped it, and the sound went bouncing from wall to wall down the steps as

195

though a stone was falling. He waited a long while before he heard any sound from within, but just as he was about to raise the knocker again there came out a grating of rusty bars which were being removed and then the latch rattled and the door swung wide and the acrid smell of burning herbs and a thick, unclean cloud of darkness rolled from the place; two bats squeaked as they flew forth, hitting Lowry with a soft, skin wing. The smell of the place and the smoke got into his eyes so that he could not clearly see the woman; he had an impression of a wasted face and yellow teeth all broken and awry, of tangled, colorless hair and eyes like holes in a skull.

"Mother, I would like to leave these stairs," said Lowry.

"Mother? Oh, so you are polite tonight, James Lowry. So you'd like to flatter me into thinking you are really going to stand there and try to come in. Hah-hah! No, you don't, James Lowry."

"Wait, mother, I don't know how you know my name, for I have never been here before, but—"

"You've been on these stairs before. I never forget a face. But now you are coming down, and then you were going up, and your name was not James Lowry, and every time you went up another step you would kick away the one below, and when you came here you laughed at me and had me whipped and spat upon my face! I never forget!"

"That is not true!"

"It will do until there's something that *is* true in this place. And now I suppose you want your hat."

"Yes. Yes, that's it. My hat. But how did you know that I was looking—"

"How do I know anything? Hah-hah. He's lost his hat. It went like a bat. Now what do you think of that? He's lost his hat? Well, now, James Lowry, that's a very silly thing to do, to do, to do. To lose your hat. You are old enough to know better, and your head is big enough to keep a hat on. But that isn't all you've lost, James Lowry."

"Why—no, it isn't."

"You've lost four hours, just like that! Four whole hours and your hat. Want advice?"

"If you please, mother, can't we come in off these *stairs?*"

"You can't leave them. You walked up them, and now you'll walk down them all the way to the bottom. You must do it, that's all there is to it. You can sag and drag and gag and wag, but you've got to go to the bottom. All the way down. All the way down. All the way, way, way, way, way, way, way down! *Down! Down! Down!* Want some advice?"

"If you please."

"Then give me your pocket handkerchief."

He gave it to her, and she violently blew her nose upon it and threw it out into the darkness. In a moment one of the bats came back, bringing it. She threw it away and the other bat came back.

"Runaways!" she scolded them. "Want some advice, James Lowry?"

"Please, mother."

"Don't try to find your hat."

"Why not, mother?"

"Because if you find your hat you'll find your four hours, and if you find your four hours then you will die!"

Lowry blinked at her as she stuffed the pocket handkerchief into his coat and reached out, talon-fingered, toward his throat. But though he felt the bite of her nails, she was only straightening his tie.

"Want advice, James Lowry?"

"Yes, mother."

"Hats are hats and cats are cats, and when the birds sing there is something awry in the world. Bats are bats and hats are hats, and when it is spring the world is only

197

bracing itself for another death. Rats are rats and hats are hats, and if you can't walk faster then you'll never be a master. You have a kind face, James Lowry. Want some advice?"

"Yes, mother."

"Go on down the stairs and you'll meet a man. If you are bound to die, then ask him where you lost your hat."

"He'll tell me?"

"Maybe he will and maybe he won't. Bats are hats are rats are cats are hats and there is no soup deep enough to drown."

"Drown what, mother?"

"Why, to drown, that's all! You have a kind face, James Lowry."

"Thank you, mother."

"And then you'll meet another man after you meet the first man. But they aren't men, either of them. They're ideas. And the first man will tell you that you are about to meet the second man, and then the second man will tell you that you have to go on down to the foot of the stairs. All the way to the bottom. Down, down, down—"

"Where is the bottom, mother?"

"At the top, of course. Hats lead to bats, lead to cats, lead to rats. Rats are hungry, James Lowry. Rats will eat you, James Lowry. Hats, you came here to bats, you go on to cats, you get eaten by the rats. Do you still want to find your hat?"

"Please, mother."

"Oh, what a contrary, stubborn, bullheaded, witless, rotten, thoughtless, bestial, wicked, heartless, contrary, stubborn, bullheaded, witless, rotten— Do you still want to find your hat, James Lowry?"

"Yes, mother."

"You don't believe in demons and devils?"

"No, mother."

"You *still* don't believe in demons or devils?"

"No, mother."

"Then look behind you, James Lowry."

He whirled.

But there was only darkness.

There was the sound of a slamming door. Far away a voice cried, "Jim! Jim Lowry!"

When he felt of the place where the door had been, for it was inky dark once more, he could find nothing but the wall. He groped upward, but the steps were gone. He groped downward and the voice, clearer now, was calling, "Jim! Jim Lowry!"

Step by step, sometimes an inch and sometimes a yard, sometimes slanting to the right, sometimes level and sometimes to the left, but always the opposite direction from what they first appeared. Another stratum of mist, white this time, curling smokily about him; it was full of something that stung his throat, but something, too, which made him walk with less fear and a straighter back.

"Jim! Jim Lowry!"

It was quite close now; it sounded hollow, as though it was being brayed by a town crier into an echo-box. There wasn't much interest in it any more than there is interest in the voice of a train caller bidding the commuters to pack into the 5:15.

"Oh, Jim! Jim Lowry!"

Paging Mr. Lowry. Paging Mr. Lowry.

The white mist was clearing as he came down into its lower levels, and he could see the stairs now. They had changed; they were clean and dry and made of polished marble, and they had an elaborately carved railing which, after the stone, was very soothing to his touch. It seemed that this case was winding a little, and that just below there was a great hall hung in banners with half a hundred guests about a board—but he did not feel that he should go near the guests. A big Great Dane came bounding up to him and almost knocked him down, and then, as though it had made a mistake, gave a sniff and walked, stiff-legged, away. Lowry kept on going down the steps.

"Jim! Jim Lowry!"

He was on a landing stage, and something had happened to the guests in the great hall, though he knew they were quite near. To his right hung a gold-and-white tapestry depicting combat in the lists, and to his left stood a stand full of lances, above which hung a sword plaque and a shield with three rampant lions upon it.

A hand tapped him on the shoulder and he snapped around to find a tall knight in full armor, made taller by the waving white plume of his visored helmet, the visor of which was down.

"James Lowry?"

"Yes?"

"Are you sure you are Jim Lowry?"

"Yes."

"Then why answer to the name of James? Never mind, we won't quibble. You know me?"

"I am sorry that I can't seem to place you. Your helmet visor is down, you know, and you are all cased in steel—"

"Well, well, old fellow, we won't equivocate about a visor now, will we? We are both gentlemen, and so there is no reason to quarrel, is there? Especially about a little thing like a visor. You think you are dreaming, don't you?"

"Why, no. I didn't exactly—"

"That's it. You are not dreaming. See, I'll pinch you." And he did, and nodded sagely when Lowry jerked away. "You are not dreaming, and this is all perfectly real. If you don't believe it yet, then look at the mark these steel fingers made."

Lowry glanced at the back of his hand and saw that it was bruised and bleeding.

"Now about this hat," said the knight. "You're bound to find it?"

"Certainly."

"It was only worth a few dollars, you know. And believe me, old man, what are a few dollars compared to the value of your own life?"

"What does my life have to do with a hat?"

"Oh, now I say, old fellow, didn't you hear the old mother tell you that if you found the hat you found the four hours, and that if you found the four hours you lost your life? Now let's look at this thing sagely, eh? Let's examine it in the light of cold and dispassionate reasoning. A hat is worth perhaps ten dollars. During the remaining thirty-five years of your life you will probably make a hundred and fifty thousand dollars at, say forty-five hundred dollars a year. Now is that anything to exchange for a ten-dollar bill?"

"Well-l-l—no-o-o."

"All right, old fellow, I am glad you see my point. Now let us probe more deeply into this problem. You are a very intelligent man. You have lost four hours. In the thirty-five years you may yet live there will be exactly three hundred and five thousand, four hundred and forty hours. Is that time sufficient to outweigh a perfectly stupid period like four hours?"

"No—but—"

"Ah, so we must still argue about this some more. You are bound to find your hat, eh?"

"I would like to."

"And you won't worry if you find your hat and then find the four hours—for they are right there side by side?"

"Well—"

"Now! I thought you'd weaken after a while. Find your hat, find four hours, find death. That's the way it will run. Hats are too numerous for you to go scrambling around looking for just one."

"I'll . . . I'll think it over."

"Don't do that. You should be convinced right here and now that it is no use finding that hat. And forget the four hours. Forget them quite completely."

"Maybe—" ventured Lowry, "maybe you can tell me what *did* happen in those four hours."

"Oh, now, come, old fellow! I tell you that if you find out you will surely die, and you ask me point-blank to tell you. And here I am trying to *save* you, not destroy you."

"You can't even give me a hint?"

"Why should I?"

"Was it that article—"

"Tut, tut, Jim Lowry. Don't try to worm it out of me, for I have no reason to wish you dead. In fact, I think you are a swell fellow, a veritable prince and the best there is. Now you just go on down—"

"Was it malaria?"

"Tut, tut."

"Was it the drink?"

"Hush, now."

"Was it—"

"I said to be quiet!" roared the knight. "If you are so determined to learn, you go on down those steps and you'll come to a man. That's all I'll say. You'll come to a man."

"Thank you," said Lowry. "And now, would you mind telling me your name?"

"Name? Why should I have a name? I am a knight, and I am full of ideals."

"But if I see you again I won't recognize you."

"I said I am full of ideals!"

"Well, what difference does that make? I am full of ideals, too." He reached out and started to raise the fellow's visor. The knight did not jerk away, but stood quite still.

The visor went up.

The suit was empty!
And there was darkness.

After a little while Lowry made another attempt to go up, but again it was futile; he almost fell through the void above him. He stood still, shivering. Did—did he have to go *down there,* after all? Down to— Swiftly he shook off the wild craving to scream. He grew calm.

There was something a little different about these steps, he found; they gave out another sound, a hollow sound, as though they were built of lumber; and unlike the others which had been above, these were regular. After a very short descent he almost fell trying to reach a step which was seemingly solid earth. Yes. He was on a flat expanse of earth! He could see nothing—

Suddenly he turned and felt for the bottom step. It was still there. The one above it was still there. The one above that was still there. Maybe the stairs were all there once more! Perhaps he could again gain the top! But again he stumbled, for where there had been a landing of marble there was now a platform of wood with a railing about it and further ascent was impossible. He went down the steps again to the flat expanse of earth.

He had not seen the fellow before, mainly because the fellow was all dressed in black. All in black. He wore a black slouch hat with a wide brim which almost covered the whole of his face, but was unable to hide the grossness of the features or the cruelty of the mouth; his powerful but hunched shoulders were draped in a black cloak of ancient manufacture; his shoes had black buckles upon them. He was carrying a lantern which threw, at best, a feeble glow between himself and Lowry; this he set down and perched himself upon a wooden seat, taking something long and snaky from under his arm. He then took out a little black book and, lifting the lantern, peered intently at the pages.

"Lowry?"

"That is I."

"Huh! Frank fellow, aren't you? Well, everybody knows better than to shilly-shally with me." He spat loudly and looked back at the book. "Nice, black weather we're having, isn't it?"

"Yes. I suppose so."

"How much do you weigh, Lowry?"

"A hundred and ninety pounds."

"Hm-m-m. Hundred and ninety pounds." He found a pencil and scribbled a note in his book. Then he lifted the lantern high and took a long look at Lowry's face and body. "Hm-m-m. No deformities?"

"I don't think so."

"Hundred and ninety pounds and an ordinary neck. James Lowry, isn't it?"

"Yes."

"Well, we won't be knowing each other very long, but that's your trouble, not mine."

"What . . . what is your name?"

"Jack. It's really Jack Ketch, but you can call me Jack." He spat loudly again. "If you want to do right by me and make it easy, why just put a pound note or two in your pocket when you come up."

There was a certain odor of decay about the fellow— decay and dried blood—which made Lowry's neck hair mount. "Why a pound note?"

"Why not? I've got to eat same as you used to. I can make it pretty easy or I can make it terrible bad. Now if you want my advice, you'll just pass over a pound note or two now and we can get down to business. I hate this waiting around. It's all built there, and we'll only get mixed up more if we keep delaying things and you'll only worry about it. What do you say to that?"

"I . . . I don't know what you are talking about."

He raised the lantern and stared at Lowry. "Hm-m-m. And you look bright enough." He set the lantern back

204

and took up the long, snaky thing from his lap. His coarse fingers became busy with it.

Lowry felt terror begin its slow seep through him. Jack Ketch. That was a familiar name. But he was certain he had never seen this man before. Jack Ketch—

Suddenly Lowry saw what the man was doing. That thing he had was a rope! And on it he was tying a hangman's noose!

And those steps. There were thirteen of them! And a platform at the top—a gallows!

"No!" screamed Lowry. "You can't do it! You have no reason to do it!"

"Hey! Hey, Lowry! Jim Lowry! Come back here! You can't run away from me! You'll never be able to run away from me Lowry—Jim Lowry—"

The hangman's boots were thudding behind him, and the whip of the cloak was like thunder.

Lowry tried to catch himself on the brink of new steps, sensing rather than seeing them, but the steps were slippery and he could not stop. He braced himself for the shock of striking those immediately below—

But he struck nothing.

Tumbling, twisting, turning, down, down, down through an inky void with the horror of falling, a lump of agony in his stomach. Down, down, down, down, through mists and the slashing branches of trees and mists again.

And then Lowry was lying in ooze, with the feel of it squashy between his fingers and the smell of it dead and rotten. Somewhere something was moving in the blackness. Brush was crackling and something was breathing hard and hot, something searching.

As quietly as he could, Lowry crept away. It was too dark for anything to see him; if he could be silent—

"Lowry! Jim Lowry!"

Lowry pressed into the muck and lay still.

"So you don't think I can see you, Jim Lowry! Wait a moment. I have something for you."

Jack Ketch's voice was growing closer, and Lowry knew that while he could not see a thing, he must be plainly visible to Jack Ketch. Madly he leaped to his feet and floundered away; brush stung him and the half-submerged trunk of a tree tripped him and, knee-deep, he somehow kept on.

"I can tell you where you can find your hat, Jim Lowry. I want to help you." And there was a sound of spitting. "You can't get away from me."

Lowry felt warm water up as high as his knees, with ooze beneath, and the steam of it smelled decayed. He hurried through it.

"I'm trying to help you, Jim Lowry!" said Jack Ketch, seemingly closer now. "All I want to do is help you. I can tell you where to find your hat. Won't you listen to me?"

Sick and weary, Lowry fell prone and pried himself out of the mud again and floundered on.

"I don't want to hurt you," pleaded Jack Ketch's voice. "I only want to hang you!" He swore and spat. "That's what a man gets for trying to help. Lowry! Come back here! I want to tell you where to find your hat!"

The ground was hard under his feet now, and Lowry fled swiftly through the velvet dark. A mighty force abruptly smote him on the chest and knocked him flat and half drowned into a mauling suction of sand and sea, turning him swiftly and snatching at him and dragging him under and outward. He was drowning!

He opened his mouth to scream and choked upon the salt water; he was being held in the depths, and all around him was a greenish light, and he could see the silver bubbles of his own breath going to the surface.

Suddenly he was on top, sucking breath into his tortured body, breath which was half sea water. He coughed and retched and tried to cry for help. And then the panic quieted in him and he found that he could stay afloat very easily. His breathing returned to normal as he tread water and he looked anxiously for Jack Ketch, but of the hangman there was no sign. Instead there was a long, jungle strand, a yellow beach bathed in white waves, green trees of gigantic size bending over the sea. And the sky was blue and the sea was blue and there was no sound in all this peaceful serenity. Lowry thankfully dragged in the beauty of the place and wondered at the comfortable warmth which spread through him. He eyed the beach again, but not for Jack Ketch; vaguely now he remembered that he had lost something—that he had lost four hours. Somehow he had to find them despite all the warnings which he had been given; somehow he had to rearrange his memory so that he would know for certain—

The darkness was settling once more and there came a wind, at first very low and then shrill, and the waves began to stir restlessly. He was beginning to feel tired.

Suddenly he knew that there was something in the deep below which was going to strike up and snatch him down, that there were many black and awful things beyond description which would haul him under and rend him apart.

He began to swim toward the shore through the thickening dark. It took all his wits to keep from speeding in blind panic and to keep from dwelling upon the things which must be under him. There was a roaring in the air and a thunder of breaking surf, and, looking closely across the waves, he saw great towers of spume appearing and vanishing, water smashed to white frenzy on a jagged reef. He turned. He would be mashed beyond recognition if he tried to land here, and yet he knew that he could not stay long in this water, for at any moment now something would reach up and gnash him in half. But he could not turn back, for the sea seemed to be forcing him in upon the jagged black teeth which thrust up through the surf. Somewhere lightning battered blue sheets at the world.

But there was no thunder beyond that of the surf. He was being raised ten feet and dropped ten feet by the surging waves, and each time he was closer to the rocks. He could not hear, he could not breathe. He was caught in a trap of water, and if he did not drown he would be smashed to a mangled mess.

Something bumped against him and he recoiled. It bumped against him a second time and he glanced toward it. A piece of wood! But even as he seized upon it he knew that it was of peculiar design, and that he had no right to touch it.

Just above the piece of wood he sensed a presence. He looked up.

He saw a book, held by a pair of hands. That was all. Just a book and a pair of hands.

"Now hold on tight," said a somewhat oily voice. "Everything is going to be all right very soon. But you must hold on tight and close your eyes and not see anything and not hear anything but what I tell you to see and hear. Believe in me and do exactly as I tell you—"

The voice was getting faint and far away, but that was because Lowry's weary face had dropped into the soothing cushion of the water while his hands, almost nerveless, still held the piece of wood.

CHAPTER FOUR

"Come on, now. You'll come around all right. A nice sleep in the jail will fix you up. Never did see why men had to drink— Why, it's Professor Lowry!"

The words came to him dimly, and the sensation of hands touching him at last reached his consciousness. He allowed himself to be helped from the wet pavement, feeling bruised and sore.

The rain was blowing under she street light in silver clouds which polished everything they touched; there was a damp, good smell in the night, a smell of growing and the rebirth of the soil.

Old Billy Watkins, his dark poncho streaming, was standing beside him, holding him up. Old Billy Watkins, who had been a young constable when Lowry was a kid and who had once arrested Lowry for riding a bicycle on the sidewalk and again on the complaint that Lowry had broken a window, and yet Old Billy Watkins could hold up Jim Lowry, Atworthy professor now, and be respectful if a little startled. The white mustache was damped into strings and was, for a change, washed quite clean of tobacco juice.

"I wonder," said Lowry in a thick voice, "how long I have been lying there."

"Well, now, I could put it at about five minutes or maybe six minutes. I come along here about that long ago and I got clear up to Chapel Street before I recollected that I'd forgot to put a call in at the box down here, and so I come back and here you was, lying on the sidewalk."

"What time is it?"

"Well, I guess it's pretty close to four. Sun be up pretty soon. Is your wife sick? I see some lights on in your house."

"No. No, Billy, I guess I'm the one that's sick. I started out to take a walk——"

"Must've been unable to sleep. Now me, I find out a nice hot drink of milk is just about the thing to put a man to sleep. Are you feeling all right?"

"Yes. Yes, I guess I feel all right now."

"You must have stumbled and fell. You got a bruise on your face and you seem to have lost your hat."

"Yes . . . yes, I guess I lost my hat. I must have stumbled. What street is this?"

"Why, your street, of course. That's your house right there, not thirty feet behind you. Here, I'll help you up the steps. I heard tell you had one of them tropical diseases. Mrs. Chalmers' maid was saying it wasn't nothing bad, though. What you want to go running off into countries like that for with all them heathens, Jimmy—I mean, Professor Lowry?"

"Oh—I guess it's exciting."

"Yeah, I reckon it must be. Like my grandpap. Fighting Injuns all night and buildin' railroads all day. Now, there you are. Want me to ring the bell for you, or have you——"

"No, the door's open."

"Well, your missis took to lockin' it while you was gone and I thought maybe she still did. You look pretty pale, Ji—professor. You sure I better not call Doc Chalmers for you?"

"No, I'm all right."

"Well, by golly, you don't *look* all right. Well, maybe you know best. Good night."

"Good night, Billy."

With fascination he watched Old Billy Watkins go hobbling down the steps. But the walk was perfectly solid and Old Billy reached the street, turned back and waved and then went on up the avenue through the rain.

Lowry opened the door and went in. Water formed a pool about his feet as he took off his coat.

"Is that you, Jim?"

"Yes, Mary."

She leaned over the upper railing and then, drawing her robe about her, came swiftly down. "I've been half out of my mind. I was just about to call Tommy and have him come over so that we could look for you— Why, you're soaking wet! And you've got a bruise on your face! And what's that on your hand?"

Lowry looked down at his hand; there was another bruise there and a cut as though he had been pinched. He winced. "I fell, I guess."

"But where? You smell like . . . like seaweed."

A chill gripped him and, all concern, she threw down his coat and, regardless of the carpet, pulled him up the stairs. It was very cold in the old house and colder still in his room. She got his clothes off him and rolled him in between the covers and then wiped his face and hair with a towel.

There was a taste of salt water on his lips and a string of words sounding in his brain: "Why, the bottom is at the top, of course!"

"I should never have let you go out."

"Poor Mary. I've worried you."

"I'm not thinking about that. You're liable to be very ill because of this. Why didn't you come back when it first began to rain?"

"Mary."

"Yes, Jim?"

"I love you."

She kissed him.

"You know I'd never hurt you, Mary."

"Of course not, Jim."

"I think you're good and loyal and beautiful, Mary."

"Hush. Go to sleep."

He closed his eyes, her hand soothing upon his forehead. In a little while he slept.

He awoke to the realization that there was something horribly wrong, as if something or someone was near at hand, ready to do a thing to him. He stared around the room, but there was nothing in it; the sun was shining pleasantly upon the carpet and part of the wall, and somewhere outside people were passing and talking, and a block or two away an impatient hand was heavy upon a horn button.

It was Sunday and he ought to be thinking about going to church. He threw back the covers and stepped out of bed. His clothes were hung upon a chair, but the suit he had worn was smudged and spotted and muddy and would have to be cleaned before he could wear it again.

"Mary!"

She must be sleeping. He pulled a robe about him and went to the door of her room. She was lying with one arm flung out across the covers, her mouth parted a little and her hair forming a luminous cloud about her lovely face. She stirred and opened her eyes.

"Oh!" she said, awake. "I've overslept and we're late for church. I'll have to get breakfast and—"

"No," said Lowry. "You aren't going to church."

"But, Jim—"

"You've earned a sleep. You just lie there and be lazy, for I'm certain you haven't been in bed more than three or four hours."

"Well—"

"I'll keep up the family honor—and I'll get something to eat at the diner. You turn over and sleep—"

"My beauty sleep."

"You don't need sleep to be beautiful." He kissed her

212

nd then, closing her door behind him, went into his room nd took out a dark suit.

When he had bathed and dressed he tiptoed to her door again.

"Jim," she said sleepily, "there were some people coming over this afternoon. I wish you'd tell them that I don't eel well or something. I don't want to go hustling about straightening up the house."

"As you will, darling."

"Tell me what the women wore," she called after him.

He was feeling almost sunny himself when he walked down the porch steps. But on the last one he halted, afraid to step to the walk. It took him some time and the feeling that he was being observed by the passers-by to make him move. But the walk was perfectly solid this morning and, again with relief and near-sunniness, he strolled to the street, nodding to people as he passed them.

The diner was nearly deserted and the blue-jowled short-order cook was having himself a cigarette and a cup of coffee at the end of the counter. He scowled when he saw someone come in and then brightened upon discovering it was Lowry.

"Well, professor! Haven't seen you since you got back."

Lowry shook Mike's soft, moist hand. "I've been pretty busy, I guess. Make it ham and eggs and coffee, Mike. And speed it up, will you? I'm late for church."

"Bell hasn't started to ring yet," said Mike, and got busy with a frying pan, grandly cracking the eggs with one hand.

"How's it feel to be back among civilized people again?" asked Mike, putting the food down before Lowry.

"I suppose so," said Lowry, not listening.

Mike, a little mystified, went back to his cup of coffee and lighted another smoke to sit broodingly, cup and cigarette both poised for use but momentarily forgotten; Mike shook his head as he gave the problem up and drank his coffee.

Lowry ate slowly, mainly because his head was a tumult of thought: Tommy's words kept passing through his mind and he could not wholly shake away the bleak forebodings Tommy had uttered, for it was unlike Tommy to jest with a man who was already worried. He had felt a gulf opening between them even as he and Tommy had talked; it was odd to seem strange and ill at ease with Tommy Williams. Why, he had even confided in Tommy that it had been he who had broken the window that time when Billy Watkins had been unable to shake the alibi; and Tommy and he had once signed a boyish pledge in blood to be friends forever.

Lowry had almost finished when he found that the food did not taste good to him; a slow feeling of quiet fear was seeping through him. Of what, he wondered, could he be afraid? The place was suddenly suffocating and he hurriedly reached for change to pay. As he placed a fifty-cent piece on the counter he caught a glimpse of the mirror between the coffee urns. There was his own face, bleak and haggard and—

Through the mirror he saw that something was behind him! A blurry, awful something that was slowly creeping upon his back!

He snapped around.

There was nothing.

He faced the mirror.

There was nothing.

"Forty cents," said Mike.

"What?"

"What'sa matter? Are you sick or something? There wasn't nothin' wrong with them eggs, was there?"

"No," said Lowry. "No. There wasn't anything wrong with the eggs."

"You forgot your change!" Mike called after him.

But Lowry was already on the sidewalk, striding swiftly away, utilizing every faculty to keep from running, to keep from glancing over his shoulder, to fight down the frozen numbness which threatened to paralyze him.

"Hello, Jim."

He dodged and then, seeing that it was Tommy, felt a surge of elation. "Hello, Tommy."

"You look shaky, old man," said Tommy. "You'd better take better care of that malaria or the old bugs will carve you hollow."

"I'm all right," said Lowry, smiling. Tommy was evidently on his way to church for he was dressed in a dark suit and a dark topcoat. Tommy, thought Jim, was a remarkably good-looking guy.

"Did you take your pills on schedule?"

"Pills?"

"Quinine or whatever you are supposed to take."

"Well—no. But I'm all right. Listen, Tommy, I don't know when I've been so glad to see anybody."

Tommy grinned. "Glad to see you, Jim."

"We've been friends for a long time," said Lowry. "How long is it now?"

"Oh, thirty-four years. Only don't say it. When one is as old as I am and still trying to act the Beau Brummell, he doesn't like to have his age get around."

"You going to church?"

"Sure. And where else would I be going?"

"Well—" Lowry shrugged and, for some reason, chuckled.

"We've been meeting on that corner, now, at about this time, for a long while," said Tommy. "Where's Mary?"

"Oh, she didn't get much sleep last night and she's staying home today."

"I wish I had an excuse like that. Parson Bates is a baron among bores; I don't think he'd ever heard of the Old Testament until I mentioned it to him at one of his wife's endless teas."

"Tommy ... Tommy, there's something I want to ask you."

"Fire away, old top."

"Tommy, when I left you yesterday afternoon, it was about a quarter of three, wasn't it?"

"Just about, I should imagine."

"And I did leave, didn't I?"

"Certainly, you left," replied Tommy, rather amused.

"And I only had one drink?"

"That's right. Say, this thing is really bothering you, isn't it? Don't try to hide anything from the old seer himself. What's up?"

"Tommy, I've lost four hours."

"Well! I've lost thirty-nine years."

"I mean it, Tommy. I've lost four hours and ... and my hat."

Tommy laughed.

"It's not funny," said Lowry.

"Jim, when you look at me with those serious eyes of yours and tell me that you're half out of your mind over a hat—well, it's funny, that's all. No offense."

"I've lost four hours. I don't know what happened in them."

"Well—I suppose that would worry a fellow. But there are plenty of other hours and plenty of other hats. Forget it."

"I can't, Tommy. Ever since I lost those four hours, things have been happening to me. Terrible things." And very swiftly he sketched the events of the night just passed.

"Down the stairs," said Tommy, very sober now. "Yes. I get your point—and I get more than that."

"What's it all about?" pleaded Lowry.

Tommy walked quite a way in silence and then, seeing that they were nearing the crowd before the old church, stopped. "Jim, you won't believe me."

216

"I'm about ready to believe anything."

"Remember what I told you yesterday? About your article?"

"You think my article has something to do with it?"

"Yes. I believe it has. Jim, you took a very definite and even insulting stand upon a subject which has been dead for a hundred years at the very least."

"Insulting? To whom?"

"To— Well, it's hard to say, Jim, in a way that you wouldn't decry the moment it was uttered. I wouldn't try to find your hat if I were you."

"But . . . but somehow I know that if I don't find it this thing will drive me mad!"

"Steady, now. Sometimes it's even better to be mad than dead. Listen, Jim, those things you said you met— well, those are very definitely representative of supernatural forces. Oh, I know you'll object. Nobody believes in supernatural forces these days. All right. But you have met some of them. Not, of course, the real ones that might search you out—"

"You mean devils and demons?"

"That's too specific."

"Then what do you mean?"

"First Jebson. Then four hours and a hat. By the way, Jim, have you any marks on your person that you didn't have when you were with me?"

"Yes." Jim pulled up his coat sleeve.

"Hm-m-m. That's very odd. That happens to be the footprint of a hare."

"Well?"

"Oh, now, let's forget this," said Tommy. "Look, Jim. Yesterday I was feeling a little bit blue and I talked crossly about your article. Certainly, it went against the grain, for I would like to believe in the actuality of such forces—they amuse me in a world where amusement is far between. And now I am feeding these ideas of yours. Jim, believe me, if I can help you I shall. But all I can do

217

is hinder if I put ideas into your mind. What you are suffering from is some kind of malarial kick-back that doctors have not before noticed. It faded out your memory for a while and you wandered around and lost your hat. Now keep that firmly in mind. You lost your memory through malaria and you lost your hat while wandering. I'm your friend, and I'll throw everything overboard before I'll let it injure you. Do you understand me?"

"Thanks—Tommy."

"See Dr. Chalmers and have him fill you full of quinine. I'll stand by and keep an eye on you so that you won't wander off again. And I'll do that for another purpose, as well. If you see anything, then I'll see it, too. And maybe, from what I know of such things, I can keep any harm from befalling you."

"I hardly know what—"

"Don't say anything. As much as anything, I've been responsible for this with all my talk about demons and devils. I think too much of you, and I think too much of Mary to let anything happen. And—Jim."

"Yes?"

"Look, Jim. You don't think that I fed you a drug or anything in that drink?"

"No! I hadn't even thought of such a thing!"

"Well—I wondered. You know I'm your friend, don't you, Jim?"

"Yes. Of course I do. Otherwise I wouldn't run the risk of telling you these things."

Tommy walked on with him toward the church. The bell was tolling, a black shadow moving in the belfry, and the rolling circles of sound came down to surround the nicely dressed people on the steps and draw them gently in. Jim Lowry looked up at the friendly old structure; the leaves had not yet come out upon the ivy, so that great brown ropes went straggling across the gray stone; the stained windows gleamed in the sunlight. But somehow he felt very much out of place here. Always it seemed to him that this was a sanctuary and a place of rest, but now—

A woman nudged against him in the crowd and he came to himself enough to see that it was the wife of Dean Hawkins. He remembered.

"Oh, Mrs. Hawkins!"

"Why, how do you do, Professor Lowry. Isn't your wife with you today?"

"That is what I wanted to say, Mrs. Hawkins. She is not feeling very well, and I believe she told you that she would be expecting you for tea this afternoon."

"Why, yes."

"She asked if she could beg off, Mrs. Hawkins."

"Perhaps I had better call and make sure she doesn't need something."

"No. All she needs is a little rest."

"Well, do tell her that I hope she will soon be feeling better."

"Yes, I shall," said Lowry, and then lost touch with her in the aisle.

Tommy usually sat with Lowry and Mary, and, as usual, their section of the pew was reserved for them. Lowry slid into the seat and glanced around, nodding absently to those about who nodded to him.

"She's an awful old frump," said Tommy in a whisper. "No wonder Hawkins has dyspepsia. It's a wonder she'd speak to you after the news."

"What news?" whispered Lowry, barely turning toward Tommy.

"Why, about you and Jebson. She and Mrs. Jebson are pals, and it's all over the place now. It's doubtful if she'd have called on Mary, anyway. I'm ruining my social status sitting with you. It's very funny, the way they carry on. As if you even felt bad about a fool like Jebson."

"I do feel bad. A little."

"Why? You've gotten a release from the sink of ennui.

You'll be free at last from teas. You don't know when you *are* fortunate."

"What about Mary?"

"Mary has been dying to travel with you, and now you can't say 'no.' If you weren't taking it so hard, she would probably be giggling like a kid. Think of telling Mrs. Hawkins not to call! Why, can't you see it, Jim? She kicked *the* Mrs. Hawkins straight in the teeth."

"We will sing," said a distant voice, "Hymn No. 197."

The organ began to wheeze and complain, and everyone got up and dropped books and shuffled and coughed; then the nasal voice of Parson Bates cut through the scrape and din, the choir lifted tremulous wails and the service was on.

Throughout the sermon, Lowry's eyes were centered upon the back of Jebson's head; not a particularly intent gaze, but one that was broken now and then by Jebson's twisting uncomfortably. However, Lowry was barely seeing Jebson at all, but, half lulled by Bates' dreary rhythm, was adrift out of himself, casting restively about in search of an answer.

An answer.

He knew he had to have an answer.

He knew that if he did reach an answer—

Four hours gone. And now he dimly realized that if he did not find them he was doomed, as Tommy had indirectly said, to future madness. And yet he knew instinctively and no matter how dimly, that he dared not find those four hours. No, he dared not. And yet he must!

He was on his feet again, staring blankly at the hymn book and singing more from memory than either the notes or the organ. And then he wasn't singing, but was oblivious of everything.

Some soft substance had touched against his leg.

He was afraid to look down.

He looked down.

There was nothing there.

Dry-throated and trying not to shiver, he focused his gaze upon the book and picked up the hymn. He glanced at Tommy, but Tommy was crooning along in his mellow baritone, unaware of anything at the moment but the glory of God.

The congregation was seated and a plate went the rounds while Bates read some announcements for the week. Lowry tried not to look at his feet and sought not to pull them up under the bench. He was growing more and more tense, until he did not see how he could sit there longer.

Something soft touched against his leg.

And though he had been looking straight at the spot—
There was nothing!

He clutched Tommy's sleeve, and with a muttered, "Come with me," got up and started up the aisle. He knew that eyes were upon him, he knew that he dared not run, he knew that Tommy was staring at him in astonishment, but was following dutifully.

The sun was warm upon the street, and the few fresh leaves made sibilant music in the gentle wind. A kid in rags was sitting on the curb tossing a dime up and down that somebody had given him for wiping off their shoes. The chauffeur drowsed over the wheel of Jebson's car, and up the street a sleepy groom held the horses of the eccentric Mrs. Lippincott, who always came in a surrey. The horses lazily swished their tails at the few flies and now and then stamped. The headstones of the cemetery looked mellow and kind above the quiet mounds of re-born grass, and an angel spread masonry wings over "Silas Jones, R. I. P." There was the smell of fresh earth from a lawn which was being sodded, and the spice of willows from a nearby stream.

Lowry's pace slowed under the influence of the day, for he felt better now out in the open, where he could see for some distance on every side. He decided not to tell Tommy, and Tommy was asking no questions.

But as they crossed the gleaming white pavement of High Street, something flickered in the corner of Lowry's eye. It was nothing very positive, just an impression of something dark and round traveling along beside him. He jerked his head to stare at it—but there was nothing there. He glanced up to see if it could have been the shadow of a bird but, aside from some sparrows foraging in the street, there were no birds. He felt the tension begin to grow in him again.

Again he caught the faintest glimpse of it, but once more it vanished under scrutiny. And yet, as soon as he turned his head front, he could sense it once more.

Just the merest blob of darkness, very small.

A third time he tried to see it, and a third time it was gone.

"Tommy."

"Yes?"

"Look. You're going to think I'm nuts. Something touched my leg in church and there wasn't anything there. Something is coming along beside me now. I can't see it clearly, and it vanishes when I look at it. What is it?"

"I don't see anything," said Tommy, muffling his alarm. "Probably just some sun in your eye."

"Yes," said Lowry. "Yes, that's it! Just some sun in my eye."

But the merest spot of shadow, so near as he could tell, or whatever it might be, followed slowly. He increased his stride, and it came, too. He slowed in an attempt to let the thing get ahead of him, so that he could find out what it was. But it also slowed.

He could feel the tension growing.

"You'd better not say anything about this to Mary."

"I won't," promised Tommy.

222

"I don't want to worry her. Last night I know I did. But you won't worry her with any of this, will you?"

"Of course not," said Tommy.

"You'd better stay over at our house tonight."

"If you think you'll need me."

"I . . . I don't know," said Lowry miserably.

They walked on, and Lowry kept edging away from the thing he could almost see, so that he almost made Tommy walk in the gutter. He was deadly afraid that it would touch him again, for he felt that if it did he would go half mad.

"Tommy."

"Yes."

"Will you walk on my right?"

"Sure."

And then Lowry could barely get an impression of it from out of the corner of his left eye. His throat was choked as if with emery dust.

When they came to the walk before Lowry's house they paused. "No word of this to Mary," said Lowry.

"Naturally not."

"You'll stay for dinner and for the night, won't you?"

"As you will," smiled Tommy.

They went up the steps and into the hall, and at the sound of their entrance Mary came out of the living room and threw her arms about Lowry's neck and kissed him. "Well! So you've been to church, you old heathen. Hello, Tommy."

He took her extended hand. "Mary, as lovely as ever."

"Don't let the current sweetheart hear you say that," said Mary. "Staying for dinner, I hope?"

"I hope."

"Good. Now you boys go take off your coats and hats and come in here and tell me what Mrs. Hawkins looked like when I forbade her to come to tea."

"She looked awful," said Tommy. "Like she had always smelled a dead cheese in this place, anyway."

They chattered on while Lowry stood near the cold fireplace. As long as there was very deep shadow he found he could not get glimpses of the thing. That is, not at first. But when he would turn his head it would briefly seem to appear in the middle of the room. Now and then he tried to catch it napping, but each time it swiftly scuttled back. He attempted to turn his head slowly so as to lead up on it, but then, too, it kept just out of sight.

He felt that if he could only find out what it was he would feel all right about it, no matter what it was. But until he saw it— He shuddered with dread at the thought of it touching him again.

"Why, Jim!" said Mary, breaking off her conversation with Tommy. "You're shivering again." She put her hand upon his arm and led him toward the door. "Now you go right upstairs and take ten grains of quinine and then lie down for a little nap. Tommy will help me put the dinner on and keep me company, won't you, Tommy?"

"Anything for a friend," said Tommy.

It made Jim vaguely uneasy to leave them together. But, then, Tommy must have been here many times while he was gone in just as innocent a capacity. What was wrong with him? To think that way about Tommy! About his best and really only friend? He started up the stairs.

And step by step the "thing" jumped along with him. He pressed himself against the wall to avoid any possibility of contact with it, but the presence of the wall, barring any dodge he might make, made him feel even more nervous.

"What was the thing, anyhow?

Why was it tagging him?

What would it do to him?

What would make it go away?

He shivered again.

In his room he found his quinine and, taking it to the bath to get a glass of water, was accompanied by the "thing." He could see it very indistinctly against the white

ile. And then he grew cunning. He guided it by slowly
turning his head, and then, springing sideways and out the
door, he banged the door behind him. He felt better as he
downed the quinine and water. For a moment he had the
inane notion that he ought to go and tell Mary not to
open this door, but then, of course, it would be a much
better idea to lock it. He found a key in a bedroom door
and carried it to the bath. In a moment the lock clicked
home. He almost laughed aloud, and then caught himself
up. That wouldn't do. Whatever the thing was, it was perfectly explainable. Something wrong with his eyes, that
was all. It was just malaria. Something the doctors hadn't
discovered about it.

He went to his bedroom and took off his jacket and
stretched out on his bed. The warm air from the open
window was very soothing, and in a little while he drifted
off into a quiet sleep, untroubled by dreams.

Some three hours later he roused himself. The sun was
shining upon his face and he felt too warm. Downstairs he
heard Mary calling to him that dinner was ready. Wasn't
dinner a little late for Sunday? It must be nearly four, according to the sun.

He got up, yawning and stretching and feeling much
better for his rest; he felt good about something he had
done, but he could not quite remember, in his half-awake
state, just what it was.

The pleasant sound of very high, musical laughter came
to him, and for a moment he thought it was Mary. But
then he knew that it could not be, for Mary had a low,
husky laugh that made him feel warm and comfortable inside, and this laugh—there was something unearthy about
it. Hadn't he heard it before?

He leaped up and opened the hall door, but it was not
coming from downstairs. He went to the window and
looked out, but there wasn't anyone on the walk or in the
yard. Where was the laughter coming from? What was it
that was laughing?

225

And then he saw a movement as though something had run down the wall to get behind him. He whirled. There was a flurry as if something had dived behind him again. He spun around.

But it was to no avail. And the thing he had so carefully locked away was still with him—and the thing was the source of the laughter.

What a mad laugh it was!

He felt very tired. Best to ignore it, whatever it was; best to walk around and not hear and not see it; best to pretend that it wasn't there at all. Would Mary and Tommy hear it?

Resignedly he went to the bathroom and washed.

"Jim? Jim, you old ox, aren't you ever coming down?"

"Coming, Mary." He'd better not appear too shaken.

When he entered the dining room the table was spread with bright crystal and silver and china, and a big capon was steaming away on a platter flanked by mashed potatoes and green peas.

"Well, sir! You look better," said Tommy.

"He didn't get any sleep last night," said Mary. "Come, Jim, m'lad, up with the tools and carve away."

He sat down at the head of the board, and Tommy sat at his right. He looked down the table at Mary and smiled. How beautiful was this wife of his, and how tingly she made him feel when she looked at him that way. To think he would wonder about whether she loved him or not! No woman could look at a man that way unless she truly loved him.

He picked up the knife and carving fork and started to pin down the capon. Then, suddenly, the knife was shaking so that he could not hold it. There was a clatter as it fell against china.

Just a shrill, musical laugh just behind him!

"Tommy," he said, trying to speak distinctly, "Tommy,

226

would you mind doing the honors? I guess I'm pretty shaky."

Mary was instantly concerned, but somehow Jim passed it off. Tommy went to work on the capon and Mary served up the vegetables—stealing quiet glances of wonder at Jim. Then everything was all served and they were ready to begin.

"Some chicken," said Tommy.

"Ought to be, what it cost!" said Mary. "The price of food can't go any higher and still let the clouds go by."

"Yeah," said Tommy in a slow drawl, "and wages stay the same. That is what is known as economic progress— get everything so high that nobody can buy so that there will be surplus which the government can buy and throw away so that the taxpayer will have less money with which to buy higher-priced goods. Yes, we've certainly improved civilization since the days when we lived in caves."

Mary laughed and, shockingly, the thing laughed, too, behind Jim. But it was an accidental combining, for a moment later, at a serious statement from Tommy, it laughed again.

Jim had picked up knife and fork two or three times. But another strange thing was occurring. Each time he started to touch his plate it moved. Not very much, just a little. A sort of easy, circular motion which ceased as soon as he did not choose to touch it again; but when he did, it did. Very carefully he found cause to help himself to more gravy, and then, swiftly, glanced under the cloth and the pad. But there was nothing wrong. He put back the plate and once more addressed himself to it. Once more it moved.

He felt ill.

"Would . . . would you two please excuse me? I . . . I guess I don't feel very well."

"Jim!"

"Better let me send for a doctor," said Tommy. "You look very white."

"No. No, I'm all right. Just let me lie down for a little while."

"I'll keep your dinner warm," said Mary.

"It was such a good dinner, too," said Lowry with a sad grin. "Don't worry about me. Just go ahead."

And then the laughter sounded again, higher and shriller, and the dark shadow scuttled along beside him as he hurried through the door and back to his bed. He flung himself down. And then, thinking better of it, he leaped up and shot home the bolt. Again he lay down, but he found he did not have sufficient control over himself. Tight-throated and half sick, he began to pace a narrow circle around his room.

CHAPTER FIVE

A clock downstairs struck eleven in long, slow strokes. Lowry, face down upon his bed, stirred uneasily and came up through the kindly oblivion of a doze. He woke to the realization that something horrible was about to happen to him, but, lying for a while in stupor, pushing back the frontiers of his consciousness, he picked up memory after memory, inspected it and cast it aside. No, no one of these things had any bearing on his present condition, there was nothing that he knew about which might have caused—

A shrill tinkle of laughter reached him.

He came up quivering in every muscle and saw the thing scurry around the bottom of his bed and get out of sight. If only he could get a full glimpse of it!

There was paper rattling somewhere, stirred by the warm night breeze, as though something in the room was sorting out his letters. And though the room seemed empty to him, after a little a single sheet, drifting on the air, came fluttering down to the carpet by his feet. He stared at it, afraid to pick it up. He could see writing upon it. Finally his curiosity overcame his fear, and he opened it and tried to read. But it was written in some ancient, incomprehensible script that blurred and ran together. The only thing legible was a time, and he could not even be sure of that.

"... 11:30 to ..."

He peered into the shadows of the room, but aside

229

from what had dived under his bed he was apparentl
alone. Had this thing come floating in with the wind?

Eleven thirty? Was this a bid for an appointment some
where? Tonight? He shuddered at the thought of goin
forth again. But, still, wasn't it possible that he migh
have a friend somewhere who was volunteering to hel
him find his four hours? And tonight he would be war
and step down no steps which he did not know had some
thing solid at the bottom.

He got up, and instantly the little dark thing got behin
him, permitting him only the slightest of glimpses. Withi
him he could feel a new sensation rising, a nervous ange
of the kind men feel in remembering times when the
have shown cowardice.

For he knew very clearly that he was being a coward
He was letting these things drag the reason out of hi
mind without even offering to combat them; he was bein
thrust about like a scarecrow in a hurricane, and th
things were laughing at him, perhaps even pitying him
His fists clenched into hard hammers; God knows he ha
never been found lacking in courage before, why shoul
he cower like a sniveling cur and allow all things t
steamroller him? His jaws were tight, and he felt his hear
lunging inside him, and he ached to join in wild battle an
put down forever the forces which were seeking to destro
him.

He took a topcoat from the closet and slipped into it
From a drawer he drew a Colt .38 and pocketed it. Int
his other pocket he put a flashlight. He was through being
a coward about this. He would meet his ghosts and batte
them down.

Eleven thirty? Certainly something would lead him t
the rendezvous. Perhaps something was waiting for him
out in the street now.

The high laughter tinkled again, and he spun around
and sought to kick the dark object, but again it eluded
him. Never mind—he would deal with that later.

Quietly he slipped out of his room. Mary's light was off, and her door was closed. There was no use disturbing her. Tommy must be in the guest room at the head of the stairs, for the door there was slightly ajar. Masking the flashlight with his fingers so that a small segment of its light played upon the bed, he looked at Tommy. Without his cynically twisted grin, Tommy was really a very beautiful fellow, thought Lowry. And Tommy, in sleep, looked as innocent as a choir boy. Lowry crept down the stairs and out the front door, to stand in the shadow of the porch and stare at the walk.

It was warm tonight, and what little breeze there was whispered faintly and sweetly across the lawns. The moon was nearly full and rode in a clear sky, from which it had jealously blotted the smaller stars.

Lowry went down the middle of the steps and dared the walk to open up. It did not. Almost smiling over this small triumph, he reached the street and cast about him. Eleven thirty was not here, but he was almost certain that if he was expected there would be a guide.

The little dark thing flicked about his legs, and the laughter sounded, gently as a child's. Lowry nerved himself to listen to it.

Tonight he would not cower and run away. These things had been strange to him before, but they were not strange to him now. Something would come to lead him, and he would be brave and carry out—

"Jim!"

He saw Tommy silhouetted in an upstairs window.

"Jim! Where are you going?"

But there was something moving under a tree ahead and it was beckoning to him.

"Jim! At least wait until I give you your hat!"

He felt a cold shudder race over him. The thing was beckoning more strenuously, and he sped toward it.

At first he could not make out what it was, so deep was the moon shadow there. But in a moment he saw that it was a cassocked little figure not more than four feet high, with a nearly luminous bald head. Beads and a cross hung about its neck, and crude leather scandals exposed its toes.

"You received my message?"

"Yes. Where are we going?" asked Lowry.

"You know as well as I do, don't you?"

"No."

"Well-l-l-l— You know me, don't you?"

Lowry looked at him more closely. There seemed to be an intangible quality to this little monk, as if he was lacking substance. And then Lowry found that he could see through him and beyond the tree trunk and the moon-bathed curb.

"I am Sebastian. You turned me out of my tomb about six years ago. Don't you remember?"

"The church tombs of Chezetol!"

"Ah, you do remember. But do not think I am angry. I am a very humble fellow, and I am never angry, and if I have to wander now without a home, and if my body was the dust which your diggers' spades broke, I still am not angry. I am a very humble person." And, indeed, he was almost cringing. But still there was a certain sly way he cast his eyes sideways at Jim that made one wonder. "I had been lying there for three hundred years, and you, thinking it was an old Aztec ruin because of the Aztec symbols on the stones which had been converted to its construction, dug me up. Where is my belt?"

"Your belt?"

"Yes, my beautiful golden belt. You picked it up and turned to your guide and said, 'What's this? A gold belt marked with the symbols of the Catholic Church! I thought this was an Aztec ruin. A week's digging for nothing but a golden belt.'"

"It is in the college museum."

"I was a little hurt about it," said Sebastian sadly. " '—for nothing but a golden belt.' I liked it because I made it, you see, and we thought it was very beatiful. We converted Razchytl to Christianity, and then we took his gold and made sacred vessels of it, and when he died on the mining gangs we went so far as to bury him with a golden cross. May I have my belt?"

"I can't get it for you now."

"Oh, yes, you must. Otherwise I won't go with you and show you."

"Show me what?"

"Where you spent your four hours."

Lowry pondered for a little while and the nodded. "All right. We'll get your belt. Come with me."

Lowry walked swiftly up the street, the little dark shadow just behind the range of his eye to the left, Sebastian a step behind upon his right. Sebastian's crude slippers made no sound upon the pavement.

It was a very short distance to the building which houses the museum, and Lowry was soon fumbling for his keys. The door opened into the blackness, but Lowry knew the place by heart and did not turn on his light until he was near the case which held the golden belt. He fumbled for more keys and, switching on his flash, started to fit one. He stopped. He played his light upon the objects within. The belt was gone!

Nervously he turned to Sebastian. "The belt isn't here. They must have sold it to another museum while I was gone."

Sebastian's head was cast down. "It is gone, then. And I shall never get it back—but I am not angry. I am a very humble person. I am never angry. Good-bye, Señor Lowry."

"Wait! I'll try to get your belt back. I'll buy it back and put it somewhere where you can find it!"

Sebastian paused at the door and then dodged aside. A beam of light stabbed down the aisle. It was Terence, the college watchman.

"Who is in here?" cried Terence, trying to make his voice sound very brave.

"It is I," said Lowry, moving into the path of the light and blinking at its source.

"Oh. Professor Lowry! Sure, and you gave me an awful scare there for a moment. This is no time to be tinkering around with them trinkets."

"I was doing some research," said Lowry. "I needed a certain inscription for a class lecture tomorrow."

"Did you find it?"

"No. It isn't here any more. I suppose they've sold it."

"Jebson would sell his own mother, Professor Lowry, and I mean what I say. He's cut my pay, that's what he's done. I was terribly sorry to hear what he did to you. I thought that was a pretty good article you wrote, too."

"Thank you," said Lowry, moving to the door, panicky lest Sebastian be frightened away.

"Course you laid it on a bit thick, Professor Lowry. Now, in the old country I could show you people that could tell you about having met a lot of things they couldn't explain. It ain't healthy to go around begging the demons to smash you."

"Yes. Yes, I'm sure it isn't. I've got to be going, Terence, but if you'd like to drop around my office some afternoon when you get up, I'd be glad to hear about your evidence."

"Thank you, Professor Lowry. Thank you. That I will."

"Good night, Terence."

"Good night, Professor Lowry."

Lowry walked swiftly toward the deepest shade of the street, and when he was sure he was out of Terence's sight he began to cast around for some sign of Sebastian. But all he could glimpse was the occasional flick of the dark object which traveled with him.

When he had searched around and about for nearly twenty minutes, a low call reached him. And there was Sebastian hiding by a bush.

"Oh," said Lowry in relief. "I hoped you hadn't gone. I wanted to tell you that if you would wait awhile I would buy back the golden belt."

"I am not angry," said Sebastian.

"But you want your belt, don't you?"

"It would please me very much. It was such a pretty belt. I made it with my own hands with many humble prayers to God, and though the metal is heathen the work was the work of love."

"You shall have your belt. But tonight you must take me to the place where I can find the four hours."

"You are determined to find them, then?"

"I am."

"Jim Lowry, I wonder if you know what it will cost to find them."

"Whatever the cost, I intend to do so."

"You are brave tonight."

"Not brave. I know what I must do, that is all."

"Jim Lowry, last night you met some things."

"Yes."

"Those things were all working on your side. They were the forces of good. You did not lose your four hours to them, Jim Lowry. Nor to me."

"I must find them."

"You could not conceive the forces of the otherside. You could not conceive so much pain and terror and evil. If you are able to find those four hours you must go be prepared to face those other forces."

"I must find them."

"Then, Jim Lowry, have faith in me and I shall show you part of the way. The rest of the way you must go alone."

"Lead and I shall follow."

Sebastian's delicate little hand made the sign of the cross upon the air and then moved out to point an upward way. Lowry found that he was upon a smoothly

235

blue roadway which would upward and onward as though to the moon itself.

Sebastian gripped his beads and began to walk. Lowry glanced around him, but for all he searched, he could not find the small black object, nor could he hear its laughter—if it was the source of that laughter.

They went a long way, past spreading fields and little clusters of sleeping houses. Once a thing with bowed head and hidden face passed them, going down with slow and weary steps, but Lowry could not understand what it was.

The way began to be broken as though it had once consisted of steps which had disintegrated to rubble; tufts of grass began to be more frequent in the cracks, showing that the way was little used. Ahead, a smoky outline of mountains took slow form and then it seemed to Lowry that they had come upon them swiftly. The road began to writhe and dip on hillsides, lurching out and then standing almost on edge toward the inside, as though earthquakes and avalanches had here been steadily at work. And even as they passed over it, it occassionally trembled, and once, with a sigh which ended in a roar, a whole section of it went out behind them, leaving a void. Lowry began to worry about ever being able to get back.

"It gets more difficult now," said Sebastian. "Have you ever climbed mountains?"

"Not often."

"Well—you look strong enough."

Sebastian headed off at right angles to the dwindling road and walked easily up a nearly vertical cliff. Lowry reached up and found to his astonishment that although the cliff had looked very high at first, it was only eight or nine feet and he ascended easily. For a way, then, they walked along its rim, and the road fell swiftly away until it was less than a white string. The wind was a little stronger up here, but it was still warm, and the moon was friendly. There seemed to be good cause for them to be as unseen as possible for now Sebastian was pressing back against yet another cliff, one which really was high.

"It is a little worse now," said Sebastian. "Be very careful."

They had come to the end of both cliffs, and here a rightangle turn folded away from them, offering only rough stone to their questing touch.

Lowry looked down and felt slightly ill. He disliked height no more than another man, but the cliff here pitched off forever and was consecutive in his sight, so that he could visualize falling through that space. Far, far down a small stream, like a piece of bright wire, wound its way through a rocky gorge, and here and there on the vertical face, trees, diminutive with distance, jutted out like staying hands. Sebastian had gone on around the turn. Lowry reached, and then reached again, but he could find no purchase.

Leaning far out, he saw a ledge. It seemed to him that if he could half fall and reach at the same time, he could grip it. He leaned out, he snatched wildly. He had hold of the ledge, and his legs were being pulled at by the drop below.

"Work along," said Sebastian.

Lowry inched himself along. It was very hard to keep hold of the ledge, for it was rough and hurt his hands and sloped a trifle outward. He tried to see Sebastian, but he could not because of his own arm. He began to be weary, and a nausea of terror came into him, as though something was staring at him, ready to pry him loose. He stared up at the ledge.

A great splotch of black was hovering there, and two large eyes peered luminously down with malevolence!

Lowry glanced down and saw emptiness under him.

There was a gentle, purring sound, and the dark object loomed higher. Something began slowly to pry Lowry's fingers off the ledge.

"Sebastian!"

There was no answer from the monk.

"Sebastian!"

The purring over his head grew louder and more pleased.

One hand was almost loose, and then it was loose! Lowry dangled in space as the thing began slowly and contentedly to loosen his left hand. He remembered the gun and snatched it from his pocket and pointed it up.

The eyes did not change. The purring was softer. Suddenly Lowry was aware of a reason he could not pronounce that he must not shoot. To do so would bring a whole pack down upon him, and it was doubtful if his bullets would take any effect. His left hand came free and he swooped away from the ledge with the air screaming past his face and up his nose, and the greedy, dark drowning him.

He was aware of stars and the moon all mingled in a spinning dance, and the cliff side rolling upward at incredible speed, and the bright wire of the stream but little closer than it had been when he had first begun to fall.

He had no memory of landing. He was lying on a surface so smooth that it was nearly metallic. Stunned, he got to his knees and stared over the edge of this second ledge, to find that the stream was still down there, but that his fall had evidently been broken by trees.

Where was Sebastian?

He looked up but could find no sign of the thing which had pried him loose. He looked to the right and left, but he could discover no descent from this place. Pressing against the cliff, he edged along. There were small caves here whose dark mouths held things he could sense but dimly. He knew he must not enter them. But still—still, how else could he ever get down?

One cave was larger than the rest, and though his resolution had ebbed considerably, he knew that he must go in. On hands and knees he crept over the lip, and his hands met a furry something which made him leap back. Something struck him lightly from behind and drove him to his knees once more. The floor of this place was furry, all of it, dry and ticklish to the touch.

A deep, unconcerned voice said, "Go along ahead of me, please."

He dared not look back at the speaker, whatever it was. He got up and went along. There were great flat ledges in the place over which he stumbled now and then. Evidently he had lost his flashlight, but he would have been afraid to have used it. There was something awful in this place, something he could not define, but which waited in patient stillness for him perhaps around the next bend, perhaps around the one after that— He came up against a rough wall which bruised him.

"Please go along," said the voice behind him in a bored fashion.

"Where . . . where is Sebastian?" he ventured.

"You are not with *them* now. You are with us. Be as little trouble as you can, for we have a surprise waiting for you down one of these tunnels. The opening, you poor fool, is on your right. Don't you remember?"

"I . . . I've never been here before?"

"Oh, yes, you have. Oh yes, indeed, you have. Hasn't he?"

"Certainly he has," said another voice at hand.

"Many, many times."

"Oh, not many," said the other voice. "About three times is all. That is, right here in this place."

"Go along," yawned the first voice.

It was all he could do to force his legs to work. Something unutterably horrible was waiting for him, something he dared not approach, something which, if he saw it, would drive him mad!

"You belong to us, now, so go right along."

"What are you going to do with me?"

"You'll find out."

239

There was an incline under his feet, and at each step things seemed to wake beneath his feet and go slithering away, nearly tripping him, sometimes curling about his ankles, sometimes striking hard against him.

The incline was very long, and there was blackness at its bottom. He must not go down here! He must not go down here! He had to turn back while there was yet time!

"Go along," said the bored voices. "You are ours now."

Ahead there was only stillness. Ahead— Lowry sank down on the ramp, too ill and weak to go on, too terrified of what lay just ahead to take another step. Everything was spinning and things were howling at him.

And then he heard Sebastian's quiet little voice speaking long, monotonous sentences in Latin.

Sebastian!

Lowry pulled himself up and staggered on toward the sound. He was not sure but what the way had forked and that he had taken another route down. He was not sure of anything but Sebastian's voice.

He rounded a corner and blinked in a subdued light which came from a stained window high up. This place was mainly shadows and dust, but little by little he made out other things. There were seven bulls, carved from stone, all along a high ledge; and each bull had one hoof poised upon a round ball as his incurious stone eyes regarded the scene below.

The floor was very slippery, so that it was hard to stand, and Lowry hung hard upon a filthy drapery on his right.

The room was full of people, half of them men, half of them women, with Sebastian standing at a tiny altar a little above their heads. Sebastian's graceful hands were making slow, artistic motions over the heads, and his eyes were raised upward to meet the rays which came down from the high window. A gigantic book was open before

240

him, and a cross and sacred ring lay upon it to hold its place. And around him, in a wide circle, filed the women.

They were lovely women, all dressed in white save for the single flash of red which came from their capes as they moved; their faces were saintly and innocent, and their movements graceful and slow.

Just outside this moving circle of women stood another circle, but of men. These were also dressed in white, but their faces were not pure; rather, they were grinning and evil. Their white capes were stained with something dark which they made no effort to hide.

Sebastian prayed on and moved his hands over their heads to bless them. The circle of women moved slowly and quietly around him, but did not look up at him save when they passed the front of the altar. The circle of men paid no attention whatever to Sebastian.

And then Lowry was made almost to cry out. For he saw what they were doing. As the circle of women passed behind the altar, the men would suddenly reach out with clawed hands, and the women, with abruptly lascivious eyes, would glance over the shoulder at the men, and then, with reformed innocence of expression, file past the front of the altar again. The men would jostle and snicker to one another, and then the next time reach out again.

Sebastian prayed on, his tender eyes upon the square of light.

Lowry tried to get away, but the floor was so slippery he could hardly stand and could not run. And then he saw what made the floor so slippery. It was an inch thick in blood!

He screamed.

Everyone whirled to stare at him. Sebastian stopped praying and bent a kindly smile upon him. All the rest muttered among themselves and pointed and scowled, an undertone of anger growing from them.

The seven bulls upon the ledge came to life with a bellow. They moved their hoofs and the balls rolled, and it could be seen then that they had had human skulls there. Again they moved their hoofs, and the skulls came tumbling down from the ledge to strike in the midst of the angry mob, felling some of the women and men, but not touching Sebastian.

Lowry could not run. He could not breathe. The mob was howling with rage now, and evidently thinking he had thrown the skulls, surged forward toward him.

Just before they reached him he was able to make the incline. As swiftly as he could he raced up it. A sinuous shape shot out and barred his way.

"Where are you going?"

Madly Lowry ripped it away and raced on.

A blow from behind felled him and a voice cried, "Where are you going? You must stay here and see it through!" But Lowry got to his feet and dashed away. He could hear the roar of the mob fading, but he knew that there were other things around him now, flying just above and behind him, striving to dive down and cut off his retreat.

He crashed into a wall, and then when he rose up and strove to find a way out, there was none. The roar of the mob was growing louder. He tore his hands as he tried to find the exit. Then there were knives flashing, and the cold bite of one against his wrist was instantly warmed by the flow of his own blood. He pitched forward and fell from a height. There was grass in his fingers and moonlight above him, and he leaped up and raced away, running through sand which reduced his speed and made him stumble. He could still hear whirring sounds above and behind him. He was outdistancing the mob, but could he never get free of those shapes?

"Sebastian!"

But there was no Sebastian.

"Sebastian!"

And just the whir of the things overhead and the blurred glimpses of things that raced with him. The moon

242

was white upon a wide expanse, not unlike a dried-up lake of salt. He was out in the open now, and there was neither hiding place nor refuge. He was out in the open and being hunted by things he could not see, things which wanted to take him back!

A shadowy shape loomed ahead, still afar. He forced himself to slow down and turn off away from it. There was something about its hat, something about the dark cloak, something about the thing which dangled from its hand—

Jack Ketch!

There was a ravine, and he scrambled down it. He crept along its bottom and went deep into a shadowy grove which he found there. Something was calling to him now, but he could not tell what the words were. Something calling which must never, never find him there! There were white mountains around him and high above him, and they offered refuge to him and he went deeper into them.

The trees were thicker and the grass was soft and protective.

Something was beating through the bushes in an attempt to locate him, and he lay very still, pressing hard against the earth. The something came nearer and nearer, and the voice was muttering.

And then the voice receded and the cackling sounds grew fainter and Lowry stretched out at length in the dewy grass, getting his breath. The moonlight made delicate shadow patterns about this place, and the night wind was warm and caressing. He began to breathe quietly, and the hammering of his heart lessened.

It was an almost triumphant feeling which went through him then. He had not found his lost four hours! He had not found them! He raised himself a trifle and cupped his chin in his hands, staring unseeingly at the white thing just before him.

He had not found his four hours!

And then his eyes focused upon the thing before which he lay. He was conscious that he was lying half across a mound, and that there was the fresh smell of flowers too late growing for spring.

There was writing upon that white stone.

But what kind of writing?

He inched a little closer and read:

JAMES LOWRY
Born 1901
Died 1940
Rest In Peace

He recoiled.

He got to his knees and then to his feet. The whole night was spinning and the high, shrill laughter was sounding again and the little dark shape dashed around to get out of his sight.

With a piercing cry he spun about and raced madly away.

He had found peace for a moment, peace and rest, before the headstone of his own future grave!

CHAPTER SIX

When he awoke the following morning he knew by the position of the sun on the wall that he still had at least half an hour before he had to rise. Usually, when that was the case, he could lie and stretch and inch down in the covers and relish his laziness. But there was something different about this morning.

A robin was sitting in a tree outside his window, cocking its head first to one side and then to another as it sought to spy worms from that ambitious altitude; now and then the bird would forget about worms and loose a few notes of joyous exuberance, to have them answered from another part of the yard. Somewhere, early as it was, a lawn mower was running, and its peculiarly cheerful whir was augmented by a careless, tuneless whistle. Somewhere a back door slammed and a pup yipped for a moment, and then evidently saw another dog and began a furious fanfare of ferocious warning. Downstairs Lowry could hear Mary singing in an absentminded way, going no more than half a chorus to a song he could not quite recognize. On the second-floor hall, just outside his door, he heard a board creak; somehow there was menace in the sound.

The knob of the door turned soundlessly and a minute crack appeared; another board creaked and a hinge protested in a hushed tone. Lowry half closed his eyes, pretending to be asleep, and saw the door come open a trifle more. He became rigid.

Tommy's face crowned by disheveled dark hair, was just beyond the opening, and Tommy's hand upon the knob glittered with its class ring. Lowry lay still.

Evidently Tommy was satisfied that Lowry slept, for he crossed the threshold with soundless tread and moved to the foot of the bed. For a little while Tommy stood there, looking out from an immobile face, as though ready to smile and say good morning in case Lowry awoke—and if he did not, then—

Lowry's eyes were very nearly shut, enough to deceive an observer but not enough to blank out Tommy. Why, Lowry asked himself, did he lie here faking like this? What strangeness was there about Tommy which bade such a precaution?

The robin evidently spotted a worm, for he let out a call and dived out of sight toward the lawn. A housewife was calling after a little boy and adding to a hasty grocery order.

Tommy stayed where he was, studying Lowry, until he seemed quite sure that Lowry still slept, and then, with a glance toward the door as though to make sure that Mary was still downstairs, he came silently up along the side of the bed.

It was Lowry's impulse to reach up and snatch at Tommy's white shirt, but some latent protective sense combined with his curiosity to let matters take their course. Tommy's hand moved gracefully across Lowry's eyes—once, and then twice. A numb sensation began to creep over Lowry.

Now was the time to move. He would awake and greet Tommy— But he couldn't move. He seemed to be frozen. And Tommy leaned over until their faces were not three inches apart. For an instant Lowry thought he saw fangs in Tommy's mouth, but before he could gain a whole impression the teeth had again foreshortened.

Tommy stayed there for more than a minute and then straightened up, a cold smile taking the beauty from his

246

face. He passed his hand again across Lowry's forehead and, with a quiet nod, turned and stole out into the hall. The door clicked slowly shut behind him.

It was some time before Lowry could move, and when he did he was weak. He sat on the edge of the bed, feeling shaky, as a man might who has just given a blood transfusion. When he had assembled enough energy he approached the mirror and, gripping the bureau top with both hands, stared at himself.

His eyes were so far sunken in his head beneath his shaggy brows that he could barely make out his own pupils; his hair was matted; his face seemed to have lost a certain pugnacity with which he had always attempted to compensate for his shyness; obviously he had lost a great deal of weight, for his cheeks were sunken, and a pallor as gray as the belly of a rain cloud gave him a shock, so much did it cause him to resemble a dead man.

He forgot the cost of his exertions and swiftly tried to wipe out the ravages of nerve strain by carefully shaving and bathing and grooming, and when he again looked into the mirror, trying his cravat, he was a little heartened.

After all, here it was a fresh spring day. Devil take Jebson; the old fool would be dead long before James Lowry. Devil take the four hours; as the knight had said, what were four hours? Devil take the phantoms which had assailed him. He had courage enough and strength enough to last them out. He had too much courage and will power to cause him to back down upon his original assertions in the article. Let them do their worst!

He trotted down the steps, buttoning his jacket, holding up his spirits with an effort which resembled the use of physical strength. The dark thing was just beside and behind him, and the high, shrill laughter sounded in the distance, but he was determined not to give them the satisfaction of heed. Despite them, he would carry on and act as he had always acted. He would greet Mary and

247

Tommy with pleasantness, and he would lecture his class as dryly and lengthily as ever.

Mary looked him askance at first, and then, seeing that he was apparently much better, threw her arms about his neck and gave him her cheery good-morning kiss. Tommy was already seated at the table.

"See?" said Mary. "You can't hurt the old block of granite. He's chipper as ever."

"Darned if you aren't," said Tommy. "By the way, Jim, eleven thirty at night isn't exactly the time for a stroll. Hope you kept out of trouble."

He felt a momentary resentment toward Tommy for mentioning it. It was as though Tommy himself wished to keep these hateful events before his eyes. But then Tommy was asking in a very friendly way which could involve no harm. Still—that strange visit, and—

"Here's your breakfast," said Mary, setting a plate of ham and eggs before him. "You don't have to hurry, but I'd advise you to start now."

Lowry smiled at her and seated himself at the head of the board. He took up his knife and fork, still thinking about Tommy. He started to take a bite of eggs—

Ever so gently, the plate moved.

Lowry glanced to see if Tommy or Mary had noticed. Evidently they hadn't. Again he started to take a mouthful of eggs.

Again the plate went slightly from side to side.

He laid down his fork.

"What's the matter?" said Mary.

"I . . . I guess I'm not very hungry."

"But you haven't eaten anything since breakfast yesterday!"

"Well—" Bravely he took up his fork. Slowly the plate moved. And as he stared at it was aware of something else.

When he was not looking at Tommy he could see from the corner of his eyes that Tommy seemed to have fangs.

He stared straight at the man, but there was nothing extraordinary about Tommy's mouth. He must be imagining things, thought Lowry. He again bent over his plate.

But there could be no doubt about the validity of that impression. The second he took his eyes from Tommy's face, Tommy possessed yellow fangs which depressed the outside of his lower lip!

The plate moved.

The little dark thing scuttled behind him.

Somewhere the high shrill laughter sounded.

With all his courage exerted, Lowry managed to sit still. He looked at his plate. As long as he did not try to touch it it was perfectly quiet.

Then he saw something else. When he took his eyes away from Mary, *she* seemed to have fangs not unlike Tommy's!

He stared at her, but her face was its own sweet self.

He looked away.

Mary's mouth was marred by those yellow fangs!

If he could only see their mouths looking straight at them! Then he could be sure!

The dark thing scuttled out of sight.

He tried to eat and the plate moved.

He sprang back from the table, upsetting his chair. Mary looked at him with frightened eyes. Tommy, too, got up.

"I've got to see somebody before my first class," said Lowry in a carefully schooled voice.

He looked at Tommy and saw Mary's fangs. He looked at Mary and she was herself, but he could see Tommy's fangs.

Hurriedly he went out into the hall and snatched up his topcoat, aware that Tommy had followed him and was getting into his. Mary stood before him and looked wonderingly up into his face.

"Jim, is there something I should know about? You can trust us, Jim."

He kissed her and seemed to feel the fangs he could not wholly see. "I'm all right, dear. Don't worry about me. There's nothing wrong."

She plainly did not believe him, and she was thinking furiously, for it was not until he was at the bottom of the steps—and glad to find the walk solid—that she called, "Your hat, Jim!"

He waved at her and strode out to the street. Tommy found it difficult keeping up with him.

"Jim, old boy, what's the matter with you?"

When he wasn't looking at Tommy he could see those fangs very clearly—and a sly, meaningful look on Tommy's face. "There's nothing the matter."

"But there is, Jim. You leave the table last night and then, at eleven or eleven thirty, or whatever it was, you go chasing forth as though possessed by a thousand devils, and now you fling away from the table. There's something you aren't telling me, Jim."

"You know the answer," said Jim sullenly.

"I . . . I don't get you."

"You were the one that started telling me about demons and devils."

"Jim," said Tommy, "you think I have something to do with what is happening to you?"

"I'm almost sure of it."

"I'm glad you said 'almost,' Jim."

"There was that drink, and then everything went black for four hours and I lost—"

"Jim, there's no poison or anything in the world that could cause such a blankness and leave no effect. Grant me that, Jim."

"Well—"

"And you know it," said Tommy. "Whatever is happening to you has nothing whatever to do with me."

"Well—"

250

"Let's not quarrel, Jim. I only want to help you."

Jim Lowry was silent, and they walked on in silence. Lowry was hungry now, and ahead the diner was full of clamor and the smell of coffee. He tried not to remember what had happened to him here yesterday.

"You go on," said Jim to Tommy. "I've got to see somebody in there."

"As you say, Jim. Will I see you at lunch?"

"I suppose so."

Tommy nodded to him and strode away. Lowry went in and perched himself on a stool.

"Well!" said Mike, relieved that he had not lost a customer through his garrulousness. "What'll it be, sir?"

"Ham and eggs," said Jim Lowry.

He was relieved to find that this plate did not move. And it began to be born in him that Tommy must have quite a bit to do with what was happening to him. He ate like a starved man.

Half an hour later he entered his classroom. It was good to be in such a familiar place, good to stand up here on the platform and watch the students pass the door in the hall. Presently they would come in here and he would begin to drone along on the subject of ancient beliefs in ancient civilizations and perhaps, after all, everything was right with the world.

He glanced around to see if everything was in place, if the board was clean for his notes—

He stared at the board behind the platform. That was strange. These were always washed over the week end. What was that sentence doing there?

"You are the Entity. Wait for us in your office."

What curious script it was! Not unlike that note he had gotten in some way, but this he could very clearly read. Entity? You are the Entity? What could that be about? Wait in his office? For whom? For what? A sick feeling of impending disaster began to take hold of him. What trick was this? He snatched up an eraser and furiously rubbed back and forth across the message.

At first he would not erase, and then, slowly, when he wiped across the first word, it vanished. Then the second, the third, the fourth! It was erasing now! He finished it so thoroughly that no slightest mark of it was left.

And then, first word, second word, letter by letter with slow cadence, appeared once more. He began to quiver.

Again he grabbed the eraser and rubbed the message out. Slowly, letter by letter, it appeared again.

"You are the Entity. Wait for us in your office."

He flung the eraser away from him just as the first two students entered. He wondered what they would think about the message. Perhaps he could trump up some excuse, include it in the lesson— No, pupils were used to weird statements on blackboards, hold-overs from past classes. He had better ignore it completely.

The class shuffled and moved seats and greeted one another the width and length of the room. A girl had a new dress and was being casual. A boy had new sweetheart and was trying to act very manly in her sight and very careless before his own friends. The rattling and talking and scraping gradually died down. A bell rang. Lowry began his lecture.

Only long habit and much reading from the book carried him through. Now and then, during the hour, his own words came into his consciousness for a moment and he seemed to be talking rationally enough. The students were making notes and dozing and whispering and chewing gum—it was a normal enough class, and obviously they saw nothing wrong.

"This fallacious belief and the natural reluctance of the human being to enter in upon and explore anything so intimately connected with the gods as sickness served as an effective barrier for centuries to any ingress into the realm of medical science. In China—"

252

Waiting in his office? What could be waiting? And what did it mean, Entity?

"—even when medicinal means were discovered by which fever could be induced or pain lessened, the common people ascribed the fact to the dislike of the demon of illness for that particular herb or the magic qualities of the ritual. Even the doctors themselves long continued certain ritualistic practices, first because they themselves were not sure and because the state of mind of the patient, being a large factor in his possible cure, could be bettered by the apparent flattery of the patient's own beliefs."

It was a relief to be able to stand here and talk to them as though nothing were wrong. And it was a normal class, for they kept gazing through the windows and out of doors, where the sun was bright and friendly and the grass cool and soft.

"In any culture, medical cure begins its history with the thunder of a witch doctor's drums, by which the witch doctor attempts to exorcise his patient." Here he always essayed a small joke about a patient letting himself be cured in a wild effort to save his own eardrums, but just now he could not utter it. Why?—he asked himself.

"Man's predisposition to illness at first acted as a confirmation of spirits and demons, for there was no visible difference, in many cases, between a well patient and a sick one, and what man has not been able to see, he attributes to devils and demons."

Strange, wasn't it, that medicine drums did cure people? Strange that incantations and health amulets had been man's sole protection from bacteria for generations without count? Strange that medicine itself still retained a multitude of forms which were directly traceable to demons and devils? And that the pile of crutches in that Mexican church indicated the efficacy of faith in even "hopeless" cases. The church! And now that people had turned from the church to a wholly materialistic culture, was it not odd that worldly affairs were so bloody and grim? Demons of hate and devils of destruction, whose lot was to jeer at man and increase his misfortunes! Spirits of the land and water and air, abandoned in belief and left, unhampered, to work their evil upon a world—

He stopped. The class was no longer whispering and chewing gum and staring out the window or dozing. Wide young eyes were fixed upon him in fascination.

He realized that he had spoken his last thoughts aloud. For a moment no longer than an expressive pause would be, he studied his class. Young minds, ready and waiting to be fed anything that any man of repute might wish to feed them, sponges for the half truths and outright lies and propaganda called education, material to be molded into any shape that their superiors might select. How did he know if he had ever taught the truth? He did not even know if the dissemination of democracy itself was error or right. These were the children of the next generation, on the sill of marriage and the legal war of business. Could he, with his background, ever tell them anything which might help them? He, who had been so sure for so many years that all was explainable via material science, he who now had wandered far and had seen things and talked to beings he had for years decried!—could he say now what he had said so often before?

"—and because of that very belief, so deeply rooted in our ancestors, none of us today is sure but what there was some truth in those ancient thoughts. Or perhaps—" Why should be back off now? These were his for the molding. Why should he stand here and lie when not twelve hours ago he had walked with phantoms, had been guided by a priest three hundred and more years dead, had been whipped on by things he had not seen, who even now could catch a glimpse of a black object which threw a shadow where there was no sun? These were his for the molding. Why should he be afraid of them?

254

"Men of science," he began again in a quiet voice, "have sought to clear fear from the mind of man by telling man that there is nothing of which he must be afraid just because he cannot see the actual cause. Men today have spread the feeling that all things are explained, and that even God himself has had his face gazed upon through the medium of an electric arc. But now, standing here, I am not sure of anything. I have dipped back to find that countless billions of people, all those who lived prior to the last century, regulated their lives with due respect to a supernatural world. Man has always known that his lot upon this earth is misery, and he has, until a split second ago in geological time, understood that there must be beings beyond his ken who take peculiar delight in torturing him.

"In this class at this very moment there are at least half a dozen amulets in which the owner places considerable faith. You call them luck charms and you received them from one beloved or found them through an incident beyond your power of comprehension. You have a semibelief, then, in a goddess of luck. You have a semibelief in a god of disaster. You have all noticed from time to time that at that moment when you felt the most certain of your own invulnerability, that that moment was the beginning of your own downfall. To say aloud that you are never ill seems to invite illness. How many lads have you known who had bragged to you that they have never had accidents, only later to visit them after accident? And if you did not have some belief in this, then you would not nervously look for wood each time you make a brag about your own fortune.

"This is a modern world, full of material 'explanations,' and yet there is no machine which will guarantee luck, there is no clear statement of any law which serves to regulate man's fate. We know that we face a certain amount of light and, disclaiming any credence in the supernatural or in any existing set of malicious gods, we still understand and clearly that our backs are against the darkness and the void, and that we have a very slight understanding of the amount of misery we are made to experience. We talk about 'breaks,' and we carry luck charms and we knock on wood. We put crosses on top of our churches and arches in our belfries. When one accident has happened, we wait for the other two and only feel at least when the other two have happened. We place our faiths in a god of good and by that faith carry through, or we go without help through the dim burrows of life, watchful for a demoniac agent or destruction which may rob us of our happiness, or we arrogantly place all faith in ourselves and dare the fates to do their worst. We shiver in the dark. We shudder in the presence of the dead. We look, some of us, to mystic sciences like astrology or numerology to reassure us that our way is clear. And no person in this room, if placed at midnight in a 'haunted' house, would deny there the nonexistence of ghosts. We are intelligent beings, giving our lips to disbelief, but rolling our eyes behind us to search out any danger which might swoop down from that black void.

"Why? Is it true, then, that there exist about us demons and devils and spirits whose jealousy of man leads on to the manufacture of willful harm? Or, despite the evidence of the science of probabilities against the explanation of coincidence, are we to state that mankind brings its misery upon itself? Are there agencies which we generally lack power to perceive?

"As a question only, let me ask, might it not be possible that all of us possess a latent sense which, in our modern scurry, has lapsed in its development? Might not our own ancestors, acute to the primitive dangers, exposed to the wind and dark, have given attention to the individual development of that sense? And because we have neglected to individually heighten our own perceptions, are we now 'blind' to extra-material agencies?

And might we not, at any moment, experience a sudden rebirth of that sense and, as vividly as in a lightning flash, see those things which jealousy menace our existences? If we could but see, for ever so brief a period, the supernatural, we would then begin to understand the complexities which beset man. But if we experienced that rebirth and then told of what we saw, might we not be dubbed 'mad'? What of the visions of the saints?

"As children, all of us felt the phantoms of the dark. Might not that sense be less latent in a child whose mind is not yet dulled by the excess burden of facts and facts and more facts? Are there not men in this world today who have converse with the supernatural, but who cannot demonstrate or explain and be believed because of the lack in others of that peculiar sense?

"I am giving you something on which to ponder. You have listened patiently to me for long weeks and you have filled notebooks with scraps of ethnology. I have not once, in all that time until now caused you to think one thought or ponder one question. There is the bell. Think over what I have said."

Half of them, as they wandered out, seemed to think it was one of Professor Lowry's well-known jokes. The other half, of more acute perception, seemed to wonder if Professor Lowry was ill.

Somehow it made no difference to Lowry what they wondered. He had seated himself in his chair and was avoiding all looks by sorting out notes.

"You are the Entity. Wait for us in your office."

CHAPTER SEVEN

For some time Lowry sat in his office, staring at the disarranged stacks of papers which cluttered his desk, wondering at the way he had finished his lecture. It seemed to him, as he thought about it, that man's lot seems to be a recanting of statement and prejudice; those things which he most wildly vows he will not do are those things which, eventually, he must do; those beliefs which are the most foreign to his nature are eventually thrust down his throat by a malignant fate. To think that he, James Lowry, ethnologist, would ever come near a recognition of extra-sensory forces— Well, here he was, waiting. Waiting for what?

Those four hours?

The thought made him rise and pace around the room with the hunched manner of a jungle brute surrounded by bars. He caught himself at it and forced calmness by stirring various bundles with his foot and looking at the address labels of the things which had been shipped up from Yucatan. There was a year's work at this classification, and even he did not know what he had here. Bits of stone, pieces of rubble, plaster casts of prints, hasty miniatures of idols, a scroll in a metal container—

To fill his waiting he unwrapped the first box at hand and set it on his desk. He lifted the cover from it. It was just a fossilized skull found beside a sacrificial block, the last relic of some poor devil who had had his heart torn, living, from his body to satisfy the priest-imagined craving of some brutal deity whose life was thought to need renewal. Just a brown, sightless skull— He had dug this out quite cold-bloodedly, so used he had become to his job. Why did it make him shudder so now?

His name—that was it. That must be it! His name engraved upon that headstone.

JAMES LOWRY
Born 1901
Died 1940
Rest in Peace

Odd that he should somehow fall upon the grassy mound of his own grave, odder still that it would be the one place he had found rest that night. And the date? 1940?

He swallowed a dry lump which threatened to cut off his breathing. "This year?" Tomorrow, next week, next month?

Died 1940

And he had found rest from his torment.

The door opened and Tommy came in. Lowry knew who it was, but he could not quite bring himself to look at Tommy's face. And when he did, as his eyes swept up he saw the malevolent smile and those yellow fangs. But when he looked straight at Tommy it was the same Tommy he had always known.

"So life is too dull for you," said Tommy with a smile. "You wouldn't want to send up to chemistry for some nitroglycerin, would you? Or do you need it?"

"What's wrong?"

"Nothing wrong, except that one of your students nearly collapsed from hysteria. And the rest of them—or some of them, at least—are walking around muttering to hemselves about demons and devils. Don't tell me you re seeing things my way now."

"Not your way," said Lowry. "What a man sees he is orced to believe."

"Well, well, well, old Witch Doctor Lowry himself! Do ou actually think those things they say you said?"

"What else can I think? For forty-eight hours I have alked and talked, pursued and been pursued by phan-oms."

"You seem quite calm about it."

"Why shouldn't I be calm?"

"Oh, no reason. You seem much less agitated than you ave been the past few days, or Saturday and Sunday, to e exact. Is . . . well, do you still see—"

"It's there," said Lowry. "A man can get used to any-hing."

The door opened a second time and they turned to see Mary. She was oblivious of any stir Lowry might have made in class, and had no anxiety to question him, evi-lently feeling that she might possibly be the cause of ome of his strange actions. She looked half frightened now for all that she was smiling, and then, seeing Lowry mile at her, she brightened.

"Hello, Jim. Hello, Tommy. I just breezed by for a very wifely reason, Jim. The exchequer, much as I hate to mention it, is at a very low ebb, and spring and an empty arder demand some clothes and some groceries."

Jim pulled out his check book.

"That," said Tommy, "is the reason I'll never marry."

"It's a pleasure," said Lowry, writing out the check.

"It's two hours to my next class," said Tommy. "May I be burdened with your bundles?"

"Such a delightful beast of burden is quite acceptable," said Mary with a curtsy.

Lowry gave her the check and she kissed him lightly. Tommy took her arm and they left the office.

Was it some sort of sensory illusion that caused Lowry to momentarily feel fangs in her mouth? Was it some way the light fell upon her face that made him see those fangs? Was it a natural jealousy which made him believe she looked lovingly at Tommy as they went out of the door?

He shook his head violently in an effort to clear away such horrible thoughts, and turned to his desk to find himself face to face with the skull. Angrily he put the top upon the box and cast it away from him; but the top did not stay on, nor did the box remain atop the pile of packages; the skull rolled with a hollow sound and finally stood on its nose hole against his foot. He kicked it and it thumped slowly into the corner where its sightless sockets regarded him in mild reproach; one of its teeth had fallen out and made a brown dot on the carpet.

JAMES LOWRY
Born 1901
Died 1940
Rest in Peace

His thoughts had gotten all tangled until he could not remember if this was Sebastian's skull or not, or even if Sebastian's grave had yielded anything but dust and a golden belt. Aimlessly, from the depths of his high-school cramming, came the words, "To be or not to be, that is the question." He said them over several times before he recognized them at all. He essayed, then, a sort of grim joke, muttering, "Alas, poor Lowry. I knew him, Horatio—"

He tried to laugh at himself and failed. He could feel his nerves tautening again, he could hear the echoes of the old mother's remarks. Cats, hats, rats— Cats, hats, rats. Hats, bats, cats, rats. Hats lead to bats, lead to cats, lead to rats. Rats are hungry, James Lowry. Rats will eat you, James Lowry. Hats, you came here to bats, you go on to cats, you get eaten by rats. Do you still want to find your hat? Hats, bats, cats, rats. Rats are hungry, James Lowry. Rats will eat you, James Lowry.

Rats will eat you, James Lowry.

Rats will eat you, James Lowry.

Rats will eat you, James Lowry.

Rats will eat you, James Lowry.

Rats will eat you, James Lowry.

Rats will eat you, James Lowry.

Rats will eat you, James Lowry.

Do you still want to find your hat?

Do you still want to find your hat?

DO YOU STILL WANT TO FIND YOUR HAT?

He threw himself away from the desk and crashed his chair to the floor. The sound of violence gave him some relief, but the second he picked it up—

Hats, bats, rats, cats. Hats, bats, cats, rats. Hats, hats, hats. Bats, bats bats, bats. Rats, rats, rats, rats, rats. Hats, bats, cats, hats, rats, hats, bats rats, cats, hats, rats, bats, cats—

Do you still want to find your hat, James Lowry?

"No!"

"Then," said a childish treble, "you are the Entity."

He glared around his office in search of the owner of the voice. But the office was empty.

And then Lowry saw a certain movement on the wall before his desk where a bookcase had been taken away, leaving a meaningless pattern of scars upon the plaster. He stared at the place intently and found that it was taking definite shape. First the vague outline of a face, and then, little by little, an extension which began to form as a body. Hair came into being upon the head, and the eyes moved slightly and a hand emerged from the wall to be followed by the rest.

"I would dislike frightening you," said the high, musical voice.

The thing looked like a child not more than four years old, a little girl with long blond curls and shapely, dimpled limbs. She was dressed in a frilled frock, all clean and white, and a white bow was slightly to one side of her head. Her face was round and beautiful, but it was a strange kind of beauty, not altogether childish; the eyes were such a dark blue they were almost black, and deep in them with an expression which was not an innocent child's, but more a lascivious wanton's; the lips were full and rich and slightly parted, as though to bestow a greedy lover's kiss. And like an aura a black shadow stood in globular shape about her. But at a casual, swift glance, it was a little child, no more than four, naïve and full of laughter. The lewd eyes lingered caressingly upon Lowry's face as she perched herself upon the top of his desk.

"No, I do not frighten you, do I?"

"What . . . what are you?" said Lowry.

"Why, a child of course. Have you no eyes?" And pensively, then, "You know, you are a very handsome-looking man, Mr. Lowry. So big and rough—" A dreamy look came into her eyes and her small pink tongue flicked out to dampen her lips convulsively.

"You wrote that message?"

"No. But I come to tell you about it. You are quite sure now, Mr. Lowry, that you do not want to find your hat?"

"No!"

"It was a very pretty hat."

"I never want to see it again."

She smiled and leaned back languorously, her little shoes making occasional thumps against the side of the desk. She yawned and stretched and then looked long at him. The full little lips quivered and the pink tongue flicked. With a seeming effort she brought herself to business.

"If you are through with all such nonsense and disbelief in us," she began, "and if you will aid us against the

264

others, then I shall tell you something you should be glad to hear. Are you?"

Lowry hesitated and then nodded. He felt very weary.

"You visited your friend, Tommy Williams, just before you lost your four hours, didn't you?"

"You probably know more about it than I," said Lowry with bitterness.

For a moment she laughed, and Lowry started as he recognized the sound which had been near him so many hours. He looked studiously at her and found that her image seemed to pulsate and that the black aura expanded and contracted like some great unclean thing breathing.

She swung her little princess slippers against the desk and continued. "Tommy Williams told you the truth. You offered us a challenge and said we did not exist, and we know more about you than you do. You see, all this was scheduled, anyway. Every few generations, Mr. Lowry, we even up accounts with mankind. Such a period has just begun. And you, Mr. Lowry, are invested with control, for we must have a human control."

She smiled and dimples appeared in her soft cheeks. She smoothed out her dress with little-girl gestures, and then, looking at him, she drummed her heels.

"That is what we mean by 'Entity,' Mr. Lowry. You are the Entity, the center of control. Usually all life, at fleeting instants, takes turns in passing this along. Now perhaps you have, at one time in your life, had a sudden feeling, 'I am I'? Well, that awareness of yourself is akin to what men call godliness. For an instant nearly every living thing in this world has been the one Entity, the focal point for all life. It is like a torch being passed from hand to hand. Usually innocent little children such as myself are invested, and so it is that a child ponders much upon his own identity."

"What are you trying to tell me?"

"Why," she said demurely, "I am telling you that this is

265

a period when *we* choose an Entity and invest that function in just one man. Your Tommy Williams, I believe, knows about it. So long as you live, then the world is animated. So long as you walk and hear and see, the world goes forward. In your immediate vicinity, you understand, all life is concentrating upon demonstrating that it is alive. It is not. Others are only props for you. This would have happened to you a long time ago, but it was difficult to achieve communication with you. You are the Entity, the only living thing in this world."

The globe of darkness around her pulsated gently. She touched her dainty little hands to her white hair ribbon and then folded them in her lap. She looked fixedly at Lowry, and that slow look of the wanton came into her eyes and her lips parted a little. Her breath quickened.

"What . . . what am I expected to do?" said Lowry.

"Why, nothing. You are the Entity."

"H-he-e i-is-s t-th-he-e E-En-n-ti-it-ty!" growled a chorus of voices in other parts of the room.

"But why do you tell me?"

"So that nothing will worry you, and so that you will do nothing rash. You are afraid of Tommy Williams. Well, Tommy Williams, as well as Jebson and Billy Watkins, is just a prop which you motivate yourself."

"Then how is it that this morning he came to me and leaned over me and stared at my face and I could not move?"

She tensed. "What is this he did?"

"Just stared into my face. And I keep seeing fangs when I don't look at him directly—"

"Oh!" she cried in shocked pain. "Then it is impossible!"

"I-it-t i-is-s i-im-mp-po-os-si-i-b-bl-le-e!" chorused the growls.

"It's too late," she stated finally. "There is nothing you can do. Tommy Williams if the leader of the *others*. And

266

you must somehow settle accounts with Tommy Williams."

"Why?"

"He has already taken from you a part of your soul substance."

"He was here just a few minutes ago."

"Every time he sees you he'll try to take some! You must prevent it!"

"How?" cried Lowry.

But the little child was gone, and the black aura turned darker and began to vanish at the top until it seemed like a small, round black thing. With a smoke puff it was gone!

"How?" shouted Lowry.

Only the echo of his own voice against his own walls answered him. And then he fixed his eyes upon the broken spot in the plaster, it was just a broken spot with no resemblance whatever to either a face or anything else.

What had that thing been?

Where was it now?

Lowry buried his face in his arms.

When the twelve-o'clock bell rang, Lowry got up more from force of habit than from any wish to leave his office. A gnawing ache of apprehension was suffused through his office. A gnawing ache of apprehension was suffused through his being as though he subconsciously expected a blow to smash him at any moment from the least expected quarter. With effort he put the feeling down; he squared his shoulders and slipped into his topcoat and strode forth with watchful eyes. But there was another feeling which was gradually coming toward recognition in him, a feeling that nothing could touch him. And as the first one was stamped out, the second one rose. It was not unlike a religious fanatic's trust in a personally interested god, a thing which seemed very foreign to Lowry. And as he walked through the hurrying crowds of students in the halls and down the stairs, he began to be conscious of his own size and strength.

He was, after all, a big fellow, but, being of a very shy nature, he had never taken much notice of the fact, thinking of his person, rather, as being somewhat underweight and undersize—without really thinking about the matter at all. Some of the athletes of the college came past him in a group, and he noticed, almost smiling, that he was taller and heavier than they. Odd he had never taken that personal quality of his into account. It was like finding a gold mine or having a beautiful woman suddenly confess her love, or hearing a million people stand up and cheer themselves into exhaustion for one.

Outside, a student had taken a seat upon the steps so that the penetrating languor of sunlight could caress his back; in his hands he held a newspaper. As Lowry passed him he wondered for a moment what was going on in the world and so glanced at the sheet.

For an instant he wondered if he were going blind.

There wasn't any printing on the paper.

It was just a white sheet, but for all that the student seemed to be reading it with avidity!

Lowry, troubled a little, went on. But as he walked, the exhilaration of exercise restored the pleasant feeling within him, and he gradually forgot about the newspaper. Several small groups of students were standing along the walk, chattering among themselves. A man was pushing a lawn mower industriously. A boy was trotting along with the yellow telegraph envelope in his hand.

Suddenly Lowry had a strange feeling about things, as though something was happening behind him which he should know about. He stopped and whirled around.

The boy had stopped trotting, but started instantly. The man at the lawn mower had paused but was now mowing again. The little crowds of students had ceased gesticulating and laughing for the smallest fraction of time but instantly went to it once more.

268

Lowry pondered the matter as he walked on. Perhaps there was something happening in his head, like false memory. Certainly it was just his imagination which led him to believe that things had paused outside his observation.

Old Billy Watkins, up earlier than usual, came limping by. He paused and touched his cap. "You feelin' better today, Ji—Professor Lowry?"

"Much better, thanks."

"Well, take care of yourself, Jim—Professor Lowry."

"Thanks, Billy."

Lowry walked on, and then again he had that feeling. He stopped and looked over his shoulder. Old Billy Watkins was standing like a limp scarecrow, but as soon as Jim Lowry really noticed it, Old Billy went on swinging down the street. And the man at the law mower and the messenger and the students—they had all stopped, too, only to resume under Lowry's glance.

That was very strange, thought Lowry.

And something else which was strange waited him when he continued on his way. A horse-drawn cart had been plodding along on his right, and both the horse and the cart had paused in mid-action when he looked away, only to start plodding along again under his scrutiny.

He had reached the small café where the professors generally took their luncheon. He opened the door upon silence. No clatter of knives and forks, no rattle of dishes, no jangle of talking. Silence. But only for an instant. Lowry stepped into the café and the rattling and clattering and jangling started in full blast like a sound track clipped on halfway through. Other than that there was nothing unusual about the place. Other professors called to him in greeting, and the sprinkling of students nodded politely, and he was forced into a chair.

"Damn shame what Jebson did to you," said a young professor in disgust. Somebody evidently kicked him, for

269

a spasm of pain went across his face to be swiftly erased
"I still think it's a shame."

"Chicken-salad sandwich and a glass of milk," said
Lowry to the waiter.

He talked, then, with the men at his table about the
petty subjects of the campus and told them an anecdote
about his latest trip to Yucatan. The feeling of self-pos-
session, coupled with an "allness" of being, put him quite
at ease. And a little later, when they were breaking up, he
was aware of the fact that he had made his friendship
with these fellows a little closer. But there had been
something odd about this place all during lunch. He had,
several times, attempted to listen in upon the talk at the
table behind him, but it had all been sounds; just a jumble
of sounds.

It occurred to him that this was Monday and he experienced a feeling of relief. He would not have to lecture
again today, for his heavy days were Tuesday and Thurs-
day. He could go out and walk around and enjoy the
clear sunshine and forget about these things which had
happened to him.

The place was almost empty when he left. He stood for
a second outside the door, wondering which way he
should go. And then it struck him that all was not well
with this familiar street.

Two cars were at a standstill in the traffic lane, their
drivers apparently asleep over their wheels. A kid on a
bike was leaning inertly against a tree. Three students
were slumped at the curb.

These people must be dead!

But no. No, the drivers were sitting up straight now
and the cars were getting in motion. The kid on the bike
was pedaling away in a rush. The students grabbed up
their books and casually strolled toward the campus.

Lowry turned around and looked inside the café. The
cashier was sprawled over the glass case beside the regis-
ter. A waiter was poised in the middle of the room with

one foot in the air and a tray of dishes balanced on his palm. A late diner was almost face down in his soup. Lowry took an inadvertent step toward them.

The waiter began to move smoothly. The cashier scribbled at a pad. The late diner began to make a great deal of noise over the soup.

Puzzled, Lowry turned away from the college and went on down the street. What was happening to him now?

He stopped at a newsdealer's stand and bought a paper. There was nothing wrong with the newsdealer, for the old man did his usual trick of stalling to keep the customer from asking for the two pennies change he should get.

Discarding the evidences he had witnessed, Lowry went along. He looked at the paper. It did not particularly amaze him that this one, too, was blank, but he felt a kindling of wrath against the newsdealer. He whirled and marched back to the stand. Another man had been standing there buying a paper, but now both the customer and the newsdealer were without motion, slumped across the stand. They did not go into action until Lowry was almost upon them and then, casually, they transacted their business. But Lowry noticed that the customer's paper was also blank. Disgustedly, Lowry tossed his own paper upon the street and returned to his way.

Lowry wandered along in a northerly direction, taking a course which would soon lead him out of town; for he felt a craving for the quieting comfort of a stream in which he had long ago swum and the sound of a breeze in the willows which flanked it. Other manifestations, just enough apparent to make him wonder at them, were met on the way, people and beasts and birds which went into action a moment late. He was convinced that he was seeing late or that his mind, being wearied by the events of the two days past, was not registering instantaneously. He did not much worry until he reached the place where

271

he had intended to rest. It had occurred to him belatedly that the spot was now the site of a cellulose factory; but, as he approached, no sign of factory or factory smoke was marring the sky.

He found the place beside the pool in which he used to dive in defiance of a sign which read: "City Water Supply. Do Not Contaminate." He stretched himself out in the cool grass and felt the sun upon him. How satisfying it was to come here and yet how different he was from the boy who had lazed in this cover throughout the long vacations. Little by little he slipped into a languorous happiness and idly reviewed the things he had thought and done as a kid in overalls. Then he had been in awe of his father, and now he was as his father had been, a professor at Atworthy.

The thought amused him that he was the image of his own early awe, and he dwelt at length upon what he would have said to the boy in overalls who had lain long hours in this very spot, how he would have told him that the mystery of the elder world was no mystery at all, but an uncertain sort of habit of dignity, perhaps grown out of the image of youth, perhaps as an excuse for diminished physical vigor, perhaps as a handy shield by which one could hold off the world. How little that boy need have worried, after all. The state of being "grown up" was a state beset by as many worries, and just as false, as those of childhood.

After a little he became aware of a swift hammering sound and the snarl of a truck engine. He tried to put the invasion aside, but it persisted and grew in volume and activity until his curiosity was aroused. What was going on in this vicinity?

He got up and peered through the willows, catching a glimpse of a half-finished wall. What was that? He moved out of hiding and was astonished to see two hundred or more workmen carrying materials and hammering nails and laying bricks with a speed which excelled anything he had ever before seen. A factory was going up a foot at a time, yard, mud, tanks, stacks, wire gates and all! And what a sweat of rushing! He drifted nearer and was conscious of the eyes of workmen upon him. The men, as soon as they glimpsed him, looked bewildered. A foreman began to bray curses at them. And within a minute, the factory was done. The workmen promptly dived in through the doors and came out bearing lunch boxes and then, as though this was wrong, the foreman flayed into them anew and a whistle blew and a siren whooped and the workmen sped inside again to send out a great clamor of machinery and the roar of steam. The plant was going full blast. The willows had vanished. The stream of yesterday was a concrete aqueduct!

Dazed, Lowry turned his back upon the place and strode swiftly back toward the town. He was beginning to feel a nausea of concern about these events. How did his own appearance so affect conditions?

The world continued to lag for him as he entered the town. People were still until he was in sight and then they moved, just as if they were props in an artificial scene.

A suspicion took form in him and he suddenly changed his course. What about all these houses?

What about them?

When he got halfway down a block that he had never traversed in his memory, he stepped abruptly into an alleyway.

Just as he had expected. These houses had fronts but no backs! They were sets!

He went on down the alley and here and there people made belated attempts to complete the false fronts and give them false backs, but they were were fumbling and bewildered, as though Lowry's presence and appearance set their knees to knocking.

What of the main street? He had never been in many of the stores. Feeling he had to put this thing to complete test, he hurried along, unmindful of the effect he seemed to have upon these puppets.

He rounded a block of the main thoroughfare of the town, but just before he turned the corner a terror-striken voice reached him:

"Jim! Jim! Jim! Oh, my God! *Jim!*"

He leaped around the corner and halted, appalled. The whole avenue was littered with apparently dead people. They were sprawled against steering wheels and in the gutters. They were leaning stiffly against store fronts. The traffic cop was a rag draped about his signal. A two-horse team was down in the traces and the farmer on the box was canted over, slack-jawed as a corpse. And through this tangled carpet of props ran Mary. Her hat was gone and her hair was wild and her eyes were dilated with horror.

He called to her and she almost fell with relief. Sobbing, arms outstretched, she threw herself upon him and buried a tear-streaked face upon his breast.

"Jim!" she sobbed. "Oh, my God! Jim!"

As he smoothed down her hair with a gentle hand, he watched the street come to life and resume the petty activity with which he was so familiar. The cop blew his whistle and swung his signal, and the horses leaped up and began to pull, and the farmer took a chew and spat. Buyers and sellers bought and sold and there was not one thing wrong with the whole street. But Jim knew that if he looked behind him those people who now passed him would be stopped again, slumped, their puppet strings slack.

A familiar figure swung along toward them. Tommy, swinging a limber black stick, his hat on the back of his head and his handsome face with its customary quirk of amusement, approached them and paused in recognition.

"Hello, Jim." And then, in concern, "Is something wrong with Mary?"

"You know what's wrong with Mary, Tom Williams."

Tommy looked at him oddly. "I don't get you, old man."

"Not that you wouldn't try," said Jim with a cold grin at his own humor. "I've had enough of this."

"Enough of what?"

"You took something from me. I want it back. I know about this, you see."

"Well?"

"I want that part of myself back."

"You accuse me—"

"Of being a thief."

"Well?"

"So long as I had all of myself, all was well in this world. Now that part of me is gone—"

Tommy laughed amusedly. "So you've caught on, have you?"

"And I'll remedy this, Tom Williams, or put an end to you."

Tommy's laugh was brittle and he swung the cane as though he would like to strike out with it. "How is it that you rate so much?"

"I don't know or care how it is. What is mine is mine. Give me back that part of myself, Tom Williams."

"And lose my own?" said Tommy with a smile.

"What is mine is mine," said Lowry.

"I believe in a more communistic attitude," said Tommy. "I happen to want that part of you and I certainly intend to keep it." And now the fangs at the corners of his mouth were quite plain.

Lowry put Mary to one side. He snatched out and grabbed Tommy's coat and hauled him close, aiming a blow. Somehow, Tommy twisted from the grasp and, in his turn, struck hard with his cane. For an instant the world, for Lowry, was ink. But he came up in an effort to lunge at Tommy's throat. Again the cane felled him. Stunned now, he swayed on his hands and knees, trying to clear his fogged senses. Once more the cane struck him and he felt the pavement strike against his cheek.

In a little while he was conscious of a face close to his own, a face from which protruded yellow fangs. A sick weakness, as though he was bleeding to death, pinned him to the walk.

Tommy stood up straight and Lowry found that he could not move. Tommy seemed twice as big and strong as before.

Mary looked at Tommy for a long while, the expression of her face slowly changing from one of wonder to one of agreeable satisfaction. And then Lowry knew why it was. She was nothing but a puppet herself, animated more than any of the rest because she had been more with a source. And when Tommy had taken part of him she had begun to divide her attention between them, for either one could animate her. And now that Tommy possessed an "allness" there could be no questions as to which one she would follow.

She gave no glance at all to Lowry on the walk. She looked up into Tommy's face and smiled tenderly. Tommy smiled back and, arm in arm, they walked away.

Lowry tried to shout after them, but they paid no heed. They were gone around the corner.

By degrees, then, the street began to slump and become still. By degrees, but not wholly. Here and there a puppet twitched a little. Here and there a mouth made motions without making sound. Lowry stared in terror at the scene.

For him the world was nearly dead!

His body was so heavy that he could scarcely move at all. But he knew that he must pursue them, find them, gain back that vital force which had been stolen. To live, an eighth alive, in a world of apparent dead would drive him mad!

And Mary!

How could— But she was just a puppet, too. A puppet

with all the rest. It was no fault of hers. The guilt was all Tommy's. Tommy that he had thought his friend!

It was agony to drag himself along, but he did, inch by inch, fumbling over the bodies which sprawled in the clear sunlight. He became aware of how hot it was getting and of a great weariness. If he could just rest for a little while, he might be able to find strength. He saw a bush in a yard where the cover was thick and he crawled into the coolness. Just to rest a little while and then to find Tommy and Mary!

CHAPTER EIGHT

It was nearly dusk when he awoke. He stretched himself stiffly, for he had become cold. For a moment he could not recall the events which had passed, and he came to his knees, aware of a thing he must do but not quite able to place it. This lethargy! Was it affecting his brain as well?

But, no, his brain was all right. Yes! Tommy and Mary and the world of the apparent dead!

And what a tremendous amount of good that rest had done him. Or else—

He peered forth from the bushes. There were people walking along the street and so it was fairly plain that Tommy would be somewhere nearby and that Lowry himself was drawing some of the force in common with the other puppets. Perhaps that would help him! If he could get close to Tommy and then, supported by Tommy's own effect, he could possibly win back what he had lost.

He lurked in the shadows of the street, watching for Tommy. But, no, he could not locate any sign of him. Could it be that Tommy was in one of these houses? Perhaps dining? In such a position that he might look out and see the street?

Perhaps there was another explanation. Perhaps, now that Tommy had all of it, these puppets would go on with their make-believe lives and Lowry along with them. But he himself knew and they—

He emerged from cover. There was a man standing

beside the letter box on the corner. Maybe he would know where to find Tommy. Lowry, assuming a careless air, sauntered up to the fellow. He was about to open his mouth and begin to question when his heart lurched within.

This was Tommy!

Tommy, with a mocking smile upon his mouth and a sly look in his eye!

Lowry whirled and sped away, but when he found that no footsteps followed he slowed down. He glanced back and the man on the corner was looking after him and there was light, cheerful laughter suspended in the air.

Why wasn't he able to face him? Did he have to find him sleeping in order to steal away that which he had lost?

Lowry stopped. Couldn't he be more clever about this? Couldn't he perhaps explain to some of these puppets what had happened to the world and thereby gain help? Many of them could assail Tommy and weigh him down and take that from him which rightfully belonged to the world.

He went along, looking for someone to whom he could broach the plan. A man was watering a lawn inside a picket fence and Lowry stopped and beckoned to him. The man, holding the hose, strolled languidly over.

Lowry was about to begin when he looked into the fellow's face. Despite the dusk that face was plain!

It was Tommy!

Lowry whirled and ran, and again the light laughter hung upon the evening air.

He slowed down, stubbornly refusing to be panicked. There was no use losing his head, for he still had a chance. Not everyone could be Tommy.

Soon he saw a woman hurrying homeward. If he told her and she told her husband— Yes. He would stop her.

He held up his hand and she dodged from him, but

seeing no menace in him she allowed him to speak. He had uttered just one word when he saw who she was.

Mary!

His heart skipped a beat. Here she was alone! And he could plead with her— Again he started to speak. But Mary's face was full of scorn and she turned her back upon him and walked away.

It took Lowry some seconds to get over that. But he would not admit defeat. Here came three students. Students would obey him certainly, and these fellows wore sweaters with stripes around the arm. He stepped out in front of them.

When they had stopped and were looking at him, he started to speak. And then he stopped. Each face into which he looked in turn became Tommy's! And each face possessed that mocking smile and slyly evil glint of eye.

Lowry stepped back and kept on walking backward. He spun about and ran away and did not stop until he had come to the corner of the next block.

A woman was there, but he knew better than to halt her, for even at ten feet, by the light of the street lamp, he could see that she was Mary. He pulled his hat ashamedly down over his eyes and slouched by and then, when she was going away from him, he began to run once more.

He fled past other pedestrians, and each one that looked at him was possessed of the face of either Tommy or Mary. And after a little they began to call to him at intervals.

"Hello, Jim," said Tommy in mockery each time.

"Oh, it's you, Jim," said Mary.

Thickening dark and the thin street lamps' glowing oppressed Lowry. It was becoming warmer by degrees and then, swiftly, turned cold. The house fronts were chill and impassive in the gloom; their lighted windows like glowing eyes that looked at him and mocked.

"Hello, Jim."

And again, "Oh, it's you, Jim."

Spreading lawns and the huddled shapes of bushes peopled the night with strange phantoms. Little shadows raced about his feet and sometimes brushed against his legs with a soft, furry touch. Once, as he stepped down from a curb, he saw a scaly thing dissolve an instant late.

And then Tommy's face, all by itself, floated eerily against the gray dark. The thing was thin and blurry, but the smile was there and the sly eyes regarded him steadily. The face faded away and left only the glinting of the eyes.

Before him a shape had begun to dance, pausing until he almost caught up to it and then scurrying to get him out of reach to dance again and beckon. There was a certain mannerism about it that brought its identity to him. Wearily he recognized Mary, her face was cold in scorn. Why and where was she leading him?

"Hello, Jim."

"Oh, it's you, Jim."

Shadows and the gloomy fronts of houses coldly staring. Shadows on the lawns and hiding at the edges of trees. Soft things which bumped his legs and a great shadow like spread wings reaching out to engulf the whole of the town.

Blurry white wisps of faces drifting just ahead. Tommy's and Mary's, Mary's and Tommy's.

Above, there was a rustling as of bats. Below, there came up a low and throaty sound. And the smells of fresh-cut grass and growing things were tinged with a perfume he could not define. A perfume. As illusive as those faces which drifted ever before him. A perfume—Mary's. Mary's perfume. Mingled with the smell of exotic tobacco. Exotic tobacco. Tommy's.

The great dark cloud spread and spread and the lamps became dim and the shadows deepened and began to march jerkily beside him at a distance. Each shadow, stationary until he came to it, coming up and marching with the rest. Darker and darker and then no sounds at all. No sounds or smells. Just the thin wisp of a mocking smile, gradually fading, forever receding.

Weakly he leaned against the parapet of a little stone bridge behind the church and listened to the water saying: "Oh, it's you, Jim." "Hello, Jim."

At the other end there stood a dark, thick shadow. A thing with a slouch hat upon its head and a black cloak draped about it which reached down to its buckled shoes. It was carefully braiding a rope, strand by strand. Lowry knew he would rest a little and then walk over the bridge to the man of darkness.

"Oh, it's you, Jim."

"Hello, Jim."

Quiet little rippling voices, almost unheard, slowly fading. And now there was nothing more of that smile. There was nothing in the sky but the vast shadow and the plaintive whimper of an evening wind.

The street lamp threw a pale light upon him and by its light he tried to see the water. The voices down there were scarcely whispers now, only a rippling murmur, a kind and soothing sound.

He caught a glimpse of someting white in the water and leaned a trifle farther, not particularly interested in the fact that it was a reflection of his own face in the black mirror surface below. He watched the image grow clearer, watched his own eyes and mouth take form. It was as if he was seeing himself down there, a self far more real than this self leaning against cold stone. Idly he beckoned to the image. It seemed to grow nearer. He beckoned again in experiment. It was nearer still.

With sudden determination he held out both hands to it. It was gone from the water, but it was not gone.

Jim Lowry stood up straight. He took a long, deep breath of fresh evening air and looked up at the stars in

283

the sky. He turned and looked along the avenue and saw people strolling and enjoying the smell of fresh-cut grass. He looked across the bridge and saw Old Billy Watkins leaning against a stone, puffing contentedly upon a pipe.

With a feeling that was almost triumph for all the weight of sorrow within him, Jim Lowry crossed the bridge and approached the night policeman.

"Oh. Hello, Professor Lowry."

"Hello, Billy."

"Nice night."

"Yes ... yes, Billy. A nice night. I want you to do something for me, Billy."

"Anything, Jim."

"Come with me."

Old Billy knocked the ashes from his pipe and silently fell in beside. Old Billy was a wise old fellow. He could feel Lowry's mood and he said nothing to intrude upon it, merely walked along smelling the growing things of spring.

They walked for several blocks and then Jim Lowry turned into the path at Tommy's house. The old mansion was unlighted and still and seemed to be waiting for them.

"You should have a key to fit that door, Billy."

"Yes. I've got one; it's a common lock."

Old Billy turned the knob and fumbled for the hall light, turning it on and standing back to follow Lowry.

Jim Lowry pointed at the hatrack in the hall and indicated a lady's bag which lay there beside a lady's hat. There was another hat there, a man's, trammeled, halfway between hatrack and living room; it had initials in the band, "J.L."

"Come with me, Billy," said Jim Lowry in a quiet, controlled voice. As they passed the living room, Old Billy saw the stumps of a broken chair and an upset ash tray.

Jim Lowry held the kitchen door open and turned on the light. The window was broken there.

A mewling sound came from somewhere and Jim

Lowry opened the door to the cellar. With steady, slow steps he descended a short flight of stairs, through newly swung strands of cobwebs. A Persian cat with a half-mad look bolted past them and fled out of the house.

Jim fumbled for the basement light. For a moment it seemed that he would not turn it on, but that was only for a moment. The naked bulb flooded the basement and filled it with sharp, swinging shadows.

A crude hole had been dug in the middle of the dirt floor and a shovel was abandoned beside it.

Jim Lowry took hold of the light cord and lifted it so that the rays would stream into the coal bin.

An ax, black with blood, pointed its handle at them. From the coal protruded a white something.

Old Billy stepped to a dark, dusty pile and pushed some of the lumps away. A small avalanche rattled, disclosing the smashed and hacked face of Tommy Williams. To his right, head thrown back, staring eyes fixed upon the stringers and blood-caked arm outflung, lay the body of Mary, Jim Lowry's wife.

Old Billy looked for several minutes at Jim Lowry and then Jim Lowry spoke, his voice monotonous. "I did it Saturday afternoon. And Saturday night I came back here to find the evidence I had left—my hat—and dispose of the bodies. Sunday I came again—I had to climb in the window. I'd lost the key."

Jim Lowry sank down upon a box and hid his face in his palms. "I don't know why I did it. Oh, God, forgive me, I don't know why. I found her here, hiding, after I had found her hat. Everything was whirling and I couldn't hear what they kept screaming at me and . . . and I killed them." A sob shook him. "I don't know why. I don't know why she was here . . . I don't know why I could not reason . . . cerebral malaria . . . jealous madness—"

Old Billy moved a little and the coal pile shifted and rattled. Tommy's arm was bared. It seemed to thrust itself toward Lowry, and in the cold fist was clenched a scrap of paper as though mutely offering explanation even in death.

Old Billy removed the paper and read:

TOMMY OLD SPORT:

Next week is Jim's birthday and I want to surprise him with a party. I'll come over Saturday afternoon and you can help me make up the list of his friends and give me your expert advice on the demon rum. Don't let him know a word of this.

Regards,
MARY.

Somewhere high above, there seemed to hang a tinkle of laughter: high, amused laughter, gloating and mocking and evil.

"Who ever heard of demons, my sister?"

"No one at all, my brother."

Of course, though, it was probably just the sigh of wind whining below the cellar door.

A GALAXY OF SCIENCE FICTION

SUPERNATURAL .OCCULT